Realms

Volume One

By Andrea Rollins

Prologue:

The crowd cheered as a dark haired woman was dragged through the square. She snarled, screaming and kicking as two large men pulled her toward a looming wooden pole. They grabbed her hands, binding them behind her back as they tied her in place.

"Witch! Witch!" The crowd chanted.

"It won't work." The woman laughed. She was ignored as a man held out a torch to the kindling below her body. "I am a god!" She screamed. "I am immortal!" She leaned forward with a toothy grin, her double canines sharp and exposed. "And when I get loose, I'm going to tear you all limb from limb." The man swallowed hard, avoiding the woman's gaze. She snickered as she watched a cold sweat form across his brow. He shook his head, however, and dropped the torch.

The fire roared up around her. It licked at her legs and chest, burning away her clothing and scorching her skin. The burnt flesh melted, but a black mist seeped into the wounds and reformed her skin into pale, undamaged patches. She cackled loudly, reaffirming her statement with a bellow, "I am a god!"

The crowd watched in horror as the ropes burned from her wrists, freeing the woman. She stepped out of the flames, unscathed. A dark tail with a spade tip and a pair of looming, black wings formed on her body. Her tail flicked playfully as she giggled, spreading her wings widely.

She flapped them, relinquishing a whirlwind of the black mist that seeped into bodies and sapped away the youth of those before her. Their flesh aged rapidly before disintegrating into dust. She stepped over the skeletons, slowly approaching a man who stood in the midst of the carnage, unaffected.

A hole in his chest glowed brightly, the light from it only slightly whiter than his pale locks. Behind him, a bright shimmering mist solidified into a long, luminescent tail with a glowing orb at its tip.

"Why?" He asked, shaking his head. The woman crossed her arms and scoffed.

"You have the audacity to ask me that?" Her wings spread once more. "I loved you, Zadkiel! I loved you and you betrayed me!" Another flap of her wings and the mist permeated through the air again. Zadkiel lifted his hand, his own mist pouring from his body. It slammed against the woman's. The two powers pressed against one another, battling for dominance over the other. "I loved you!" She screamed once more, tears rolling down her face.

"You know you can't win." He called out. "Don't make me kill you, Circe." The woman shook her head as mist flooded from her body, joining her power as it assaulted the bright midst opposing her. Zadkiel sighed. "You know," he lifted his other hand, "I really did love you too." A blast of light shot from his palm and engulfed Circe. She screamed in agony as she was devoured by the force, the bright mist shining more brightly than anything the townspeople had ever seen. When the light faded, there was nothing left of the young woman – not a skeleton or even dust. She was gone. Dead.

Chapter One:

The morning sun glittered down on the bustling figures crowding the market. Crimson eyes watched their movements, taking in every subtle twitch of their muscles. Their owner, a dark haired woman with pale skin and a short stature, slunk between bodies, weaving through the mass as she relinquished wallets and coin purses from their owners. She snickered as she snatched a particularly fattened purse, brimming with satisfaction as she sauntered through the sea of people. Shoving her haul up her sleeve, she easily made her way deep into the crowd, her long black locks flowing behind her as she avoided interaction. She passed by a guard, glancing at him from the corner of her eye. He didn't know. He hadn't seen. She smirked. Everything was going perfectly. Today was going to be a great day.

She paused abruptly as she felt something creep up her spine; a chilling realization. She felt eyes on her. They burrowed into her back, watching everything she did. She jolted around, catching sight of a hooded figure whispering to a guard on the opposite end of the marketplace.

The dark haired woman cursed, staggering back slightly as her heart began to race. Did they know? Had they seen? Under the hood, glowing blue eyes stared at her. Another whisper and the guard's eyes narrowed. They knew. A wicked smile formed on the hooded figure's face as the guard drew his sword and started through the crowd, trudging toward the dark haired woman.

She ducked between bodies and she scurried away as quickly as she could. Civilians screamed and darted out of the guard's path as he bellowed after her.

"Criminal! Stop!" His booming voice echoed over the commotion. He was gaining on her - quickly. She would never escape at this rate. She bit her lip. She had to think of something, but only one option appeared in her mind. She crouched behind an abandoned stall and drew in a deep, shaky breath. Peeking out, she saw the guard lumbering toward her hiding spot – coming to hack off her hands at the wrist.

"Damn it." She muttered as she recoiled.

It had been two weeks since she had needed to do this, but it seemed she had no choice. She held out her pale hands in front of her. Black mist drifted from her fingertips, slithering into the crowd like a snake. It seeped into flesh, penetrating skin and pouring into bodies. The attendees of the morning market were slowly becoming infected with her power.

Those who were touched by the mist soon began pacing, agitatedly muttering to themselves and pushing others aside. They argued with each other about nothing and everything all at once. Slurs filled the air as they grabbed at one another, screaming threats and insults.

The guard glanced around at the citizens who seemed to have become irritable at nothing at all around him. Confusion painted his face. He grabbed at people, commanding them to calm down, but he was ignored as they jerked away and continued their frenzy. He frantically tried to silence some of the arguments with threats of stocks or hanging, but nothing worked. He was outnumbered by the mob of angry inhabitants. His pleas were drowned out by the shouting around him, ignored and forgotten the moment they left his lips.

The woman smiled, creeping out of her hiding spot and slithering into the crowd, dodging attention as the arguing escalated. Everything seemed perfect as she made her way to the edge of the crowd; right until a man boiling with rage pulled a knife from his belt. He lifted it high into the air, plunging it over and over into the neck of the man he had been arguing with. Screams of horror erupted as the crowd began to clamor over one another, stampeding like cattle to get away from the ongoing murder. Then, another and another began. People all around fell into fits of violent rage, attacking anyone nearby. Murders were occurring everywhere the dark haired woman looked.

Blood sprayed through the air, splattering across stands and people. It seeped onto the ground in puddles. Guards plunged their swords through frenzied individuals, killing civilian after civilian – the only solution they had to end the pandemonium. Children fell to the ground, crushed beneath the feet of the crowd as the clamoring to escape persisted. Their tiny skulls were crushed and their blood turned the dirt road into a crimson, muddy mess. The woman's mouth fell agape. She backed against a wall, clinging to it as the mass of bodies began running by her.

"I…didn't mean for this – I didn't want *this* to happen." She muttered, backing into an alley. Tears threatened to roll down her face as she looked upward and swallowed a lump in her throat. "It's all my fault. Damn it! It's all my fault!" She glanced once more out of the alley, looking back at what she had caused.

Blue eyes stared through the crowd at her. Calmly, they cut through the madness. They didn't waver, not even for a moment. They were cold, unfeeling. The wicked smirk worn by the hooded figure was a knowing one. Did they know she was the cause of the madness? The woman shuddered, darting down the alleyway without looking back.

It's okay. She thought as she made her way out of the alley's opposing exit and onto the street. Screams were still filling the air and the blue eyes were burned into her mind. She increased her pace, snatching an apple from a distracted vendor. *It's okay. The mist will dissipate just like always. Everything's going to be okay. It'll go back to normal. I need to calm down.* Her thoughts drifted back to the hooded figure, but she shook it from her mind. *They don't know. They can't know. I don't even fully*

Despite what she told herself, she felt like letting out a
frustrated scream. Who was that person? Did they see what had
happened? They must've seen. How could they not? She had
caused countless people to die by losing control. Was that why
the figure had smiled? Why would that make them smile? She
sighed as she shook her head, rubbing her temple. These powers
were evil and nothing would be okay so long as she lacked
control of them, but it endangered everyone when she used.
Now, it seemed someone else knew about that. She lacked
control. She had barely any semblance of it, honestly. While it
wasn't as bad as it had been before, it wasn't as though she
hadn't just killed more than fifty people in a matter of seconds.
She was a monster.

She groaned. Even leaving the town to practice using
these ungodly powers was out of the question. Samba Forest
surrounded them on all sides and everyone knew it was home to
a wide array of dangerous creatures. Every citizen had been
taught at an early age that they shouldn't wander off into its
depths unless they intended to die. A few hunters would
venture out to get food for the town, but fewer had returned.
They told stories of cackling and howling near Hell's Lake in the
midst of the Samba Forest; it spelled death for anyone who went
out into it. Meaning, if she wanted to practice, she had to do it in
town. Without complete control, however she threatened to
decimate the population.

Every part of her strange power clawed at her insides,
constantly begging to be released. She rounded the corner into
another alleyway and bit into her stolen apple, the blood on her
hands decorating its skin with a liquid crimson, candying the
apple with its irony taste. It slightly placated the pressure inside
of her, but only a little. Every day of her life, she fought against
an insatiable thirst – a desire for blood that she could never quite

satisfy. She wanted to pour buckets of it down her throat. The violence she caused didn't help the matter. Whenever she caused blood to be spilled, it was as though her senses heightened and she could smell every drop. She wanted it. She wanted it more than air or water. Sometimes, it was almost maddening to her. She trembled with satisfaction as the bite of blood-candied apple slipped down her throat.

She held the next bite in her mouth, appreciating the sweetness of fruit mixed with the savory decadence that coated it. A shiver ran up her spine. *So good.* She tore into the fruit again, tossing away the reminder when the blood had all been eaten. Rats scurried from their homes in the alley, swarming it almost instantly. They occasionally looked between the food and the woman, squeaking with pleasure. With a halfhearted wave to the vermin, she exited the alley and began to make her way down the street.

"Astrid!" She jolted, jerking around to see a tall man behind her. He was built like a wall, huge and muscular and he was adorned in the same armor as the man who had pursued her in the market – a guard. A smirk crept onto her face as he joined her on her way down the dirt street. He was at least two foot taller than her with shaggy brunette locks that hugged his face. His bones were sharp, his jaw square, and his auburn eyes burned like the fires that had purged those who were blamed for her deeds. His eyes were the spectacle that drew her in again and again. They made her heart flutter. They were gorgeous and yet filled with anger and destruction. She could feel her hands getting clammy as she walked beside him. Her heart beat faster and her cheeks burned as she walked by his side. He was magnificent to her – always saving the day when she was caught in her antics. He was her knight in shining armor when she needed him most. She smiled softly until words left his lips.

"There was a commotion in the square." He stated plainly. She jolted. Her smile faded and she turned to him, crimson eyes wide as she recalled the chaos she had caused. Word had spread quickly. "Are you okay? I know you like to spend time there in the mornings." The words he picked were precise, careful to avoid admitting he knew of her crimes. He did. He always had. There had been many times when he had been the guard chasing her – times when they played a game of cat and mouse in the crowds. He always caught her, slamming her against a wall before telling her to move along. He would always find her later, telling her how gorgeous she had looked pinned against the brick walls of the buildings, telling her what a fine wife she would make for him once he tamed her. She had the bruises to remind her.

"I'm fine." She lied, the images of the massacre still playing over and over in her mind and the taste of blood still fresh on her palate. Her stomach twisted as the thoughts danced in her mind, the screams still ringing in her ears, and the craving for blood still boiling inside of her. She tried not to let any of it show. "People must have just been a little excited or something." She shrugged. "I'm sure you can calm them down in the stocks, eh? I mean, aren't you becoming a bit liberal with your punishments anyway? What better time to exercise that?"

"Don't push it." He warned with a glare. "You're guilty of plenty of crimes. If anyone needs to be in the stocks, it's you." He leaned closer, roughly grabbing her face and pulling her closer to him. He smelled of firewood and smoke – of a cold night by a fire. She gulped. "You're just lucky you have me to keep you safe." He released her face and she rubbed her cheek gingerly.

"Did you get it all settled?" She asked, turning away so that he couldn't see her grimace as she stretched her jaw.

"Oh, of course." He bellowed. Relief washed over her. It seemed as though her powers had evaporated from the area much more quickly than usual. There would be no more murders today; or at least none that were her fault. "The man responsible for starting it all is in our custody and will be dealt with accordingly." He patted the hilt of his sword, a wide smile on his face.

"Dealt with?" A twinge of guilt wormed its way into Astrid's stomach. Nausea began to swirl inside of her. "I mean, I'm sure he didn't *mean* to start all of that, Dane. Couldn't you just, I dunno, lock him up for about forty-eight hours?"

"Hell no! He's a menace to society! Anyone who causes a panic like that should be lynched the moment we get our hands on them, but that's not what the rest of the guard wants, you know?" Rolling his eyes he added, "They like to ask prisoners a hundred questions before we string them up." He scoffed, adding, "He deserves to die."

"He didn't mean to do it!" She argued as her stomach threatened to spill its contents on the street. She gripped the fabric of her shirt, hoping the feeling would lessen as she clenched her hand around the wad in her hand.

"He tore open loads of people!" Dane screamed inches from her face. She could feel his spit splashing on her skin as he roared his words. "I think he meant to. People watched their families die today, Astrid. Besides, did you see the commotion he caused?" He crossed his arms, shaking his head. "He's a monster." Astrid's heart sank. It wasn't that man's fault and he was going to die for it. He was a victim of her power – he was innocent. Tears formed in her eyes. She could taste the acidic vomit in the back of her throat.

"I have to go."

"Astrid, I'm not being cruel. I just –" As he reached out to her, she ducked away from his grasp, turning away with a light whimper.

"I'm gonna be sick." Before Dane could react, she dashed down the street.

It was all her fault. Tears rolled down her face as she rounded a corner, falling into the dirt before scurrying to her feet and taking off again. She could feel the vomit rising up, pushing its way into her mouth. She could feel the squirming and burning in her. It was going to pour out at any moment. She clasped her hand over her mouth as tightly as she could as the squirming pushed harder inside her. She couldn't vomit here – she would be burned alive if she did. *Just a little farther.* Her heart pounded. She could see her shack – her sanctuary.

She burst through the door, allowing herself the release she needed. Black sludge burst from her lips. Spiders and snakes fell from her mouth onto the floorboard, dissipating into a black mist soon after coming into existence. Astrid fell to her knees, panting before spitting out the last of the goo and a lingering spider. She wiped her face, watching as the mist vanished. She groaned, climbing to her feet and walking over to the corner of the shack that served as her bedroom. It was all one room – that was all she had ever needed. A bed in one corner, a small, cozy stove in another, and a bath tub in a third. She was barely here anyway. She only showed up to drop off her stolen goods or to hide away from the eyes she feared might see her misdoings.

"Disgusting." She muttered as she flopped down on her bed. "The sun hasn't even been up that long and I'm already done with this shit." She glared at the wall, her body exhausted from the anxiety and fear she had felt all morning. "I swear, this is too much." She rolled over, rubbing her stomach and closing her eyes. "I'll just," she yawned, "sleep. Yeah, sleep. It'll be better tomorrow." She closed her eyes, snuggling into her pillow. "This'll all go away by tomorrow."

* * *

Astrid's heart pounded as she ran through the forest, the trudging of the mob chasing after her. Where was it? She shook her head. What was she even looking for? Whatever it was, it was screaming for her, calling out to her. She clasped her hands over her ears. Her stomach felt aflutter with excitement and anxiety about potentially finding this…thing.

She darted through the undergrowth, pushing back leaves and branches. *Where is it?* She slipped in the mud, falling on her rear. As she looked up. She saw herself surrounded by mirrors. She shuddered as a crimson-eyed reflection of herself stared blankly back at her. *Where is it?* She ran through the maze of glass as she was followed by the field of torches and swords. Something in the distance was beating – a heart. It was close. She could hear it so clearly. She held her breath as she looked over the dark water of a lake before her, cackling echoing in the distance. Where was it?

She took another step, but, as she did, a pounding echoed in her ears. It wasn't the beating of the heart she searched for. She paused, glancing around. It sounded much more like someone was beating on a door. What was that? It rang out again. She cocked her head to one side, confused. Again.

* * *

Astrid growled as the loud banging at her door stirred her from her slumber. Groggily, she glanced around the dark room. It was night. The mirrors, the mob, the running – it had all been a dream. She winced as the pounding rang throughout the shack once again.

"Hold your horses!" She called out to the door, swinging her feet over her bed. Her boots had barely touched the floorboards when the door burst open with a 'crash.' She yelped, flinching as wooden shards from the doorframe scattered across the room. "What the hell?!" She screamed as Dane clamored into her domain, glancing over his shoulder occasionally as though he expected someone to follow him.

"We need to go!" His voice dripped with authority.

"Get lost, Dane! You can't just bust into someone's house–"

"We need to *leave!*"

She squeaked as he roughly grabbed her arm, yanking her from her bed and dragging her toward the door. She staggered behind him, hardly able to keep up with his long, hurried stride. He leaned out the hole that had once housed her door and assessed their surroundings. "Seems to be clear. They aren't here yet." He muttered as screams rang through the air. He pulled her out of her home and onto the dirt path. She could see a glowing in the distance – a fire. The town was on fire.

"They?" Astrid asked as she desperately tried to pull away. His grip was too strong as he yanked her along behind him. He pulled her to his side.

"The angels." He breathed out with a shudder.

"Angels?" She blinked dumbly at the word. "What are angels doing here? Don't most of them live in the East?" She sighed in relief as Dane's hand finally released her bicep. Pain still shot through her arm. It was going to bruise for sure, but at least she wasn't being dragged anymore.

"They came here looking for a demon."

She staggered back slightly. *A demon?* Her heart pounded. Was that what she was? It was bad enough before, but being a demon would be something else entirely. The same nausea she had felt earlier in the day revisited her. The world seemed shaky and like it might melt away. She staggered slightly, grabbing Dane's arm to steady herself. Her mouth was dry and she felt numb – like reality was slipping away. A lump formed in her throat, but she could feel her breathing getting faster.

"Wh-Why would they think that Crimson Barrow had a demon problem?" She couldn't force herself to look into Dane's burning eyes. She felt her own crimson orbs might betray her – that Dane might see the truth behind her twenty-five years of lies.

"They've had reports." She shuddered, remembering the hooded figure in the marketplace. They *had* known. They knew exactly who had caused the issue and, worse yet, they knew even more than she did about herself.

"From who?" The words sounded as though they came from somewhere else entirely – as though they hadn't left her own lips.

"Who knows? They just think all the random violence we've been having over the years has been caused by a demon. They said it can make some kind of cloud to spread vice energy or something like that." He shoved her back as a few citizens clamored by as a building collapsed in the distance. "We've got to get out of here. We don't have time for anymore stupid questions."

"Wait!" She all but screamed, dodging his grip. It was her. The angels were there because of *her*. Her heart had never beat this fast before. "Why do we have to leave? I mean, they're *angels*! They're good, right? They should listen to reason."

"They're killing everyone!" The words crept slowly through her brain, repeating over and over again. "They're going to keep killing until they find the demon!" They'd keep killing until they found *her*. People were dying because the angels were looking for a demon that the people didn't even realize existed.

"You want me to leave?" It was all her fault. Her breathing seemed so fast. She couldn't control it and it felt like it was getting shallower and shallower. "You want me to let everyone just get slaughtered?" Her voice was weak, squeaking as she spoke. Her body felt as though it was sinking into a void. Everything except for what was in front of her seemed like a blur. Nausea rested in her chest again.

"We don't have a choice here!" Dane growled.

"We don't have a choice?" She glanced toward the town as another scream rang out. Flames roared up, dancing as though they were celebrating the fall of the town. Homes fell to the ground. Families deep in the maze of buildings were watching as their loved ones were exterminated. They wouldn't be able to tell the angels anything about the demon because they didn't know anything about one. She had managed to wiggle out of trouble for twenty-five years. She seemed normal to them by all accounts – no one would think to identify her as the demon.

She imagined the townspeople cowering below the winged figures as they were helplessly executed. How were they supposed to defend themselves against trained soldiers with powers that humans could only dream of? She bit her lip. They would all be killed if she didn't do something. Everyone she had ever known would die and it would all be because of her.

"Look," she began, turning back toward Dane, a passion boiling in her eyes, "if you wanna run away, fine! I'm not leaving these people to some homicidal, glorified pigeons though! We have a choice! *I* have a choice! I'm not leaving these people with no way out!" Dane snarled at her words and lunged at her, only to miss by inches.

"You're making a mistake, you dumb bitch!" He called after her as she disappeared into the rubble and destruction.

Astrid tried not to look around. The bodies that littered the streets wore familiar faces. The shops that had been reduced to rubble were all places she had known. Her home was being reduced to nothing before her eyes. It was all going to be gone soon and she wasn't sure what she could do about it. A scream pierced her mind, peeling her away from her thoughts.

She turned, catching a glimpse of a man in shimmering armor standing over a young girl. She was no more than seven or eight but he stood over her with a blade drawn, cackling. He wasn't a Crimson Barrow guard. Instead, he wore metal that looked pristine and white with a symbol in the midst that resembled a sun pointing in all directions at once. He wasn't an angel, but he was certainly a member of their ranks. He lifted his sword up as tears rolled down the girl's face. She was pleading for her life, pinned and unable to flee.

The girl looked over, catching Astrid's gaze. The world seemed to fall silent as her small mouth formed one word. *Please.* The soldier grinned above her, his sword falling toward the child. The rage inside of Astrid grew, inching through her veins like a virus. Her own words formed a chorus in her mind. *I have a choice.*

It was automatic. She hadn't even willed the movement. She tackled the soldier, pushing him to the ground. He let out a grunt as they tumbled down onto the debris together, rolling over stone and broken glass in a tangled heap.

"Run!" Astrid screamed to the girl. "Get out of here!" The child nodded, frantically staggering to her feet and taking off through the streets. As the small figure disappeared through the smoke, Astrid smiled softly. She had saved her. For once, she had saved someone rather than causing the panic and death.

"Bitch!" The soldier growled, slamming the hilt of his sword into Astrid's head. She yelped, falling back. A gasp flew from her lungs as his foot collided with her stomach, launching her through the air. She crashed through the wooden wreckage, gasping for the air that had been knocked out of her body.

She had barely filled her lungs again before he yanked her up by her dark locks. He laughed as he lifted her off the ground, watching her squirm in his grasp. She gritted her teeth, clawing at his hand, but he didn't relinquish his hold in the slightest.

"You're going to die here, little girl." He cackled out. She grunted as she swung forward, knocking him squarely in the jaw with her knee. Astrid fell back to the ground as the soldier grabbed his injured face and stomped in pain. He let out a frustrated roar as she inched away from him. A twinkle of shining metal caught her eye. He had dropped his sword upon being kneed in the face.

Her heart raced as she glanced at the soldier. She dove for the blade. He swung his fist at her, plowing through the air just above her head as she rolled away from him, sword in hand. He opened his mouth, crude words on his tongue, but was quickly silenced.

Blood trickled down to the ground in front of her as Astrid pulled her shaking hands away from the weapon's hilt. The soldier fell to his knees, the blade penetrating his forehead. His mouth seemed to be trying to find words, but the only sounds that come forth were gags and gargles. He collapsed on the ground, a heap of flesh and blood.

Astrid's stomach twisted as a red puddle formed around the man's body. She panted, stepping back from the corpse, her hand sliding down to her sore stomach. The bruise that was forming was nothing compared to the craving that was stirring inside of her as the aroma of blood invaded the air. She cringed away from the body, turning the other direction, taking a deep breath before starting back through the streets.

She winced as her cravings cried out, louder and louder as she passed the corpses strewn throughout Crimson Barrow. Her head was spinning. She could smell it everywhere. The town was a sea of blood and her insides wanted nothing more than to absorb every drop. She gripped her stomach as it cramped with desire. She rubbed her eyes, attempting to will away the blurry vision that was starting to set in. *What's happening?* She shook her head, her hair flopping around vigorously with the movement. The hunger was only growing.

"Ah. Perhaps you can answer my questions." Astrid jolted as a voice echoed off of the walls around her. It seemed to be coming from everywhere and nowhere at once and her blurred vision wasn't aiding in finding the source. Her stomach cramped again. This time she had a specific target she wanted, however. She wanted the man speaking to her. She wanted to rip out his insides after she found him. She wanted to devour his organs and drink up his blood. She shuddered at her own urges.

"Who are you?" She called back to the voice, unsure of where to face as she spoke.

"That's irrelevant." The voice stated. A large, looming figure landed atop a pile of rubble in front of her, silhouetted by the burning wreckage. The metallic shimmer of the armor was almost blinding as the figure stepped down, revealing himself to her.

Astrid cursed under her breath as the urge to murder the man intensified. Large white wings fluttered behind him as he slowly walked towards her, his sword still dripping with the blood of his last victim. She wanted to taste the red liquid, but she felt something even stronger in the moment. Wrath. It burned inside of her. It consumed every numbed part of her body. She felt hot – fiery. She gritted her teeth and clenched her fists as her heart raced. She tried to shake it away, but it was persistent.

"Where is the demon?" The angel demanded, closing in on her. She winced as a sharp, stabbing pain shot through her brain. She could barely stand it. It felt as though someone had taken their sword and sliced through her mind. He smirked, spinning his sword in his hand and splattering the blood across the ground. "If you don't speak, little girl, I'll kill you too." She glared at him. His words seemed so distant, but there was something that sounded close enough to touch – his heart. She could hear each beat in his chest, each pump of blood. The thumping pounded again and again in her head. Everywhere she looked, everything seemed to have a red film over it. It all seemed unreal – like a dream. "Can't speak?" The angel scoffed. "Then you're of no use to me."

His blade rose into the air, sparkling in the flame's light and reflecting in Astrid's eyes. Still shaking, she stood transfixed by the blood dripping from it. The world seemed to be in slow motion as it dripped from the cold metal, falling toward her. It splashed down on her cheek, warm and revitalizing. As it touched her, the rage inside her overcame the cravings and the fear. It exploded, overtaking her.

She slammed her body against him, throwing him off balance slightly. He staggered back, laughing at her attempt. He soon was silenced as he noticed that his breastplate was rusting and fading away into nonexistence. He snarled, ripping it off of his body and throwing it to the ground. "Demon!" He howled, launching himself into the air through the smoke.

He was out of her sight. She had no way of knowing where he would come from and she no idea how to repeat what she had done. Taking in a shaky breath, she hazarded a quick glance down to her hands. The black, translucent mist that she had released only hours ago was swirling around them.

"Damn it! What did I do now?" She muttered as she tried to hold her sleeves over the shimmering, black mist that encircled her hands. It was no use. They weren't long enough. She cursed, recoiling slightly as she glanced around.

She yelped, jumping out of the way as the angel suddenly pelted down from the sky. His sword swept by her face, slicing open her cheek. She stumbled back, falling to the ground to stare helplessly up at him as he laughed and licked some of her blood from his blade.

"You know, you're lucky my orders are to take you alive…for now. Otherwise, I'd make it a point to make your death as painful as–" His smile faded. The metal of his blade began to corrode. Her blood rusted the steel, burning it away as she and the angel stared. They glanced at one another, horror on the man's face.

"Uhm, you might want to induce vomiting." She pointed out. Frantically, he threw the bladeless hilt to the side and tore open his shirt. Blood poured from a hole where his stomach had been. He screamed as his flesh burned away and his insides fell to the ground. She scurried backwards as he fell to his knees, reaching out to her.

"I…have…to take…the de…mon…back…." The pounding of his heart finally faded from Astrid's ears as he fell to the ground, his body half corroded in a puddle of blood and organs. She panted heavily as she pulled her knees up to her chest. She had done it. She had taken care of one of the angels to help the town. She almost smiled, but her joy was shattered by a familiar voice behind her.

"What the hell?" She groaned, turning to see Dane standing over her. His face was twisted in disgust and horror, but he wasn't gawking at the angel or the carnage. His gaze was fixed on her.

"Dane, I can explain." She started as she staggered to her feet. Her stomach was cramping so badly now that she nearly doubled over. She had never wanted blood so badly in her life. She clenched her teeth, whimpering as everything inside of her screamed at her to turn around and eat the mangled corpse behind her.

"I think everyone can at this point!" Dane shouted as he drew his sword. "Stay back, you filthy demon!"

"Dane, please just listen to me!" She pleaded, taking another step in his direction. She yelped as he lunged forward, bashing her in the face with the metal bracer on his arm. She coughed up a mouthful of blood as she fell to the ground. Tears welled up in her eyes as she opened her mouth to plead with him, but she couldn't find any words that would rectify everything she had done. She winced as the bracer collided with the back of her head before corroding into nothingness. She was the monster.

Dane raised his sword above his head, bloodlust and malice burning in his auburn eyes. She stared into them. They raged like the flames around them. It was like a nightmare as his lips formed the words 'you deserve to die.' Her tears soaked her face as his sword sliced through the air.

Everything blurred together as she let out a scream. Dane dropped his weapon, covering his ears as he screamed in pain. Blood dripped down the side of his face.

"Damn monster! Even your voice is unholy!" He fell to his knees, hands clasped over either side of his head. As he struggled to regain his composure, Astrid staggered to her feet and darted through the street, glancing back at the only person she had ever trusted.

She moved through the streets as quickly as she could. Dane knew. Everyone would. The worst part of the whole thing was that she had *just* found out what she was. She had lived her whole life knowing that she wasn't normal. She knew there was something in her being that wasn't there for everyone else, but she had never expected the brand of 'demon.' She jolted as the small girl she had saved earlier caught sight of her and let out a shrill scream.

Astrid nearly tripped as she rushed away as quickly as her feet could carry her, slipping into an alley. Panting she glanced back before leaning against a stone wall. It didn't seem as though anyone had seen her hide. She dropped down to the ground with a groan, glancing over beside her. Her hand flew over her mouth. In a puddle, she saw what she had become.

Her shaking fingers reached up to her head and lightly touched the black horns that swooped back. Her fingers ran across the small ridges in them as tears rolled down her face. As she sobbed, a black tail with a spade tip wrapped around her legs. She screamed, jumping up and stumbling to the opposite side of the alley. To her horror, it followed her every move. She looked behind her, realizing it was attached to her body. She groaned, flopping down on the ground and covering her face with her arm.

"What am I supposed to do?" She asked the emptiness around her.

"Astrid!" She jolted to attention as Dane's voice rang through the streets. "I know you're around here! Come out and face your death with dignity!"

She crouched behind a barrel as Dane passed by, shouting his demands in all directions. She withdrew from his presence before darting away. The other end of the alley led her to the edge of Crimson Barrow. Samba Forest loomed over her, its foreboding foliage daring her to enter as the sounds of angry citizens began to fill the air. Dane had told everyone. He had told them that it was all her fault – that she was the demon.

Her throat felt as though something large and sickening was stuck in it. Crimson Barrow was all she knew. It was her home. She had never left before, but she would die if she stayed. She rubbed the tears from her face and took a deep breath before starting into the maze of trees.

Years of avoiding the forest were instantly transformed into regrets. Everyone in Crimson Barrow had described it as a place to be feared and avoided – a place where nightmares and monsters grew. Astrid couldn't see any of those things, however. It seemed that the sounds of the mob forming in Crimson Barrow couldn't penetrate the lush greenery that surrounded her. Their anger couldn't drain the beauty from the black, velvety flowers that grew on vines swirling up the trees. As she reached out and touched one of the petals, she noticed that the aura around her hands had faded. Her tail, however, was still flicking happily around her as the moonlight sparkled down on the moist foliage.

As she trudged deeper and deeper into the forest, minutes turned into hours and everywhere she looked she saw the spectacular visions. It was gorgeous; a true show of how wonderful nature could be. Fireflies fluttered around like stars in the darkness of the forest. Pixies landed on flower buds and coerced them to bloom. It was entrancing until a realization seeped into her mind.

"Shit. I'm lost. Like, really, really lost." She sighed as she plopped down on the ground. Her hand slowly drifted down to her stomach. The bruising and the cramping still throbbed away. To make matters worse, the look on Dane's face was still clear in her mind. Her heart sank.

She had thought that maybe, somehow, they would have some inkling of a future together, that he would make good on his promises. Seeing his reaction to what she was had firmly destroyed those hopes. Wherever he was, he hated her and everything she was.

She groaned before climbing back to her feet, trudging and pouting through the woods. After three sorrowful steps, however she felt a sharp jerk against her ankle. A tightly knotted rope dragged her through the grass and mud unforgivingly, slamming her head against a rock and sending her into a void of darkness as she dangled upside-down from a tree.

Chapter Two:

The darkness around Astrid faded away as sunlight aggressively burrowed through her eyelids, waking her. It felt as though it was penetrating her brain. Her head was pounding. She groaned, opening her eyes. The lush forest still surrounded her, but it was upside-down. She glanced at her feet, scoffing at the noose around her ankle before looking ahead again. Before her stood a looming figure – a man. He had honey colored eyes and auburn hair that hugged his jawline. His skin was tanned from years of working in the sun and scars riddled his bare chest.

He had to be a hunter. Of that much, Astrid was sure. His attire looked as though it was made with scraps of hide. It was handstitched and, by the looks of it, by someone rather unskilled. It was certainly an undesirable look.

"Who the hell are you?" She asked, narrowing her eyes at him.

"I should be asking you that." He all but growled. Astrid squirmed under his intrusive gaze. She assumed some of his attitude was probably stemming from the fact that her horns still adorned her head and her tail still danced behind her. She feared this might become the new norm. After all, news would have to travel from Crimson Barrow eventually. This man might even know. She had no idea how long she had been hanging there after all. News could already be here. She groaned. The man raised an eyebrow at her. "What are you even doing in this forest?"

"Oh, ya know doin' some demon stuff." She quipped, rolling her eyes at the question. Part of her felt put off by how quickly his tone had lost its aggression, but it soon regained its seriousness as he stifled a smile and continued his interrogation.

"Demon stuff, huh?" The way his lips curved into a smile was reminiscent of the way Dane would smile at her. She cringed. The last thing she wanted was for anything to remind her of the guard hunting her back in Crimson Barrow. Those lips reminded her of every horrible word Dane had said to her – they reminded her of lips that had hissed out threats and promises to kill her. "What, pray tell, does that include exactly?"

Shrugging, Astrid remarked, "Long walks on the beach, dances in the moonlight, hanging upside-down from trees while trapped in snares – the works, really." The man crossed his arms. "What?" Astrid continued. "Don't I look like a vicious demon to you?" She gave a half-hearted, phony snarl. "You'd have to be a moron to not be terrified of me. That or just someone who is aware of how dense someone has to be to get caught in a snare." She sighed. "Either way, think you could let me down?" His smile faded as he narrowed his eyes.

"I don't know about that. I barely know anything about you. "

"Scared I'll do demon stuff to ya, huh?" She asked. "I assure you: I have no idea how."

"You don't know how to use your powers?" He asked, eyes wide. Astrid fell silent for a moment. She glanced away from the man, suddenly feeling embarrassed by her own incompetence.

"Look, can you just–"

"Yeah, yeah. Hang on." He gave a wave of his hand to silence her before heading off behind the tree. After a moment of silence, Astrid toppled to the forest floor with a loud 'oof.' The dewy grass caressed her body for a moment as she muttered a profanity. Climbing to her feet, she straightened her clothes as the hunter reappeared, a wide smile on his face.

He had clearly been uncomfortable being so serious before, but, even now, Astrid didn't feel the need to trust him. After all, the last person she had trusted had tried to run her through with a sword.

"So! How did you come to be here?" He asked with a bit more pep than Astrid appreciated. She ignored him, turning away and starting in the other direction. "Where are you going?" He called after her. "You can't just wonder off in the woods! Wait!" His hand slipped around her wrist, but she quickly jerked away from him and increased her pace. "Hey, lady, wait! Look, there's a town nearby! I can take you!"

Astrid rolled her eyes. She didn't need to be in another town. An angel could easily find her there. Worse than that, an angel might not find her. She shuddered as she thought of the countless lives that had been lost all because the angels couldn't find her in Crimson Barrow.

The thought of Dane screaming at her raced through her mind again. He hated her now. She gripped the fabric of her shirt. When did her heart start beating this fast? She shook her head and tried to continue on, but her breathing soon matched her heartbeat. Nausea rolled around in her stomach. It burned her throat. It was like all the air was gone around her – as though something was stuck in her throat, blocking her breath. Her hand flew over her mouth as tears slowly began to form, rolling down her cheeks. What was happening?

The same hand grabbed her bicep, yanking her to a halt. More memories of Dane pooled into her mind as the man touched her bruised arm. She gritted her teeth as the hunter pulled her back toward him. She collided with his muscular chest just as the nausea peaked. Black sludge and snakes poured from her mouth, splashing across the man's chest and on the ground between them.

"O-Oh, wow." He remarked, the smile finally fading from his face. "That's…uh…a new one. Can't say I've seen anyone do that before."

"It's a…a demon thing." Astrid stated between gasps. She spit out a spider before wiping her mouth. The vomit vanished into mist as she turned away from him once again.

"Ah." The man cringed, looking down at his chest where the black sludge had been. "Anyway! So, as I was saying," he rapidly continued, ignoring Astrid's attempts to escape him, "there's a town you can rest at."

"I don't need to rest. I need to…," she paused for a moment, measuring her response before finishing, "get somewhere. I need to get where I was going."

"And where is that?" The only thing that was as annoying as his smile was his questioning and that damned attitude he had – like he knew what was best for her even though they had just met. She glared at him. "Okay, so you're not going to tell me?" *How observant*, she thought as she continued on through Samba Forest. "Well, if you're going on a trip, you can at least stop by town and prepare. You don't have to stay. Just come and get some supplies." The silence persisted. "Look, I don't know why you don't want to come with me, but you're not doing too well in this forest alone. Just…let me help." He smiled again. She wanted so badly to punch him, but she restrained herself. "Besides, you could at least get a bite to eat there." Silence fell between them for a moment before Astrid spun around on her heels. Her crimson eyes narrowed at the man and she leaned forward with a glare plastered on her face.

"Just for food and supplies." She muttered.

* * *

The town of Doewood was a small hunting village with log cabins that lined the dirt streets. The petite cabins were nothing compared to the large, stone fort the town circled around, however. It loomed largely over the other buildings, casting a shadow around its base.

There looked to be hunters everywhere. They went in and out of the forest as they pleased, seemingly without concern. They laughed and smiled as though Samba Forest was nothing to fear – a drastic difference from the hunters of Crimson Barrow who ventured out with tears streaming down their faces and their final goodbyes having been said. Despite these differences, the only thing that held Astrid's interest for any significant time was her own lack of spectacle. It seemed no one was bothered by her sleek horns or her wiggling tail. In fact, most of the citizens didn't even cast a look in her direction. They remained fixated on their tasks, ignoring the demon in their midst. Even a pair of burly looking guards sauntered by her as though she looked utterly normal to them.

"What is this?" She asked as they rounded a corner. Her crimson eyes scanned the crowds for some sign of panic but it was absent.

"Well," the hunter started, gesturing toward some stalls, "this is the marketplace. This is where you–"

"I know what a marketplace is." Astrid barked out. "What I mean is: what's up with these people? It's like they don't even care about me."

"Should they?" The question baffled her. Crimson Barrow's citizens would have been attempting to hack off her head by now, yet this town was acting as though her demonism was no big deal. She considered this anomaly for a moment, before shrugging. This was lucky if nothing else and she wasn't about to argue with having a little luck for the first time since her demonic appendages had formed.

"I suppose not."

As they continued, Astrid glanced around, sizing up the citizens. They were tanned and chipper people, workers who stayed out in the sun for most of the day and appreciated small joys. A woman passed by her with a set of three children who smiled at her as they darted down the street. She gave a slight wave back. The mother smiled softly at her before calmly following after her children. *So normal*, she thought. *It's perfect*.

She paused, stopping in her tracks as she caught sight of something new to the scene. In the midst of all of the people happily exchanging wares stood a man like none she had seen before. Her jaw fell open as she gaped. The lower half of his body looked like that of a muscular, brown stallion while his upper half was that of a tanned man. The vendor he spoke to seemed unfazed by the man's strange body – he acted as though it was a normality he saw daily. Astrid stuttered out a few syllables, but couldn't quite form a coherent question as she watched the man trot to another stall.

"Hm?" The hunter rejoined her, looking in the direction of her gaze. "What's up?"

"That man…he's…he's a horse." She muttered, cocking her head to one side.

"Well, not exactly. He's a centaur."

"A what?" Astrid asked, jerking her head toward the hunter and narrowing her eyes. She had never seen a man who was half horse before. It hadn't even been in her imagination before now. Crimson Barrow had been a place where only humans and angels were welcomed, and, since angels tended to stay in the East, she had only experienced humans before.

Her reality had always been that humans hated anything that wasn't human, but, here in Doewood, her perception of the world was being shattered. It was awe-inspiring. Awe-inspiring and also, in a way, unsettling. Everything she knew had come crashing down around her in what felt like such a short amount of time. Her whole reality had been wrong. She jolted as the hunter gave her a nudge, cuing her to follow him and leave the centaur to his business.

"There it is." He stated, gesturing toward a large building nestled in the market. Like most other buildings in Doewood, it was wooden. Two large, green doors adorned the front and through the huge windows on either side, Astrid could see what looked to be drunken patrons downing mead inside. "The tavern. We can eat here." Astrid rolled her eyes at the explanation, but followed none-the-less.

The interior of the building was rustic, illuminated by the soft glow of candlelight. Hunting trophies littered the walls. Astrid shuddered at the dead eyes of the animals that stared at her as they made their way to a wooden table. It was filled with notches and carvings from hunters who apparently didn't know how to keep their knives sheathed. She groaned.

These were the places that Astrid had tried to avoid during her life, bustling and full of people ready to be infected by her powers. She squirmed in place as she took her seat on a hard, wooden stool.

A busty woman appeared by the table, hands on hips and staring expectantly. Astrid glanced up at her for a moment before quickly avoiding the woman's gaze. Her face looked stern, annoyed. She wondered for a moment if it was about her horns or her tail that drooped behind her, but her fears were soon placated by the hunter who sat opposite of her.

"This is Rose." He introduced. He smiled widely adding, "She's not human either." He turned back to the woman as Astrid looked between the two rapidly in disbelief.

"She what?!" She was ignored as the hunter spoke to Rose on her behalf.

"I found this girl in the woods. She could use a good meal." Rose nodded before disappearing into the mob of people bouncing around the tavern. Astrid's gaze followed the seemingly human woman's path, wondering what in the world she might be. Half of her wondered why the hunter had bothered with introductions despite the fact that she had insisted she wouldn't be staying. She knew she couldn't – it could spell disaster for Doewood. "So!" The man leaned back in his chair. "Do you have a name, mystery girl?"

"Everyone has a name." Astrid snarled as she glanced around the tavern. Everyone seemed human. Had the hunter lied about Rose or were they just like she used to be: someone who looked human but wasn't? Her heart dropped a bit as she realized she was the only one who looked like a monster in the tavern. Her tail drooped further.

"Well, could you grace me with yours?" The hunter asked coolly, bringing Astrid's attention back to the conversation.

"Why?" She spat, sparing a moment to scowl. "I told you – I'm not staying here."

"Then does it really matter if I know?"

"Tell me this," Astrid began, shooting her glare at him again and slamming her hands down on the table, "how the hell is everyone here be so calm about a demon? Do they not know what demons do?"

"Everyone here knows good and well what demons can do." His statement was simple, almost emotionless. He leaned forward, resting his arms on the table.

"Then why are they so calm?" She demanded, her tail flicking behind her in agitation. Was he purposely avoiding giving her answers or was this really how annoying his personality was? Either way, she hated it.

"They realize that demons are no more likely to be killers than humans. Demons are just people like everyone else." He shrugged as he made his comments. Astrid's brain whirled as she thought about the day before and about how her powers had caused a mob and countless deaths. *No more likely than a human? Bullshit.* "So…your name?" He asked again as Rose placed two heaping plates of roasted meat and vegetables in front of them. She glanced over at Astrid and gave a smile that looked forced and out of place on her face before instructing them both to enjoy their meal. The crimson gaze of the demon followed after Rose again as she vanished into the crowd. What the hell was she?

Ignoring the hunter's question, Astrid stabbed a fork into the meat and shoved some of it into her mouth. She devoured the seared morsel quickly, barely chewing it at all. It wasn't as tantalizing as the blood she had consumed, but it was food.

The hunter sighed, rubbing his fingers through his auburn locks. "Okay, well, I guess I can start then: my name is Rilis." She glanced at him as she continued to shovel food into her mouth.

"I told you that I'm not staying. Introductions are a waste of time," she swallowed another bite of meat before adding, "but it's Astrid." She opened her mouth to say something further, but stopped short. From across the room, she saw a familiar visage. A chill ran up her spine and she dropped the fork. Her tail froze behind her, no longer flicking with excitement over the food.

A hooded figure stood among several men. It leaned against the wall, glowing blue eyes watching those nearby. Astrid muttered a profanity before jumping to her feet and scuffling out the door and into the street. Taking a deep breath, she rushed into the busiest sector she could find. *Hide,* she thought. *Hide in plain sight if you need to, but just hide.* She could hear Rilis calling after her, but she ignored him.

She collided with a woman, apologizing as they asked her if she was okay. *Run,* she thought. *Don't let them see you. They'll kill everyone.* She panted as she darted down the street, only stopping when a large shadow consumed her, darkening the area around her. She looked up to see the stone fort looming above her. Still panting, she nestled into a small crevasse in the stone wall.

Her heart raced and her breathing was shallow. She could feel her body shaking. Her stomach turned. She wracked her brain about what the figure's presence could mean. Was Doewood about to suffer the same fate as Crimson Barrow? She tugged at a strand of her hair and bit her lip. What could she even do to stop it?

Her eyes shot up, scanning the crowd for any sign of halos or fluttering white wings. Nothing stood out, but that didn't mean anything. Perhaps they could hide their wings and halos just as she had managed to somehow hide her horns and her tail.

"Hey, kiddo. You okay?" A smooth voice drizzled down over her. Astrid turned to see a woman, only a couple of years older than herself, bending down beside the wall, offering a sweet smile. She smelled like salt water and a crisp breeze. Her brunette hair flowed down over her shoulders in waves. Glancing up slightly, Astrid caught sight of the brown tricorn hat decorated with tropical flowers and feathers. It sat atop the woman's head like a crown.

"You're…," she muttered, her tail drifting away from the stranger. The woman cocked her head to one side, her seaweed green eyes looking up toward her own hat.

"Ahhhh, yeah. This?" She pointed to the accessory. "Yeah. I'm a pirate." She paused for a moment, waiting for Astrid's response. The demon wrapped her tail around her legs, maintaining her silence as the woman's smile faded. "Can't say I blame ya for not trusting me. People can be shitheads." The woman plopped down on the ground. "Name's Valentina by the way." She flashed another smile at Astrid before adding, "You can call me Val though." Valentina leaned over, eyeing where Astrid's gaze landed. She looked over the crowd before turning back to the demon and nudging her. "Which one?"
"What?" Astrid muttered.

"Which one bothered you?"

"I…uhm…none of these people bothered me." She scooted away from the pirate and pulled her knees to her chest, hugging her legs tightly.

"You sure? Cause if one of these losers did, I could make 'em hurt." Valentina winked at her and slammed her fist into the palm of her hand. Something about her was refreshing compared to the others.

"There's someone here," she admitted before she knew what she was saying. "They destroyed my home." She looked down as she thought about the massacre the night before. "They're after me – hunting me."

"Hunting you?" The woman's eyes widened a bit. "Why would they do that, kiddo?"

"I think," Astrid pulled her knees close to her chin, "it's because I'm a demon." She furrowed her brow and made herself as small as she could.

"Well, shit." The woman stretched before hopping to her feet. "C'mon. Let's check it out." She offered her hand to Astrid, pulling the demon to her feet and locking their arms together.

"I don't think that's a good idea."

"It's a perfect idea!" Valentina chirped loudly. "If there's someone hunting demons," she smirked, a blue mist forming around her before solidifying into a thick, blue tail with fins at its tip and a swirling, pearl-like horn from her forehead, "I feel like maybe we should both know about them." Astrid yanked her arm from Valentina's grip. Her eyes widened as she took in the sight of the horn and tail.

"Y-You're a demon!" She exclaimed.

"Got it in one, kid. So, about that demon hunter…."

"How are you a demon?!" Astrid circled around Valentina, reaching out toward the woman's scaled tail. Before her fingers could make contact, the blue extremity snapped to life, knocking up dirt from the street. She flinched, finding herself soaked rather than coated in dust. Confusion filled her as she looked up at the laughing pirate. "Wha…How did you–" Valentina patted Astrid's head, earning herself a glare.

"I'm a water demon." She pointed to her tail. "Hence the fins. I can turn stuff to water." She kicked up more dirt with her boot, turning it to water and watching it drizzle back to the ground. "It takes a lot of energy to change something into something else though, so I tend to not do that much – way easier to just manipulate the water that's already around, ya know?"

She grabbed Astrid, pulling her close and directing her gaze to a man stepping out of a building with a tankard of mead. She moved her finger only slightly but it was enough to cue the liquid to spray up into the man's face. He screamed profanities and blamed the tankard for the event, throwing it to the ground before staggering off in a drunken rage.

Astrid bit her lip to try to contain her laughter, but Valentina made no such attempt. She burst into a fit of giggles as her tail wiggled behind her. "See? Easier and much more fun!"

"That's amazing!" Astrid shouted, her tail wagging behind her. "How do you have that much control?!" She couldn't help herself. Valentina could use her powers so precisely. Astrid had never even considered having that much control over her own powers.

"I've been practicing since I was little." The pirate shrugged, pausing before adding, "Do you not have your powers all squared away?"

"I'd hardly call anything about my being a demon 'squared away.'" Astrid sighed, rubbing her arm as she looked away. "I…I sort of just found out what I was…like…yesterday." Valentina's tail drooped down as her eyes widened again.

"Oh. That's rough." She grinned widely, wrapping an arm around Astrid. "But, hey, you got someone to help ya now, kiddo!"

"Uhm…" Astrid wiggled uncomfortably, her tail wrapping around her ankles. "You don't even know me. And besides, I don't think we have the same types of powers. Mine sorta' kills people."

"Not knowing someone is a technicality in friendship that is easily rectified and I don't know what you're talking about with that second bit." Valentina released the smaller demon from her hold, lazily gesturing toward the bottom of the wall. Dirt melted into water and surrounded a small rat that attempted to scurry away. It was no use though. It was quickly trapped and lifted into a tiny water filled bubble. It wiggled in the liquid, squirming and flailing as it attempted to reach the bubble's edge. It had no such luck, however. Valentina kept it suspended until it floated motionlessly in the water. "My powers kill things too."

The rat fell to the ground, lifeless, in a puddle. The pirate flicked one finger up and the rat's corpse dissolved into water that swirled around her hand. "Now!" She smirked. "Where is this person who's hunting you? Let's do a little recon."

* * *

The hooded figure slipped out of the tavern as the two demons watched from a distance. Valentina led the way, holding Astrid closely behind her. They weaved down streets and between people, keeping an eye on their target. Astrid's tail perked as they rounded a corner. They were nearing the edge of town.

"Maybe they're leaving for good?" She suggested as she and Valentina began to navigate between the branches in Samba Forest.

"Do you think they're just going to cut and run if they're really hunting you?" She grabbed Astrid's arm and pulled her down into the foliage as a large, armor-clad man stomped through the leaves. He had blonde locks that were almost white and brown eyes that looked like the dirt of the town's roads. On his breastplate, he wore the same sun-like sigil as those who had attacked Crimson Barrow. He trudged over to the hooded figure, a smile on his face.

"Aurora." The figure turned to the man, pulling off the cloak. A woman with a curvy figure stood before him. Blond locks fell gracefully over her shoulders, freed from the hood. Her blue eyes reflected in his armor like jewels. She was dressed in a black, leather shirt that exposed her stomach and a tiny pair of shorts that matched. Her boots extended up to her knees, out of place with the rest of her outfit.

"Forfax." She greeted him dryly despite her sweet expression. "Why are you here? You should be helping the men prepare."

"I was getting worried." He admitted, taking a step toward the woman. "You were gone for so long."

"Well, that's what happens when people scout, stupid." She spat sharply, rolling her eyes.

Astrid and Valentina exchanged uncomfortable looks as the man looked down at the ground. He looked like a pup who had just been scolded by its master.

"Aurora, I just –"

"Can't you just do your job? Remiel's demon is in that trashy little hunting village, but who knows how long she'll stay. That town has monsters crawling all over the place too. This could be a real troublesome mission," she put her hand on her hip, "and here you are just being worthless in the forest."

"Aurora, we can handle it. I'll get the demon for you." He smiled brightly at her, but she didn't return the gesture. Instead, she stalked over to the man, glaring at him as she positioned herself only inches from his face.

"You'd better get her for *you*. If you fail me like my Crimson Barrow team did, I'll be sure to punish you myself."

Valentina grabbed Astrid from behind and pulled her through the undergrowth, dragging her through the vines and branches and dense grass until they reached Doewood once again. They slunk their way back into the town, blending back in with the crowds that plagued the street. Valentina didn't seem satisfied with that, however. She continued pulling Astrid along behind her, her stride too long for the shorter demon to comfortably keep pace.

"Valentina," Astrid muttered, jogging to keep up, "where are we going? The demon hunter lady is the other way."

"I know." The pirate stated, her expression more serious than it had been during their entire time together. She looked determined – even menacing.

"Shouldn't we, uh, I dunno, liquefy them or something?"

"They said they were getting their men ready, right?" Valentina asked as she pulled Astrid around a corner, leading them through an alleyway. She glanced back, finally realizing her pace was far too much for Astrid to keep up with and slowing down to match the smaller demon's pace. Her tail wrapped around Astrid, keeping her close as they made their way toward the stone fort. "That means it's more than just the two of them."

"I lived north of here – about a day or so away. When they came there, they had a whole slew of soldiers and angels." Astrid tried to recoil but was forced onward by Valentina's tail. "They destroyed the whole town."

"Crimson Barrow?" Valentina asked, finally taking a moment and stopping.

"What was it you said earlier? Got it in one?" Astrid half expected to be shunned in the same way she had been before. After all, everything was out in the open now – it was her fault that Crimson Barrow was in shambles. It was her fault that everyone was dead. It was all because she existed.

"Right." Valentina muttered. "Well, they'll be bringing the same here. We have to let Saffron know."

"Saffron?" Astrid questioned, still wiggling in the grip of Valentina's tail. There was no point. Even though it was soft and gentle against her body, it was solid muscle and nothing she did would force it away.

"The Baroness of Doewood. Her name is Saffron Wulf." Valentina gestured toward the fort. "She lives here."

"She lives in a fort?" Astrid looked up and down the imposing stone walls that loomed over them. "Damn. Color me jealous." She glanced back at the pirate. "But what's she gonna do? They had angels attacking us when they raided Crimson Barrow. Humans are no match for angels."

Valentina laughed. "You've just not been around the right humans, kiddo."

They circled around the structure until they reached a large, wooden door. Two men adorned in armor stood on either side. They didn't seem even slightly interested in their positions. In fact, they seemed poorly trained and, if anything, eager to get off duty to visit the brothels. Astrid grimaced. Her stomach turned. *This is a bad idea.*

"Hey, boys!" Valentina chirped, shifting her mood back to her happy-go-lucky attitude rapidly. Astrid blinked dumbly at the shift, wondering how the hell she could shift her personality so quickly. "Just gonna slink in here to see Saffron, okay?" She leaned over to a guard with a huge smile on her face. "Keep up the good work."

Astrid stared at the pirate in shock and disbelief as the guards stepped aside and allowed her to saunter through the front door. She tried to process what had happened, but couldn't quite get anything to add up. Why would a noble's guards just allow a *pirate* to walk in? She glanced back at the men, narrowing her eyes in confusion as she followed after Valentina.

The two demons' steps echoed through the stone halls as they quickly made their way through the fort. Banners representing the families if Doewood were clumsily strung across tables as tablecloths rather than hanging regally above their heads. Dust coated the broken heirlooms that littered the shelves and the floor. Astrid stumbled over a loose chunk of cobblestone, only saved by Valentina's tail swiftly sliding under her body when she fell face first toward the floor. It pushed her back to her feet.

"Thanks." Astrid muttered, blushing at her own clumsiness.

"What're demon friends for?" Valentina smiled. "Here we are." She stated, pushing open a large, wooden door.

Astrid wasn't prepared for what awaited her. A slew of soldiers and pirates mingled together, drunkenly singing and dancing in what looked to be a throne room. She ducked as a tankard flew through the air and slammed into the wall behind her.

"What is this place?" She asked, not daring to take her eyes away from the crowd for fear of another stray beverage being thrown in her direction.

"This is the baroness's throne room." Valentina stated as though the wild party wasn't happening right in front of them. "She should be hanging around here somewhere." She craned her neck, looking through the sea of bodies for the hostess. Astrid, meanwhile, stared in horror.

"All the guards are drunk with pirates and the town is about to be invaded. They're gonna die." She leaned back against the wall, sliding down to the floor as Valentina slipped through the crowd to look for her target. "They're gonna be getting stabbed by angels and they're gonna think it's a party game. Holy shit. They're so drunk that they're not even going to know. Holy shit."

"Kid!" Valentina's voice broke through the ranks, grabbing Astrid's attention as she waved at her from a large, stage-like area. She stood beside a woman with a tight, brunette bun. The woman's forest green eyes matched her gown and complimented her tanned skin. She had a less muscular build than Valentina, but the two seemed to be the same age. A soldier at the woman's side rubbed her tanned shoulder sensually despite his eyes remaining vigilantly on mass of bodies before him. He seemed more armored than any of the other guards they had run into – a captain for sure.

Astrid ducked through the crowd, flinching as those around her swung their drinks, singing and dancing clumsily.

She cringed as one soldier fell backwards off a table, landing in front of her with a loud crash. He smirked up at her as she stepped over him and made her way to where Valentina stood.

"Valentina, I don't think that this is going to work out so well." She admitted, glancing back at the crowd. She paused for a moment, catching the gaze of a man staring back at her. His eyes were like water. They were entrancing. His black locks spiked around his head in an unkempt and yet flattering manner. He wore a blue shirt that brought out his eyes and a black duster that extended down to his ankles. He was entrancing. She felt her heart fluttered slightly in her chest and her cheeks burned.

"Kid!" Astrid jumped as Valentina screamed almost directly beside her ear. She stammered, looking between the man and the pirate who eyed her in confusion.

"I…er…uhm…"

"Are you blushing?" Valentina grinned wickedly, poking Astrid's cheek.

"Why are you mocking me when the town is about to be invaded and destroyed by an army of angels?!"

"You like him!" Valentina chided, giggling as the woman in the green gown turned to Astrid.

"Invaded and destroyed?" She asked, ignoring Valentina's mockery.

"Uhm, yeah." Astrid answered, trying to also ignore Valentina who continued chanting 'you like him, you like him' behind her. "You're Baroness Saffron Wulf, correct?"

"I am." The woman confirmed as Valentina grinned widely at the man in the crowd, waving eagerly to him. She mimicked kissing on her hand and let out a mocking moan, cuing Astrid to groan and blush more deeply. She grabbed the pirate's arm and pulled her back to the group.

"We overheard a plan to invade Doewood – I think angels are involved."

"What she means," Valentina interrupted, finally paying attention to the conversation, "is that we *know* that angels are going to be involved. They're trying to catch a certain little demonic shorty." She pointed down at Astrid, earning another sharp glare.

"I didn't mean to attract them here! I just...I was trying to get away from them. They said something about taking me somewhere when I was back in Crimson Barrow and after everything happened, I couldn't..." She bit her lip and looked down at her feet. "I just..."

"You couldn't stay in Crimson Barrow." Saffron finished Astrid's thought, nodding. "Crimson Barrow isn't exactly agreeable to demons. Many try to avoid it and end up boarding here instead. I get it." She stood up, glancing back at the guard that kept his hand on her shoulder. "Beau, get everyone ready."

"Just like that?" Astrid asked, raising an eyebrow. "I mean, we don't even have proof."

"Val vouches for you, right?" Saffron smiled at Valentina who nodded. "She's been a friend and valuable ally for years now. She doesn't lie to me. If she says there's a threat, then we prepare for battle."

Chapter Three:

Moonlight glimmered down on the wooden cabins and the dirt streets of Doewood. The bustle from the day was missing as silent shadows crept through the town. A horde of shimmering armor followed after Aurora. She led them into the midst of several cabins.

Astrid gritted her teeth as she watched from her perch atop a building. This woman was following her, stalking her and killing everyone Astrid knew. It was torture to crouch silently on the rooftop, watching as the small army marched into Doewood. She didn't want to be doing nothing. She wanted to attack, to make this threat vanish, but she knew it was counterintuitive to their plan – to their trap. She had to stay put. Her tail flicked as she caught sight of Valentina crouched atop the opposing roof.

The pirate seemed just as eager, her fingers drumming on her knee repeatedly as she watched the soldiers below. It made Astrid feel better about her own impatience to see someone with such control and confidence struggling with the same eagerness. She wondered for a moment if Valentina struggled with other issues. Did she feel guilt for something in her past like Astrid did now? Was she terrified she would lose control at any moment? Valentina's seaweed green eyes didn't betray her. No such feelings shined through them, but perhaps the feelings were buried deeply within the pirate. Astrid shook her head, shaking the thoughts free and redirecting her attention back down to the angelic army.

In the street below them, Aurora stopped, spinning back and smiling cutely at those who stood behind her. The army halted on her mark, ready for a command.

"Ready?" She asked, twirling a strand of blond hair around her finger.

So ready, Astrid thought, clinching her fist and leaning forward. Her crimson eyes didn't shift from the woman below her.

"You know the drill. If they don't know where the demon is, they're worthless to us." She pulled her hood over her head, masking her face once more. "Get to it." Swords left their sheaths, sparkling under the moonlight. Astrid's muscles tightened. She wanted to pounce, but she knew better.

The soldiers stalked up to the houses that lined the street. Each stood in front of a door with their weapon drawn. Astrid's heart pounded as she shifted in place. This was it. It was almost time. Her excitement nearly dissolved, however. From the corner of her eye she noticed a strange movement. She glanced down at her hands and cursed under her breath. Black mist circled her fingers as it had before, swirling like ribbons. Valentina spotted the issue and flashed a reassuring smile. Outwardly, it did nothing to assist, but internally Astrid felt calmer. If such an experienced demon wasn't worried, should she really be? She smiled back before looking down at the soldiers again.

Doors were kicked in. The crashing of wood and the sound of shattering glass filled the air. Aurora smirked, turning and slowly sauntering away from the scene, starting on her way toward Saffron's fort. She stopped dead, however, as screams rang through the air – the screams of her men.

She jolted back. Her jaw dropped as blood sprayed out of their bodies and metal clashed against metal, sword against armor. The meek villagers they had expected weren't the ones waiting for them inside the homes. Instead, they had been greeted by the blades of the Doewood guard. Forfax staggered back, barely dodging Beau's blade before retreating to Aurora's side.

"T-they knew!" He stammered. Aurora glared as Saffron smoothly strolled out of the building and joined her captain at his side. She wore the same armor as her guards and held a blade dripping with the blood of one of Aurora's men. She smiled, leaning against Beau as she twirled her blade carelessly.

"So it would seem. How about that?" Aurora growled as she scowled at the baroness. "This makes it easy, though. We can handle them all here and now."

"But–" Forfax was silenced as Aurora's stern gaze turned on him.

"Kill that woman." She demanded. "Bring me her head and–"

Water collided with Forfax, slamming him through one of the tiny buildings. Wooden debris showered down on Aurora. She brushed it off, stomping her foot in anger before turning to see Valentina jumping down from the building and landing in front of Saffron and Beau. A swirling, glistening whirlpool danced around the pirate as she smugly smirked.

Forfax limped from the wreckage, quickly rejoining his commander. He gritted his teeth, looking Valentina up and down.

"A water demon." He stated as the pirate mockingly mouthed his words in unison.

"It would seem so. I was hoping to only deal with one demon at a time. No matter." Aurora glanced over at Forfax. "Capture her. I'll find the one that fled from us." Forfax nodded as a twinkling silver mist swirled around him, forming metallic, large wings and a matching halo.

Valentina narrowed her eyes and Astrid twitched, nearly falling from her hiding spot. She bit her lip as her suspicions were confirmed – the angels were like demons. They were all different with different powers and looks and they could hide themselves in plain sight by melting their body parts into a mist. Her tail wrapped around her ankles.

Aurora turned on her heels and started back on her path toward the fort. Forfax launched himself into the air, flying at Valentina. He crashed through her watery vortex, colliding with the demon and slamming her into the ground. Saffron lunged forward, sword slicing through the air, but Forfax dodged, jumping back. He narrowly avoided her blade as it whizzed by his chest.

Aurora was nearly out of sight now. Astrid gritted her teeth, glancing at Valentina. The pirate directed water to chase Forfax as he fled into the air. Plenty of Aurora's men had turned into angels now and were fighting the Doewood guards. None followed after the angels' commander, however. She was going to get away. Astrid's heart raced in her chest as she leaned forward more. Aurora was going to get away.

Just then, something slammed against her body. She groaned, rolling over to see the blue-eyed pirate from Valentina's crew on top of her. Panic roared in her stomach as she quickly examined where her hands were located. She sighed with relief when she realized she hadn't touched him, that the black mist around them was far from his body.

His eyes narrowed as he grabbed her by the back of her shirt and threw her aside, blocking an angel's sword with his own cutlass. The angel above him smirked, but the blue-eyed man cleared the expression when he slammed his knee into the angel's gut. A quick slice rendered the being flightless as one wing was amputated, blood painting the roof before the man kicked the angel off the building.

"Are you okay?" He asked, offering Astrid his hand. She glanced at her own, the black mist still swirling around them.

"I...I can't touch you right now."

"Demon powers a bit out of sorts?" He asked, pulling her to her feet by her bicep. "No big deal." Astrid looked by him. Aurora was gone. "The bitch commanding them – that's who you were going after, right?" He slid down the roof, jumping down onto the street below. "Let's go together. It's dangerous one-on-one. There's a reason she must be in charge, after all." Astrid blinked blankly for a moment before looking back at the fight between Valentina and Forfax.

The metallic-winged angel grabbed the pirate demon by her neck and slammed her into the dirt. Astrid winced, but before she could move in their direction to offer Valentina her aid, another stream of water shot through the air and launched Forfax through a building. The pirate jumped to her feet and straightened her hat before running toward the wreckage. "She'll be fine." The blue-eyed man assured. "Trust me – she's my captain. I've seen her go through worse than that. She's resilient to say the least."

"If you say so…." Astrid muttered. She felt a pang of guilt as she turned away from the fight and jumped down from the building, landing beside the man. The two darted off after Aurora. The buildings blurred together as they scoured the streets.

"She was walking. She couldn't have gotten that far." Astrid whined out, ruffling her hair in frustration. The man suddenly grabbed her arm and yanked her to the side as a blur of pink and black swooped by them. Astrid watched as Aurora smirked, fluttering above them after her failed assault, bright pink wings keeping her airborne and her matching halo sending its glow down her blond locks.

"Oh, lookie!" Aurora chided. "The demon is friends with a sea rat. How fitting. The rabble all plays together!"

"Ready?" The blue eyed man asked his companion, ignoring the angel overhead for a moment.

"I have to be." Astrid mumbled.

The angel swooped down, barreling toward them in a streak of pink. Rolling to opposite sides, Astrid and the blue eyed man evaded as quickly as they could. While the man landed gracefully, Astrid collided with a wall. She rubbed her head tenderly as she winced. "Damn it," she muttered.

The pirate gave chase, jumping from stalls to rooves with cat-like dexterity, swinging his cutlass at the angel. The swipe of his sword came too late. Aurora was out of his reach, flying just overhead as she laughed.

"Aw. Poor little sea rat. What's wrong? Can't fly, pirate? Must be horrible." She giggled, looping around in the air.

"Aw. Poor little winged slut." The pirate mocked in the same tone Aurora had used. "What's wrong? Too scared to fight anyone without your army? Maybe that's your only skill – getting weak-willed men to do your bidding." He let out a laugh. "How pathetic."

Aurora let out a shrill squeal of frustration before darting through the air, tackling the man before dragging him into the sky. His cutlass dropped to the ground with a 'clang' as they disappeared into the clouds overhead.

Astrid stared at the area where they had vanished, pacing below. She huffed, looking down at her hands as her tail drooped. The black mist was still there, circling around her palms. She groaned loudly before looking up at the sky again. She tapped her foot, waiting for some sign that the two might reemerge. Nothing.

"Are you kidding me? I'm literally the one they're after and I'm the only one standing around doing a crap ton of nothing. Cool. Great. Awesome even." She rolled her eyes, putting her hand on her hip and pacing a bit more before finally resolving that she would be waiting a while and flopping down on the ground in a huff. She crossed her legs and rested her head in her hands as she pouted.

It seemed like an eternity of nothingness as she waited on the ground. She wasn't sure how much time had passed, five minutes or fifteen, but, just as she was beginning to wonder if she should go elsewhere, she heard the sound of a faint screaming. She glanced up to see a small form falling through the sky. Her stomach turned as she realized that the figure was the pirate who had been helping her.

"Shit!" She bit her lip. What am I supposed to do?! I can't save him! Her heart raced in her chest as her breathing began to shallow. She felt her muscles shaking as she clamored to her feet and ran toward the would-be point of impact. With every step she took she felt as though she was getting higher – as though the ground was growing distant. Looking down, she gasped. It was more than a sensation. She was floating in the air, flying higher and higher.

"Wh-What–" She squirmed in the air, wiggling in place. "What's happening?!" She screamed. Just then, the man collided with her, knocking the both of them down to the ground. "…Ouch…."

"You okay?" He asked, rubbing his head as he climbed off of her. "Oh, and thanks for breaking my fall." He winked and flashed her a smile.

"No problem, guy. I love having people collide with me at high speeds and knocking my face into the dirt. Best pastime ever." Astrid groaned out, rubbing her aching head.

"Davy." He stated. He offered his her his hand, but grimaced, realizing he couldn't take hers. He mouthed out a 'sorry' as he patted her head and stepped back.

"What?"

"My name is Davy – not 'guy.'" He paused for a moment, smiling. "Nice wings by the way."

"Wh-what?!" Astrid jolted, looking over her shoulder. A pair of huge, black, furry wings loomed elegantly behind her, fluttering with her every movement. "You have got to be kidding me!" She screamed, stomping her foot. "First the horns and the tail and now I have damn wings?!"

"I take it this is new." Davy stated, absent-mindedly glancing up at the sky, scanning the clouds for Aurora. "I wouldn't worry too much about it."

"'Wouldn't worry too much'?! I have absolutely no control and I'm turning into some kind of monster!" Her eyes burned as tears threatened to form, but she leaned her head back and forced them away.

"Don't worry. Sometimes Val–" Before he could finish his thought, a pink blur slammed him into a wall. He gasped as Aurora's hands wrapped around his throat, her maniacal cackle filling the air. Astrid reached out for a moment, faltering as she caught sight of the black mist around her fingers. She cursed, recoiling from the situation. She'd end up killing someone if she got involved and she wasn't sure that was what she wanted – even if Aurora was responsible for all those deaths in Crimson Barrow.

Davy's hand tore at Aurora's arm as he fought for air. His eyes met Astrid's. It was as though time slowed to a halt. Astrid felt the swirling sickness in her stomach fighting with another feeling – a fluttering. Her heart was pounding in her chest, but her muscles wouldn't move. She felt short on breath as she watched him writhe in the angel's grasp.

The panic in her chest subsided as Davy grabbed Aurora by her blond locks, yanking her head back. She yelped, her hands instinctively reaching up to the hand holding her by her hair. A kick landed squarely in her ribs, sending her falling back.

Astrid stared in shock as Davy grabbed the angel and slammed her face into the ground. Again and again she collided with the dirt and stones. Blood dripped down her face more and more with each collision. After several impacts, Aurora's wings sprang to life, smacking the pirate away. Astrid stood, rubbing her arm nervously as the pirate and the angel both clamored to their feet. They both panted, glaring at each other as Astrid watched.

"Guess your little demon friend isn't going to help you." Aurora mocked with a smirk. Astrid flushed with embarrassment. The pirate was giving this fight his all and she was doing next to nothing to assist him.

"Oh, shut it." Davy spat. "You should be grateful. I mean, what kind of pathetic angel has this much trouble with a human anyway? I could only imagine how screwed you'd be against a demon." Aurora opened her mouth to retort, but before she could find the words, Forfax appeared over the buildings. His metallic wings and halo glittered in the starlight as he landed beside Aurora. He was soaked, battered, and beaten. Blood dripped from his face and body.

"We need to go," he panted out. He stared at Davy and Astrid despite directing his words at Aurora.

"Go? We haven't accomplished the goal!" She sounded like a child ready to throw a tantrum. Her octave had gone up considerably while she had squealed the words. Davy and Astrid cringed at the display.

"Aurora, our forces aren't doing well." He gulped as the pink-winged angel narrowed her eyes at him.

"Excuse me?"

"L-Let's get out of here and then we can talk about it." He flashed a smile at her, but it wasn't reciprocated. She turned back toward the pirate and the demon.

"I'll be back for you, demon. No matter where you run, we'll find you. There's no hiding from the Holy Light." Her wings spread widely before thrusting her into the air. Forfax sighed with relief before joining her. Within seconds, the two had disappeared through the clouds. They were gone.

The Holy Light? Astrid thought. *What is that?* She sighed. She still had no answers about what was happening. At least the town hadn't been destroyed though. She looked over at Davy. He was considerably disheveled and a bruise was forming on his throat.

"You okay?" She asked, walking over to him. He grabbed his cutlass from the dirt, sheathing it.

"Yeah. I'm fine. It's a shame we lost her though. What was she talking about at the end there? Holy Light or something like that? What is that?"

"I'm not sure to be honest." Astrid admitted, trying to ignore the tingling in her stomach as she pulled on her sleeve and shifted uneasily. What was this feeling? She felt it every time her eyes met his. Her cheeks darkened with a blush once more. "I've never heard if it."

"Me neither." Davy sighed, rubbing the back of his head. "Val or Saffron may've though." Astrid nodded, following Davy through the streets. As she watched him walking ahead of her, she couldn't help but notice the confidence in his stride. He seemed so sure of every movement. The light sway of his hips was fluid and flowed with each step. His figure was slim yet muscular. She clenched her teeth, urging herself not to look any longer, but she couldn't turn away. She bit her lip as her eyes drifted down. Even his ass was nice to watch.

He glanced back at her, smiling. The tingling in her stomach intensified. It tickled and sent a spark of energy blazing through her veins. Did he know she had just been looking at his ass? No. That couldn't have been it.

She wasn't sure what to do with her new feelings and it seemed her new appendages were unsure as well. As her eyes met his, her wings suddenly flapped. She yelped as she was launched into the air slightly, falling down onto her pirate comrade. Gasping, she jumped to her feet as Davy rubbed the back of his head.

"S-Sorry! I didn't mean to! They're still new and–" She fidgeted as he hopped to his feet. Her cheeks burned as he laughed, patting her head.

"It's all good." He leaned closer, whispering, "If you wanted to be on top of me," he winked, "all you had to do was ask." Astrid jumped back, squealing as her face turned red.

"Kidding!" He chirped, chuckling at the demon's reaction. "You're a fun one, you know that?"

The two jolted as a large crash echoed through the town. In the distance, a building crumbled. Dust flew into the air, a cloudy memorial to what had fallen.

"I guess some of them are still going at it." Astrid muttered.

"It seems that way." Davy glared at the wreckage in the distance. "Let's go." He grabbed her wrist, avoiding the dark mist around her hands, and darted off in the direction of the battle. She panted as she ran behind him, glancing down every alley they passed, scanning their surroundings for hidden enemies.

"Do you think they're in trouble?" She asked as he pulled her down the street. They were almost there.

"I'm not sure." He admitted just before they rounded the final corner. They stood before a wall of dust that shrouded the battlefield. Straining their eyes, they searched for any sign of Saffron or Valentina. "Stay here." Davy stated, releasing his grip on Astrid.

"But what about–" She started, ready to protest leaving Davy's side. He was still battered and beaten thanks to Aurora. Her heart sank as she thought of him alone, blinded by dust and surrounded by the opposition.

"Don't worry about it – I'm sure they're fine." As the words left his mouth, a figure launched itself through the dust. A rage-filled angel screamed a battle cry as he began to swing his sword toward them. Davy threw himself over Astrid, blocking her from the blade with his own body.

Before it made contact, a small tidal wave intervened, slamming the angel through one of the few structures that still stood. Valentina emerged from the dust and smoke, glaring at the winged man as blood dripped down from a gash on her arm.

The angel coughed up some of the water before attempting to climb to his feet. The water demon stomped on his chest, the heel of her boot pressing down on the fractured armor just over his heart. She glanced back to Davy. His arms were still wrapped around Astrid, holding her petite body tightly against his own muscular physique.

"Saffron is in the fort with Beau. Take her," she gestured to Astrid, "and go."

"Are you sure you don't need some help?" Davy asked, finally releasing Astrid. The demon sat blankly staring at him, her cheeks burning as she thought of his warm, muscular chest pressed against her only seconds before. Her tail flicked around rapidly and her wings twitched over and over.

"I've got this handled." Valentina stated, her seaweed green eyes shooting back to the angel. "This is nothing but cleanup – taking out the last of the trash."

The angel's jaw tensed. His sword was well out of reach and he couldn't move thanks to the boot on his chest. Davy nodded, gently pushing Astrid in the direction of the fortress. Valentina watched them until they turned the corner and a large stone wall obstructed her supervision.

Astrid was fairly certain that she knew exactly what was going to happen to that angel. She wanted to feel bad for him, but she just couldn't find it within herself. The images of those from Crimson Barrow dying at the hands of angels still plagued her and that put her pity in short supply. She glanced down at her hands. A wide grin formed on her face. Finally, the mist had vanished.

"Looks like your powers are calming down a bit." Davy stated as they neared their destination. His expression was soft and the way his lips subtly turned up into his smile made her legs feel wobbly. Her tail flicked upward at his words and her wings twitched out before refolding themselves.

"Seems like it." Astrid muttered, replaying the memory of Davy throwing his body onto hers over and over in her mind. The blush on her cheeks darkened as she remembered the feel of his muscly chest pressed against her back and the security that his arms offered as they wrapped around her.

"Well, that must be good, right?"

"Good?" Astrid blinked blankly before pulling herself back to reality. "Oh, yeah. *So* good." She assured as they made their way into the dreary, stone fort. Astrid tugged at her sleeve as they made their way through a maze of cobwebs.

"You're tough on yourself, huh?" Davy bluntly asked after some silence.

"I'd say I'm not tough enough on myself." They stopped at two large doors. He looked over at her. He seemed so genuinely confused.

"Why?" She held her breath as she stared into his ocean blue eyes. *Why does he think I shouldn't be?* She shook her head, pushing open the door. *I have to be. Someone will die if I'm not.*

Beau sat in the throne as Saffron tenderly bandaged his arm. They laughed with other warriors and with Valentina's pirates, downing ale to celebrate what Astrid assumed had been deemed a victory.

"Oh, hey!" Saffron chirped, glancing back at them with a beaming grin. "Val is finishing up, but I'd say it was a rousing success!"

"A huge part of the town was destroyed in the battle." Astrid pointed out.

"Rousing," Saffron declared again with confidence, "success."

"Well, she's easy to satisfy…."

Davy stepped forward, leaning on the arm of the chair. He waited as Saffron finished dressing her guard's wounds, crossing his arms and watching silently. She glanced up at him, but rolled her eyes with a smile upon seeing his expression.

"Oh, don't look so glum, Davy! We won! What's that mopey face about?"

"The angel we confronted mentioned something called 'The Holy Light.' Any idea what they were referring to?" Saffron raised an incredulous eyebrow at the name before shaking her head. She glanced over at Beau, but he merely shrugged. "I see." Davy stated. "Well, it would seem as though 'The Holy Light,' whatever it is, is responsible for the attacks. Before leaving, they told us that there was no hiding from it."

"Whatever it is," Saffron started, leaning against the opposite arm of the throne, her expression hardening, "it can't be good."

"And what's the point in rounding up demons anyway?" Davy wondered aloud.

"No idea." Saffron admitted. "But I don't think it's a solid idea for Val to stay in one place for too long." She looked up at Astrid. "Or you."

Astrid's heart sank. Though she had been planning on leaving anyway, it was different to hear it from someone else. It felt as though she was being kicked out – shunned. She was beginning to wonder if she would ever find a place to truly call home.

"Oh…right." She looked down at her feet as she spoke.

"Do you have anywhere else?" Saffron asked, cocking her head to one side and exchanging concerned looks with Beau. She stood up and took a step toward Astrid, but before she could say anything more, Davy interjected.

"She does."

"I do?" Astrid questioned.

"She can stay on the ship. We're going to have to hit the waves here soon anyway, so it makes sense to take her with us.

Besides, Val knows how to control her powers pretty well. Astrid could learn from her."

Chapter Four:

Astrid groaned as she stared up at the looming ship. She had never been on the ocean before; she had never even seen it. She hadn't given a thought to how huge it would be or to how huge the ships floating in it would be either. Worse yet, she had never considered how important swimming could be. As she took in the crashing waves, the smell of salt on the wind, and the cawing seagulls overhead, she was becoming painfully aware of her mistake.

Valentina flashed a reassuring smile, but Astrid did not return the gesture. Why was she doing this again? Wouldn't being in the middle of the ocean while unable to swim be just as dangerous and life threatening? She sighed, dragging her feet through the sand as she neared the vessel. Better control over her newly-formed wings would've made her feel at least somewhat better, but she lacked even that.

"Aw. Someone looks gloomy." Astrid jolted, spinning around to meet Davy's smile. "What's up, sunshine?" He stepped closer to her, sending a tingling that was somewhere between panic and jubilation through her body. *What the hell is wrong with me?! Why do I keep freaking out around this guy?!* She cleared her throat and tried to act disinterested, but she could feel her cheeks burning red. "You okay?" He continued, stepping even closer. Yelping and hopping away from him, Astrid turned away.

"I-I'm fine! It's just…I dunno. Uhm, I've never seen the ocean and, uh…."

"Oh!" Davy cooed. "I get it. It's bigger than you expected."

"B-bigger?"

"Yeah," he continued, "I've known loads of people who didn't expect to be so awe-stuck when they saw it – sailors even." He reached out and grabbed her arm, pulling her close to his body. She could feel his muscular chest pressed against her back as he gestured out toward the water. "Don't you worry though. All of that – that's our friend. Remember, Val is a water demon. She and the ocean are tight." He twirled Astrid around, holding her face between his hands. "Nothing's going to hurt you. Okay?"

Nothing's going to hurt you. The words echoed in her mind for a moment as she stared into his deep, oceanic blue eyes. She gulped heavily as her body instinctively leaned closer, the distance between their faces getting smaller and smaller. Her heart raced. Her hands shook. She closed her eyes.

"You two ready to board?" Valentina's voice was an unwelcome intrusion, but Astrid tried not to let it show as she yanked away from Davy.

"I'm ready." She stated, the dark-haired man before her smirking.

"Me too." He nonchalantly shrugged, waving to Astrid before heading to the ship. Valentina grinned, watching as Davy walked away to bark orders at the crew.

"I think he likes you."

"Wh-What?!" Astrid squeaked.

"He doesn't take to people too fast." The pirate stated, smiling sympathetically in the direction of the man who had left them. "He gets a sense for who he likes pretty quick though." Her smile turned on Astrid. "You should be proud. Davy's an excellent judge of character. If he likes you, it means you're going to be a stellar pirate!"

"I never agreed to become a pirate!" Astrid called out as Valentina whistled a tune and headed toward her ship, completely ignoring the smaller demon.

* * *

It wasn't just The Clover that was huge – it was the crew as well. There were so many bodies bustling around that Astrid felt she was in the way at every turn. She apologized to one of the men as she backed into a banister, leaning on it to stay out of the way. The open sea was sprawled out before her – no land as far as her eyes could see. She sighed, her wings folding close to her body and her tail wrapping around her legs.

She wondered what Aurora was doing – if she was invading another village and searching for her or if she was regrouping. She had no way of knowing, no way of gathering intel. She was stuck, impatiently waiting, the expectation of being attacked looming in the back of her mind.

"Kid!" Astrid looked back to see Valentina's brimming smile greeting her. "What're you up to?"

"Just thinking." She muttered.

"Ah. About the angels I'm assuming." Too accurate. She had seen right into her mind without even a follow up question. "There's something about that, something I wanted to talk to you about."

"Yeah?"

"Your bits." Valentina pointed to Astrid's horns. "Your demon bits." It was at this moment that Astrid finally realized that Valentina looked all too human again. Her swirling horn and aquatic-looking tail had vanished. *How?* She wondered. *How can she make them vanish?* "I noticed you, uhm, ya know, still got 'em."

"You don't. Did you make them melt away into that mist?" Astrid asked, circling the pirate and examining her lack of demon parts. Valentina nodded.

"They fade away when you 'undo' your transformation. You can go back and forth between forms; that way so people don't know you're a demon. It'll help you out loads in all kinds of situations." She took a step toward Astrid, taking the dark-haired demon by the arm and leading her across the deck. They headed up to the helm where Davy lazily steered the ship, pouting about something or another.

"Oh, don't do that, Davy. It's not like you can teach her. You're human, after all." She turned back to Astrid. "I can though."

A bolt of energy shot through the shorter woman's spine. She smiled widely. All her life she had been guessing about how to control her powers, but now she had a teacher. Control had always been one of her desires and now it was finally being presented to her.

"Please!" She pleaded. "I *need* to know how to work my powers!"

"No need to beg." The captain giggled. "I intended to help." She shrugged. "Let's begin."

Davy mocked the pirate's words before leaning on the wheel with a huff. Valentina rolled her eyes, but proceeded to ignore Davy afterwards.

"Step one is the same for about everything."

"Acceptance?"

"Uhm, no." The pirate chortled. "Calm. You have to stay calm."

"Is that a joke? You realize what my powers do, don't you?" She crossed her arms, popping a hip out as she rolled her eyes.

"Oh, don't be like that. You could at least try."

"Fine. I'm calm, so what's step two?"

"You're not calm." Valentina pointed out, pointing up and down Astrid's body. "You're pissed and worried."

"I'm fine." Astrid spat.

"Your tail is wrapped around your leg. It's like how dogs tuck theirs."

"I know you didn't just compare me to a dog." Astrid growled out the words, leaning forward slightly. Behind them, Davy chuckled, earning himself a glare.

"It's not cause you're a dog; it's a tail thing."

"Whatever."

"Why not just focus on your breathing for now?" Valentina suggested.

"I know how to breathe."

Several hours of bickering passed by as Valentina tried to help Astrid relax. It seemed to be failing as her tail never unwrapped from her leg and her wings stayed close to her body. The two pirates at the helm seemed astounded by the lack of progression as night slowly fell over The Clover.

Astrid couldn't blame them for being shocked – she was as well, to an extent. She had always thought she was a calm person, but now she wondered if she ever had truly been relaxed. As the stars shimmered overhead and the ship drifted through the dark waters, Davy decided he'd had enough.

"This is getting ridiculous. Why don't you let me show her, Val?" He turned to face them, leaning his back against the wheel as he spoke. "Clearly you two aren't jiving on the same idea of 'calm.' Let someone else have a crack at…," he smirked, "making her feel good." Astrid blushed, wings perking and her tail flicking at the comment, earning herself a snicker. Valentina grimaced.

Davy sauntered over to the smaller demon. His hand slipped onto her waist and pulled her close against him. A shiver of excitement coursed through her body. His touch was sure, secure and yet gentle. He was warm like the ocean air around them. She wondered for a moment if he was truly human. Her thoughts were interrupted as Valentina scoffed.

"Keep her safe. They'll be no shenanigans on The Clover."

"Val," Davy sighed, "when have I ever partaken in shenanigans?"

Valentina looked shocked that her first mate even had the audacity to ask such a question. He released Astrid from his hold and gave a wink.

"Let's go, sunshine."

Below deck was a sight that Astrid was only vaguely familiar with. A party. Booze, food, and dancing were abundant among the men. They laughed and fell over onto each other, so familiar with one another – familial almost. She glanced back at Davy as he gestured for her to join.

"I, uhm, er…" She muttered, unable to fully form the words to convey that she had purposely avoided alcohol up to now in fear of what it might cause her powers to do. After all, if she could barely control them sober, she could only imagine what it would be like otherwise.

"Don't be nervous." He took her by the hand and led her to a table to join several of the crewmates. They waved and toasted as their two new comrades joined them. One of the men poured out two overflowing goblets and passed them down the table. "Like I told you before," Davy repeated, handing the dark-haired demon the goblet and pulling out a seat for her, "I'm not letting anything hurt you." Astrid glanced down the table at the smiles and happiness before turning back to the pirate. An image flashed through her mind. The image of the square the day she had lost control of her powers; the commotion, the carnage, the death.

"I'm not worried about *me*." She admitted. She reached out to hand him the goblet, but he pushed it back toward her. Davy smiled, looking mischievously sinister.

"They'll be fine. Trust me." He leaned close to her, pushing the goblet to her lips. It burned in the strangest and most satisfying of ways as it slipped down her throat. She wanted to cough, to choke on it, and at the same time she wanted to down the whole cup. Against her better judgement, she decided on the latter, tilting the goblet back and draining it. She lightly coughed, but smiled up at the pirate.

"Good?"

"Great." She confirmed. Davy laughed, screaming a cheer and pouring another round into her goblet before downing his own. Astrid took in the contents of the glass freely this time. A man beside her topped off the goblet again with a booming laugh.

"Let's dance!" He suggested happily to her, offering his hand.

"Oh, uhm, no." She smiled at him, pushing his hand back. "I don't dance."

"Nonsense!" Davy interjected, pulling Astrid atop the table and wrapping his arm around her waist. Music began being played as he swung her elegantly around. She laughed as he twirled her to the lively beat. "See? It's fun!"

Soon the lower level was full of pirates dancing and jubilantly twirling and stomping. They screamed out shanties of which Astrid had never heard, but, as she downed two more goblets of whatever she had been drinking, her swimming head felt as though she must know the words. She loudly sang with the man who had initially requested a dance, much to Davy's amusement and pleasure. She was happy to see that everyone was content to simply make up words to songs as they went along. Another goblet was downed and she staggered over to Davy, sitting beside him and leaning into his arm. She beamed brightly at him with her glowing cheeks and hazy, crimson eyes.

"Let's get you some fresh air." He suggested, helping her to her feet.

"Aw, but the party."

"It's okay. We party every night."

"But tonight!" She whined.

"Shh. It's okay." He petted her head, kissing her forehead and leading her above deck.

She laughed, leaning against Davy's arm as she stumbled across the deck under the moonlight. Had she really danced on a table in front of the crew or had that been a dream? She giggled. Had it always been this warm on the ship?

Astrid glanced up at Davy. Her fingers stroked the muscles under his duster as her tail swayed behind her and her wings fluttered. She couldn't tell if her cheeks burned from the alcohol or from the view.

"You're cute." She slurred, leaning closer and biting her lip.

"You're drunk." Davy laughed, twirling her before wrapping his arms around her waist as her wings stretched out, fluttering with her giggles. "See? I knew this would help you relax."

"You got her trashed." Valentina observed from the top deck, leaning on the banister and shaking her head judgingly.

"Someone had to." Davy shrugged.

"Oh, really?" The captain scoffed. "And where are you taking her?"

"To bed." He stated matter-of-factly. "If you're implying something, Val, then don't. She's staying in my bed and I'm staying in the floor." He gave Astrid's head a pat as he took her by the hand and led her toward a room next to the captain's quarters, adding, "I'm a gentleman."

"You're a dirty sea rat and you know it." Valentina screamed after him as the door closed.

* * *

Astrid yelped as the ship shook violently, knocking her out of the bed. She blushed deeply, staring at the man she had landed on before they jumped away from each other.

"Wh-What was that?" She asked, turning away from Davy as he pulled on his pants. She cursed her own lack of a shirt, wondering where the hell she had left it and how the hell she'd even lost it in the first place.

"Nothing good." The pirate stated, tossing her one of his garments from his bedside table. "Put that on."

"Wings." She pointed back to her additional appendages. He quickly took the top and sliced it open in the back, creating two openings for her wings.

"Hurry. They might need—" Before he could finish the thought, the door burst open. A sneering angel stood before them. His eyes and halo glowed a toxic green as his powder blue wings spread widely behind him. He held a shimmering blade that dripped with blood. "Are you fucking kidding me?" Davy muttered as the angel swung at him. He blocked with his own weapon, the blood splattering over their faces upon the impact of the two blades. "Who are you and how the hell did you find our ship?" He demanded. The stranger ignored the question, kicking Davy back and advancing with another swing of his blade.

Astrid's wings flapped harshly, launching her into the man and knocking him out of the room. She slammed the door and pulled the shirt on before running to the pirate's side and helping him to his feet.

"Are you okay?"

"Fine." He answered, rubbing his gut and brushing the boot print off the fabric of his shirt. "You think that guy is with—" The door burst open again, the man entering once more with a growl. "He really doesn't know about knocking, does he?" The pirate muttered before launching himself at their foe, cutlass slicing through the air, only narrowly missing the dodging angel with each swing. Their blades collided once more. Davy winced as his cutlass shattered on impact, shards of metal scattering about the floor. "What the hell?!"

"My power." The angel muttered. He stated the words as though he wasn't even in the fight. They were hollow, lifeless. It was like he was absent from his own body. "I can harden any of my weapons." He held up his blade as it shimmered with a powder blue glow. "You'll never be able to beat me in an armed fight."

"Sounds like a stupid power." Astrid called out, slicing into her hand with a fragment of the shattered metal. She prayed she was able to make her own abilities work as she swung the blood at the angel. Just as expected, he blocked his face with his sword. Unlike expected, however, her powers seemed to actually be on her side. The metal began smoking as the blood corroded it. The angel glanced from his weapon to the demon.

"How dare you." He stated, monotonously.

"The hell is wrong with this guy?" Astrid muttered, inching closer to Davy, her tail flicking behind her as she silently and inwardly celebrated the slight control she had exhibited. "It's like he has no emotions what-so-ever."

"I know." The pirate agreed. "I feel like it has to do with the lack of color coordination."

"What?" The demon raised an eyebrow, confused. "What does matching have to do with emotions?"

"Angels and demons – their halos and wings and tails and such all match; at least somewhat if nothing else. Your tail and wings and horns are all black. Valentina's demon parts have an oceanic color scheme. It's part of how you can exist in certain environments – it's your natural camouflage for the places you would live in the wild. Like how certain fish are different colors based on where they live." He pointed to the man's halo. "He's got that green though. It looks almost like an infection when you compare it to the color of his energy and his wings."

"You're right." Astrid observed. "So, you think something's wrong with him?" Davy pulled a dagger from a sheath at his side, readying himself as the angel before them flapped his wings aggressively.

"Well, I don't quite think something is *right* with him."

* * *

Valentina jumped back, blocking an angel's attack with her sabre while directing water through the air to topple over a wall of soldiers advancing on her. Aurora launched herself at the pirate. The sabre collided with her pink wings but did no damage. It was as though they were impenetrable.

"This your power?" Valentina asked, kicking Aurora back. It seemed the defense extended to the angel's whole body as the kick did almost nothing to assist.

"Your water isn't going to affect me, demon! My defense is—" Before Aurora could finish, a tidal wave burst over the side of the ship, bashing the angel down to the planks and washing her across the deck.

"That's rough." The pirate muttered, wincing. "I didn't even try hard." The angel scurried to her feet but was quickly put over the banister as a blue winged angel crashed through a wall and collided with her. Valentina glanced back at Astrid and Davy, both of whom flashed her a smile. "Good of you two to join me." She looked the other demon up and down for a moment, smirking. "Nice top." She added.

"Sh-Shut up! It's all I had!" Astrid screamed, blushing. Davy didn't argue. Instead, he brimmed as though he had accomplished some great task. "Oh, knock it off! Nothing happened and you know it!"

"Get out of my way!" The trio turned to the sound of the voice that growled out the words to see the angel with powder blue wings throw Aurora aside. She yelped as she fell to the planks.

"Damn it, Oran! That hurt." She squealed out. The other angel ignored her.

"The demon – give her to me." He demanded, holding out a hand. Davy smirked.

"You really think after all this fighting we'd do that?" The angel glared, his feathers frizzing out and sharpening until they were blade-like.

"Do it or die. Your choice, human."

Davy yanked the sabre from Valentina's hand, pointing it at his opponent with a cocky smirk. Before he could speak, however, Oran had already darted by him, his wings slashing open his arm and blood spraying into Valentina's face. Astrid screamed as Oran's fingers tangled into her hair. He dragged her into the air with him. They were getting higher and higher. Toxic eyes flashed down at her, filled with insane malice. Oran sneered. "You're his now."

* * *

Aurora's fist collided with Valentina's face after the angel rolled through the air, dodging a blast of water. Davy slashed through the liquid, nearly slicing through the angel. He cursed. He had only missed by a little.

"Call your friend back down here." He demanded. "Or is he too much of a coward to join us?"

She snickered, jumping at the pirate and automatically blocking with her steel-like wings. Davy pulled back before the blade connected. He growled, remembering his broken weapon before angrily kicking the cocoon of feathers. "You're a fucking coward too! Stop blocking with your damn wings and fight me!" He continued kicking the mass, chanting, "Fight me! Fight me! Fight me!"

"I don't think she's gonna come out." Valentina stated with a sigh. She was proven wrong, however, as Aurora's wings burst open, slapping Davy back and into the banister. His lip dripped blood as he rubbed his jaw and winced. Aurora grabbed Valentina by the arm, preparing to launch herself into the sky, but was consumed by a torrential wave crashing over the deck and washing the two of them into the ocean.

Bubbles swirled around them as Valentina's elbow collided with the angel's neck. The water whirled, circling rapidly. Aurora gritted her teeth as the pirate vanished somewhere in the dark waves. The swirling water pulled her deeper, obstructing her ability to swim as it dragged her down. She squirmed, struggling to reach the surface. Glancing down, she realized where the demon had vanished to. Arms outstretched and eyes glowing an oceanic blue, Valentina floated below what quickly became a whirlpool.

Aurora couldn't scream. She was gobbled up by the spinning vortex, tossed around as the tower of water breached the surface and extended into the sky with Valentina at the center. The pirate exhaled a mouthful of sea foam as she was lifted into the air by her creation.

Oran's eye twitched as he glanced down and saw what was coming for him. He cursed, darting higher and weaving through the clouds. Astrid squealed as the puffy masses around them melted into liquid and whizzed after Oran. Water rushed them from all sides, surrounding and engulfing them. It squeezed itself around Oran's throat as Valentina appeared behind them, standing atop a fountaining mountain of salt water.

As she reached out, the liquid around Astrid shoved itself back, forcing Oran away from the younger demon and releasing her from the watery prison. Valentina quickly took her in her arms and pulled her close, holding her against her body. She wrapped an arm around the smaller demon, securing her so that she didn't plummet to her death in the ocean below.

The watery bubble that Oran squirmed in reminded Astrid of that which Valentina had killed the rat with before. Oran even squirmed in much the same way, desperately fighting to reach the edge and take in air but getting nowhere.

Unlike the rat, Valentina didn't let him drown. The watery prison shot through the air, slamming into the deck of The Clover and sending water splashing all over, washing away soldiers who fought her crew and the blood of those exchanges. Valentina's whirlpool sat them down gently, dissipating and leaving a choking, gagging Aurora on the deck, crawling on her knees.

"I'm done with your shit. You think you can injure my crew and then kidnap one of us on my watch? Get over yourself and get off my fucking ship." She demanded. Aurora glared at her, turning to Oran to spout a command. She flinched. He was unconscious on the deck, soaked and beaten. She cursed, shakily climbing to her feet.

"You're not going to get away forever." She began, eyeing Astrid.

"Then I should end this now and drown you." Valentina interrupted. Water flicked around her like tentacles, threatening to attack at any moment. Aurora scoffed, turning to where the soldiers had washed off the ship.

"Forfax!" She called out. Her lackey appeared almost instantly, his metallic wings shimmering beneath the stars. "Grab Oran and let's go. This is a lost cause with these slackers." She gestured toward the men in the water.

Astrid couldn't help but notice the freshly forming scar over Forfax's left eyelid. His eye was missing, the lid of it dipping in slightly. She cringed as she remembered Aurora's promise to punish him if they didn't retrieve her in Doewood. She supposed losing an eye was better than death.

The man nodded, throwing Oran over his shoulder before taking to the sky. Aurora's wings spread, but, before she could leave, Astrid called out to her.

"Aurora! Wait! I have to ask you something!"

"Pft. What?" She turned, annoyed.

"What's with Oran's halo? Why is it green?"

"That's none of your concern. Oran is my brother, so I'll be the one concerned with him. I don't need some demon in our affairs."

"Is there something wrong with him?" She persisted. "He didn't seem…, uhm, well –"

"Right." Davy finished the sentence for her.

"It's not your business!" The angel screamed before taking to the air and joining the fluttering members of her army. Valentina sighed as the small fleet disappeared into the sky.

"Guess we'll never know."

"I guess." Astrid muttered, turning to look at the human members of the army who were left behind. "What about them?"

"I'll adjust the tide to help them get to shore," Valentina shrugged, "but I'm not doing any more. Those angel worshipping sods aren't setting foot on The Clover again."

Chapter Five:

Astrid leaned over the banister and sighed as the evening sun shimmered down over the crew, casting its orange glow upon The Clover and the waves that crashed against it. The battle a few days before had taken a toll on the ship and the repairs had been long, extensive, and tiring. It had been an arduous task to say the very least. She had never worked with repairs before – she had always just pickpocketed enough to hire someone else to do it, so she was glad to have the patience of Valentina and Davy as they instructed her. She yawned, wings stretching widely and tail perking up as she outstretched her arms.

"Exhausting, huh?" Davy smiled as he joined her at her side. "Sucks, but Val wants me to get you to practice controlling your powers now too." He glanced over at the demon's confused expression. "She's busy with the repairs and some captain-y stuff so it's just you and the first mate for now, sunshine." He leaned over, wrapping his arm around her shoulders. A spark of excitement and panic shot up Astrid's spine. Her tail flicked rapidly behind her. "Ready?" She was *so* ready for time alone with him.

Davy might not have been a demon, but Astrid couldn't deny that he was a good teacher. He had already taught her how to repair many things on the ship and now he stood before her explaining something he couldn't feel or experience as though it was as natural to him as breathing. She supposed years of working with Valentina had made demon subjects common knowledge to him, but she was impressed none the less. He didn't come off as nervous or unsure of anything. He was suave, cool, relaxed. It made her feel something in her stomach, a fluttering. It tickled her insides and sent sparks through her body. At the same time, though, she felt so assured; she felt as though she had security. Davy had already proven he'd risk his life for her. The bandage on his arm and his bruised neck were reminders of that. She was safe here.

"Well, nearly there!" Davy excitedly praised. The comment interrupted Astrid's thoughts.

"Wh-what?" She muttered. The pirate smiled widely, pointing back to where Astrid's wings had been before. They were gone and a black, shimmering mist was dissolving into the air behind her. She stared, wide-eyed for a moment before screaming in joy and happily dancing around. "I did it! I did it!" She sang out, hugging Davy while bouncing up and down. "They're gone! I can't believe it!"

"Well, you should." He stated, patting her head tenderly. "Cause you did a great job." A blush crossed her cheeks as she let go of him.

"Only cause you're such a good teacher, Davy."

"That's not true at all. This was all you, sunshine." He paused for a moment before placing a small kiss on her forehead. She squeaked, jumping back, away from the sudden affection. "You did great." He assured again, brimming. She felt like a million thoughts were screaming through her head all at once and she could feel her tail flicking around in excited panic behind her.

"I, uhm, uh…uhm…er…."

"We should work on your horns and tail next." He stated, ignoring how flustered she was. "What do you think? Wanna do that now, or should we take a break?" There was no way she was going to be calm enough to concentrate now. She glanced around for a moment before deciding on the calmest and most rational thought in her mind.

"Bye!" She screamed, darting away and ducking into the captain's quarters. Valentina glanced up at her from behind a desk. A map was spread out before her, various locations marked with pins.

"You're red." She observed. "Too much sun?"

"Too much Davy." The demon admitted, melting into a chair across from the captain's desk. "He…he kissed my forehead." The words came out much more squeakily than intended. *What the hell?* She half wondered if something was wrong with her, but assumed it wasn't when Valentina burst into laughter.

"Oh, wow. You two are too much."

"What do you mean?" Astrid asked, narrowing her eyes at the water demon.

"Just that you two get along well." It was a lie, but a lie that Astrid accepted. After all, what else did she expect the water demon to say? "More importantly," the woman before her leaned over the table slightly, "what are you planning on doing?"

"What?" Astrid jolted upright. Valentina's expression conveyed more than what her words did. Astrid technically wasn't member of the crew, so it made sense that she would be departing from The Clover at some point. "Oh, uhm…well, I guess, er…" She had declared that she had never decided on being a pirate, but she had been on The Clover for a week now and it was beginning to feel right – like where she was supposed to be. The thought of leaving made her heart sink.

"That's what I thought." The pirate captain smirked. "You don't really have a plan." Her smirk transformed into a large, beaming grin. "I do though." The captain stood from behind the desk, stretching. "I know what you said before, but why don't you join us?"

"I'm already here." Astrid stated bluntly.

"No, no. I mean, what do you think about becoming a member of my crew – my family?" She walked around the table, sitting on the edge as she spoke. "You've been with us for a while now. We've fought together a few times. We all like you. You're one of us as far as we're concerned. Plus," she continued, looking back at her map, "there's something I've been planning, an expedition of sorts. Another demon on my crew would make it easier. You could really be an invaluable member of this crew."

"What are you planning?" Astrid asked, ignoring the invitation in favor of what was surely the reason she was receiving it. "And why won't Davy do? He has more experience. Demon or not, there's not much I can offer you that he can't."

"You're more naturally resilient than a human – even without much training." Valentina explained. "It takes more to injure a demon or an angel than it does a human. If I take Davy, he could die. If I take you, we could be a-ok by the end."

"So you need a punching bag?" She raised an eyebrow and crossed her arms. "And you want one that won't break."

"No, no. I just need someone who won't die if we run into problems." Valentina glanced to the side nervously. "Demon problems." Astrid perked up at the words.

"Demon problems?"

"I know you don't have much control now and you're just fully coming into your demonic powers, but this'll be a good chance to practice. Plus, I'll be there to assist if anything goes wrong." She smiled wider. "Which it won't."

"And what are we doing?"

"Well," Valentina continued to explain, "I've been having a sense in this part of the sea – a demonic sense."

"Really? I don't sense anything." Her shoulders drooped. Maybe she was just too inexperienced?

"I figured." Valentina turned, looking at the map. "See, I think it's a me kinda' thing, or at least a water demon thing. It came to me in a dream first. I just knew I needed to find…something."

Astrid froze as she remembered the dream she had back in Crimson Barrow; how she had felt as though there was something she needed to find. Valentina ran her fingers over a section on the parchment on her desk. "I need to figure out what it is that's calling out to me." She turned back to Astrid again. "So! What do you say? Will you help me?"

Astrid looked down at her boots for a moment, considering. It could be dangerous and maybe even deadly, but Valentina had taken her in. They shared in so many of the same experiences – the dreams, the demonic powers, and now they were even both being hunted. She had welcomed the chance to teach her, to help her to become more in control and more powerful. She had pursued Aurora when she had appeared in Doewood to save her and accepted her into her family afterward. How could she say no? This woman was more of a friend than even Dane had been. Astrid leaned back in the chair, glancing to the side and sighing.

"I'm in. Where are we going?" The taller demon perked up at Astrid's agreement.

"Really?! That's great!" She snatched up the map and held it in front of her comrade. "This place!" She said, pointing to a tiny island. "It's called Sucrose Isle."

"Okay, what's there?" She took the map and looked at it in confusion. "And where the hell are we on this thing? And how far is that?" She grimaced at the illustrations. She understood almost none of it.

"Erp. Right…you haven't really had a reason for maps being that you've lived in that tiny village your whole life. Guess you wouldn't know how to read one. Well," Valentina started, tipping her hat back slightly and leaning on the table again, "Sucrose Isle is mostly deserted other than this teeny village in the northern part. That's not really super important to us cause we're headed south. That's where I keep feeling this at. Problem is, there're a lot of obstacles in the southern part.

"Heading down from the North isn't an option either. Davy scouted for me once and the village is…less than welcoming. He barely made it out with his life."

"What happened?" Astrid inquired.

"Cannibals." The pirate shrugged. "He's been a bit grumpy about the whole plan ever since he almost got eaten. What a baby, right? Anyway, heading in from the South is the best plan to avoid massacring the whole population of the isle, but we're going to run into lots of things – in the water and otherwise."

"Such as?"

"Sharks will be the least of our worries, but they are definitely in abundance. I've seen a couple of sirens lurking as well. It makes me think the place is a haven for aquatic monsters. Mermaids, selkies, krakens – they're all probably there."

"I have no idea what half of those things are, but it won't matter if we just don't bring the ship, right? We can be stealthy about it. I can try to carry you and fly us over and we'll avoid the water and village completely."

The captain smiled brightly. Her arms wrapped around Astrid as she pulled her into a hug and ruffled her hair.

"I knew you'd be a great crewmate! Bright as can be, kiddo!"

"N-not really." Astrid muttered, blushing at the flattery, but brimming proudly at her own plan. "When should we plan to head out?" She asked as she was released from the embrace.

"No time like the present." Valentina shrugged. "We're close enough and it's best we do it when we're not too far off since you're still new to those wings of yours. We don't want you to tire yourself out before we get there. I could probably fight off some of those monsters, but I'd rather not have to. So long as you can reform your wings, we can go now."

Astrid nodded, taking a deep breath and focusing for a moment on the calm feeling Davy had helped her discover. The black mist emerged from her body and began swirling behind her, however, before her wings formed, she remembered something – something that made her blush and had her heart racing. The kiss. The kiss the pirate had planted on her pale skin, how he referred to her as 'sunshine,' the way he smelled like the ocean, how he had been alone in a bedroom with her after their drunken night together. She squeaked, hiding her face in her hands. The black mist all but rammed itself into her back, sending her toppling over the desk. She fell in a tangled mess on the floor, groaning and glancing to the side.

"Thank the heavens...." She muttered as her wings fluttered behind her. "At least they formed in all that."

Valentina burst into laughter on the opposite side of the table. She all but fell into the floor in a fit of giggles as Astrid staggered to her feet.

"Nice. Real graceful!" She commented between laughs.

* * *

Astrid's flight time had been limited since she had become a demon. That much was obvious from the moment she lifted Valentina from the deck. Their journey was precarious and rather turbulent as they headed toward Sucrose Isle. Astrid occasionally fell toward the shark infested water, cuing a sharp inhale from her pirate passenger until she rapidly fluttered upward again. Flying was much more difficult than all the birds had led her to believe over the years. Aurora and the other angels made it look so easy. She groaned. It was so unfair.

They could see the shadowy silhouettes of the monstrous creatures below the surface. Huge, beings made their way through the water, devouring even the largest of sharks and squids that terrorized the tiny fish. Astrid bit her lip, remembering that she couldn't even swim, much less fight underwater. Relief washed over her as a small island, lush with foliage came into view. Sucrose Isle.

"Straight ahead." Valentina confirmed. "We'll land on the beach. You won't be able to fly through that jungle anyway." She was right. The edge of the Isle was shimmering, white sand, but the jungle was dense – far too dense to fly through. Thick vines draped down and the trees seemed to be only inches apart.

The canopy was so thick that Astrid couldn't even hazard a guess about what was below, hiding in the jungle.

"I have to admit," the smaller demon began as she and Valentina plopped down on the sand, glancing back at the blue waves, "this place is gorgeous."

"Danger has a way of presenting itself that way." The pirate stated, grimacing upon noticing her sabre was still missing from her possession. "Remind me to kick Davy's ass when we get back."

"I won't, but okay."

The two demons started into the jungle, the waves crashing on the beach behind them. It was different than Samba Forest. Most of the colors were rich green and Valentina had to slice through foliage with a whip of water to allow them to pass through. Roots and vines tripped them every few steps. Snakes slithered on the jungle floor and in the trees. Lizards and spiders scurried from them as they passed through. Everywhere there was something alive.

Both demons paused after only about an hour of navigating through the foliage, noticing a strange sound that was new to the air. To Astrid it sounded as though thunder was rolling through the jungle, refusing to dissipate. She glanced up to where the sky should have been, forgetting for a moment about the roof of greenery that blocked her view. She cursed, glaring at the leaves. They couldn't even check the clouds.

"It's a waterfall, kid." Valentina explained after seeing the smaller demon's conundrum.

"A waterfall? I didn't realize they were so loud." She paused. "Not that I would've seen one anyway."

"Yeah. They can be super loud." Valentina took Astrid's hand as she spoke and led her further through the thick greenery. "I think it's this way."

"Why are we even heading towards it? Is that sense of yours telling you to go that way?"

"Yeah. I know it sounds weird, but I think I passed by here in my dream too." She said as she led Astrid through the thick undergrowth. "Look!" Valentina was almost screaming her words now just to be heard over the thundering sound. "There it is!" Astrid glanced up. She had never seen a waterfall before. It was huge, crashing down into a shimmering, clear lake, a constant rainbow at the base. The waterfall was giant – so high that she could barely see the top, splitting in several areas due to the rocks that blocked the straight flow. The lake it poured into was surrounded by plants and flowers she had never seen before. They were every color – green, blue, pink, and yellow flowers all dancing in the mist that the waterfall exuded. Frogs and turtles entered the lake at will, swimming peacefully through the waters.

"It's gorgeous." The smaller demon observed as they headed down to the water's edge, her words drowned out by the crashing water. Valentina flicked her wrist, water squirming up from the lake at her will. Astrid watched as it glistened, forming a bubble around them as Valentina took a step forward, marching into the shallows of the lake.

"I think whatever is calling me is below the surface." She glanced back, smiling reassuringly at Astrid. "I made the bubble so that you can breathe down there, kid. You won't drown." Astrid faltered for a moment. Despite Valentina's words, she was definitely still feeling off about going to the bottom of a lake. She couldn't swim and she wasn't sure what to expect underwater. She shook the fear from her head, casting a smile at Valentina, and stepping into the shallows, hoping to feel better about the escapade upon reaching the destination. After all, she was part of the crew now. She was a pirate. She couldn't remain out of the water forever, right?

Chapter Six:

As the water washed over the bubble, Astrid could feel her anxiety roaring up again. Each step she took on the lake's floor increased the feeling of dread in her chest, but she followed in Valentina's footsteps despite it. She flinched as several fish darted by. They were colorful, like nothing she had seen before. Their scales were highlighted by the glistening sunshine breaching the surface. She cursed under her breath, ashamed that some damned fish had startled her.

"Look at that." Valentina gestured towards the ground. It was littered with dark shells. "Oysters."

"Oysters?" Astrid poked one with her boot.

"They're good eatin'." Valentina picked one up, popping it open to expose its innards. Astrid cringed. "See?"

"People actually eat that? Disgusting." Sticking her tongue out in disgust, Astrid turned away from it.

"It's better than it looks." She dropped the creature as they resumed their journey.

"Well that's—" Astrid paused as a shadow sped by overhead, covering the entire area in darkness for a moment. "What the hell?" She glanced around but saw nothing.

"The fish are gone." Valentina observed. "They're hiding. That's not a good sign. Let's move."

"Right." Both demons hastened their pace. Seaweed and oysters littered the lake bottom as they made their way deeper into its depths. The amount of light was lessening. They could barely see anything when Valentina finally came to a halt.

"What is that?" Astrid asked, cocking her head to the side as she stared at the small wooden structure before them. It looked like a shack and had barnacles and coral all over it. Seaweed tangled around its supports and oysters littered the roof. It sat in the water just a few feet away. Somehow, it felt natural – as though it belonged there despite it being a building. There were no windows and there was only a single wooden door that looked as though it had been taken from something more fortified and plopped onto the building.

"I think it's a shrine or something." Valentina answered as they approached. Her fingers traced the door as she spoke, stopping on a large metal knocker. It twirled in much the same way that the water demon's horn did and glistened like a pearl. "Let's go."

"Wait. What?" Astrid asked, cringing as she poked a barnacle. Without any further warning, Valentina pulled open the door. Water poured out, washing by them.

"C'mon."

"Next time I get to be the one dragging you around," Astrid grumbled as she obeyed the order given to her.

The inside was bigger than either had expected. Treasures littered the floor, coins and jewels of every size and color were everywhere they looked. Chests of gold and pearls overflowed. Diamond necklaces and rings sparkled around them, glittering even in the darkness. Centered in the back of the room was a huge mirror, taller than either demon. Its rim was constructed of pearls that glimmered with a blue tint. They were held in place with a golden trim. Crowning the mirror was a blue gem that rippled like the water around it. Both demons exchanged confused looks before approaching it.

"This is it." Valentina confirmed. Her breathing was heavy and her hands were shaky. Astrid had never seen her so excited before.

"A mirror?"

"Something about it is weird. I guess you could call it demonic. I don't know," she shrugged, "I just feel like it's somehow the same as me – like it shares my energy or something." She reached out, a single finger touching the glass. Both demons jolted when the mirror rippled like the water around them, moving at the touch.

"What the hell?!" Astrid reached out and poked the mirror, watching the glass move. "What is this?"

"I have no idea." Valentina shrugged before placing her hand on the glass. She stumbled forward, her hand drifting through it. She glanced over at Astrid with a smirk. "It think it's a portal or something!"

"We're going in the mirror, aren't we?" The smaller demon groaned out her words as the pirate beamed. "I can't change your mind?" Valentina shook her head.

"Nope!"

"Are you sure?"

"Positive!"

"Fine." Astrid groaned. "Let's just get this over with." Valentina clapped excitedly before diving through the mirror. Astrid glanced behind her. Water was pouring into the air bubble in Valentina's absence. She yelped, scurrying into the glass after the pirate. "Wait up!"

* * *

Water rushed around Astrid as she flailed. She gagged as the liquid filled her. She searched for air, but there was nothing. No surface in sight. Her lungs burned and her heart raced. She couldn't feel anything but the pain. Just when she thought she would die, the water drained away. She fell to the floor, gasping and choking up water.

"Sorry, kid." Valentina patted Astrid's back as the smaller demon coughed up the last of the water. She glared, but allowed the pirate to help her to her feet.

"Where…the fuck…are we?" Astrid panted. The hall they stood in was pearlescent. On one side there was the mirror they had passed through, but on the opposite end was a door with a whale shaped handle.

"I don't know." The pirate captain shifted and glanced around, wide-eyed. "But we won't figure it out by just standing around." She nodded toward the door, triggering a groan from her comrade.

"Are you sure about this? Shouldn't we be, like, I dunno…careful?"

"Maybe," Valentina shrugged, "but I feel like this place is safe. I feel," she paused for a moment, considering her words before glancing back at Astrid and continuing, "connected."

"What do you mean? Like the same way you felt connected to the mirror? You seriously feel like that about this whole place?"

The pirate gave a nod and started toward the door, forcing the bubble and Astrid to follow after her. Valentina pushed it open. Another pearlescent hall shimmered in front of them. This one, however dazzled with the colors of the stained glass windows on either side of it. "It all seems so…," Valentina muttered.

"It seems like a palace." Astrid finished. The pirate nodded. They cocked their heads at the extravagant, silk curtain at the end of the hall. It fluttered with the flow of the water, dancing while hiding where the doorway led. They shrugged at one another, ducking through the curtain and heading into the next room. They froze instantly.

This room wasn't empty. It was a huge, round room that bustled with activity. The two squeaked, ducking back behind the curtain and peeking out. Astrid couldn't believe her eyes. Half human, half fish creatures swam around the room. Their long, fishlike tails propelled them as the gills on their necks pulsated. Their bare bodies were decorated with strings of jewels and pearls dangling loosely around their necks and arms. Their hair danced in the waves behind them as they moved through the water.

"Merfolk." Valentina murmured before smiling over at Astrid.

"You think they're friendly?" Astrid asked skeptically. She had never met merfolk and wasn't sure what to expect.

"Dunno. Only one real way to find out though, eh?" Before Astrid could object, she had been dragged into the open. "Hey there!" Valentina called out in her usual chipper voice. The merfolk turned, staring at the strangers wrapped in an air bubble. "Hey, all. Name's Valentina!"

"You're insane!" Astrid whispered aggressively. She was ignored.

"We're a little lost, friends. We were wondering if you could –"

"A water demon!" A merman cooed as the crowd excitedly clamored. The two demons exchanged confused looks before backing away slowly.

"Er. Sup? Yeah. That's me alright." Valentina's flashed a false smile. "We were wondering if you could tell us where we are. We'll hit the waves after that."

"Calm yourselves." Astrid and Valentina jolted as a man joined their side. He was different than the others. While he was also mostly naked, his body seemed fully human. His only covering was a seal pelt around his waist. He had inhumanly large brown eyes and matching hair. "If she is our mistress, she has no memory of this place." He addressed the crowd as he spoke despite his gaze never turning away from the two demons. Remember, everyone: the demons are reborn." He gestured to Valentina. "She has never been here."

"What the hell are you talking about?" Astrid finally demanded. His gaze had started to make her uncomfortable. It reminded her of an animal. She squirmed uncomfortably.

"Yeah," Valentina added, "what the hell *are* you talking about?"

"Pardon me. I should explain." He gestured toward the room. "This is Atlantis of the demon realm, kingdom of the apex water demon."

"Excuse me? *Demon* realm?!" Astrid screamed the words. She felt the feeling in her legs drain away. She wasn't sure if she should be terrified or excited.

"Yes. This is the realm where most demons and inhuman creatures reside. Apex demons can pass through using a mirror portal."

"You mean that mirror?" Astrid pointed in the general direction of where they had come from.

"Yes. You two passed through it? That would mean you are our mistress," he smiled at Valentina, "the apex water demon." He turned toward the crowd as the citizens bowed down to the pirate captain. "Welcome back to your kingdom, my liege."

"My kingdom?!" Valentina staggered back slightly at the words. "Woah, woah, woah. I think you're making a mistake here."

"It's no mistake, my lady. You're the water demon, yes?"

"There're plenty of water demons." Valentina stated, shrugging. "How can we say for sure that I'm the one you're looking for?"

"Cause you used that portal." Astrid pointed out. "Plus you had that magic demon dream, remember?"

"A dream?" The man perked up. "That happens when apex demons are near their portals. That settles it! You must be the apex water demon!" He took a step towards the two, closing in on the line that separated water and air. "Though there are more water demons in the world, only the most powerful of their caste can be led to the demon world portals and only that demon can activate them. You did all this, and you even manipulated the water so that this girl wouldn't drown. You are our queen."

"Well," Astrid muttered, glancing up at Valentina, "he certainly has a point. You *did* do all that stuff, Valentina." The pirate groaned, turning back to the man in the seal pelt.

"Whatever. Uhm, so where is this place exactly?"

"Your palace, my liege." As he spoke, he and the two demons began to walk through the castle. The merfolk bowed deeply as Valentina passed by, only going back to their tasks after she had passed.

"So," the pirate muttered as she lifted her hand in the direction of another group of merfolk without even casting a glance in their direction, "you mentioned a kingdom, huh?"

"Yes, my leig-"

"That's enough with the 'my liege' crap." Valentina cringed. The phrase even sounded unnatural coming from her lips. She gave a shudder and stuck out her tongue at the words. "Just call me Valentina or Val or something like that."

"But-"

"No. No calling me 'my liege.' I'm not anyone's 'liege.' I hate the way that word sounds."

"Yes, Lady Valentina." He glared over at Astrid who was giggling at the interaction. His eyes were too large to be menacing to her, however. He looked more like a puppy than he intended, cuing Astrid to fall into a fit of laughter. The man growled, stomping on as they proceeded through the castle.

"Drop the 'lady.'" Valentina instructed sternly as they descended a flight of stairs into the mass of merfolk. "Though, while we're talking about names, you've yet to tell us yours."

"You needn't bother with a name for me, Valentina."

"I want to." She flashed him a smile, earning an eye roll from Astrid. "You've been hospitable to us thus far. It's natural I would want to know your name."

"Calder." He stated as two mermen adorned in pearlescent armor opened a pair of looming doors. Beyond them was a bustling underwater city. Coral lined the streets and shells made up the walkways. Sunken treasure was strewn about as though it were nothing more than litter. Fish darted by in schools, led by mermaids.

Above them, a large eel obstructed some of the light that glistened down into Atlantis. Astrid gapped at it, recognizing the shadow as that of one she had seen in the lake. She gulped, inching closer to Valentina as the creature swished through the water.

"Ladies and gentlemen," Calder called out to the crowd. Their attention turned towards him as they put their tasks on hold. "I give you your liege – I mean, Valentina. Our apex demon has returned!"

A cheer erupted and, as though it had been planned for years prior to their arrival, a celebration commenced. The merfolk began to dance as music blared through the water. Strings of pearls were thrown like confetti. Fishes twirled in whirlpools of color. Even the eel seemed to squirm with excitement.

Valentina and Astrid followed Calder through the impulsive party, smiling at those who passed near their bubble. The smaller of the two demons felt somewhat like a third wheel, like Valentina should have been alone for all of this. Her eyes wandered over the crowds of aquatic citizens as she considered her intrusion. Most were merfolk, but, sparse in numbers and sprinkled amongst the fishtailed people, there were people who seemed to be like Calder. They seemed human other than animal-like eyes. They all wore seal pelts draped around them. She looked over to Valentina, but the pirate seemed busy with her own staring as merfolk swam by and schools of fish shimmered in the light above them.

"So how do you know our mistress?" Astrid felt herself almost glaring up at Calder as he spoke. She glanced back to Valentina, but the pirate had taken to speaking to some children.

"We're friends." She answered as Valentina manipulated the water to form a palm sized whirlpool for the children around her to gawk at. "She's been helping me to control my demon powers." Astrid smirked, challenging Calder with her gaze. "That's not an issue, is it? Another demon here?" Their eyes challenged one another as Valentina waved good-bye to the children and rejoined the group with a smile across her face. She glanced between Astrid and Calder.

"Hm?" She cocked her head to one side. "Is something wrong?"

"Is it an issue, Calder?" Astrid asked again with a bit more aggressive tone.

"Of course not!" His answer was much more cheerful than Astrid had expected. "You're more than welcome here, but there is a small issue." He looked her up and down with a snarky grin painted on his face. "A very small issue, really."

"An issue?" Astrid virtually spat out her words. *He's totally implying that I'm the issue. What a cunt.*

"Yes," Calder continued. "This." He gestured to the bubbled of air that surrounded Valentina, Astrid, and, at present, himself. "You clearly can't breathe water. Surely you would be more comfortable if we took you to the beach?" Astrid opened her mouth to retort, but didn't have the time.

"The kid doesn't leave my side." Valentina had been so silent up until this point that Astrid had almost forgotten that she'd rejoined them.

"Understood, Valentina. We could all go." He suggested with a smile that only made Astrid want to punch him. *What a kiss ass*, she thought. "I only meant to make her more comfortable; I know how sensitive air-breathers can be." He grinned widely, exposing animalistic canines in his mouth. "We wouldn't want her drowning, now would we?"

"Pft. Would you?" Astrid muttered. She was met with a disapproving glance from Calder, but she felt her point had been made. She shrugged at his look as they continued on.

"The edge of Atlantis," he continued, "is beach. Your tiny companion will feel comforted by the air there." He shot her a falsely sympathetic look. "Now wouldn't you?"

"I'd be more 'comforted' by you not being a pretentious prick." Astrid snarled.

"He's right though. You're gonna be better off up there." Valentina flashed her an apologetic smile before nodding at Calder. "Take us."

He led them through the city, happily making subtle jabs at Astrid as they walked. He went with everything from how he believed water demons were superior demons, how Astrid was lucky to be friends with such a powerful apex demon, how sad it must've been to be someone who could only breathe air, and even how easily she must almost drown because of her height.

None of it mattered, however. She was far too busy being amazed by the colorful piece of artwork it turned the city into. Hues of pink, blue, green, orange, and red dazzled her eyes as they proceeded down streets that were lined with beds of seaweed, coral, seashells, and golden coins. Houses were made of coral and seashells. They had pearls lining their doorways. Every ray of light shimmered off of scales or pearls and reflected gorgeous colors onto the city. It was all fantastical and radiant. That was, until her eyes caught sight of the eel again. It slithered through the water overhead, watching, waiting.

"What is that?" She asked as it passed over. The water was becoming a bit shallower, but the creature still followed. She wondered how low the water would have to be to make it leave them.

"Just an eel." Calder stated, shrugging.

"A big one." Valentina narrowed her eyes at the area where the creature had been. "We saw another outside of this realm."

"There is one guarding the mirror on both sides." Calder stated plainly. "Most of the mirrors have guardians. The eels are yours. They won't attack you," he looked Astrid up and down, "or whatever you bring with you."

The pearl and seashell lined streets were crowded with aquatic creatures that gawked at the group, some bowing to Valentina as they passed, some sobbing and praising her arrival, but all of them seeming rather pleased by her arrival. Gazes cast at Astrid were filled with confusion and concern. Her tail flicked with agitation as many whispered and stared at her. Her eye twitched. She assumed they must be wondering why their dear Valentina was with some ratty little air breather. "Maybe the seagulls will like me better." She muttered.

As the water began to lose its depth, the crowds thinned out. The closer they got to the surface, the more they saw merfolk with tattered fins and missing scales. Astrid observed the familiarity of the rabble living on the outskirts of town. The tatters reminded her of the scars and injuries that she'd seen on Crimson Barrow's homeless. They were the unwanted, living where she would have if she had been born in Atlantis. Their homes, what few there were, were made of sunken trash – from nets and large cages. She shifted uncomfortably, wishing she could do something for them. Calder didn't spare a glance, but Astrid found she couldn't tear herself away.

"Well, there it is." Calder interrupted Astrid's thoughts, gesturing toward the surface only a foot or so from the top of the air bubble. "We're essentially there."

"Great!" Valentina chirped, a bright smile on her face. "Let's go!" Astrid nodded, eager to get to a place where she would be able to move freely.

The surface was equally as magical as the underwater world. Mermaids lounged lazily on rock structures crafted for exactly that, women and men who were like Calder walked around the small village on the sand, their pelts draped over them but only barely. Music filled the air, a strange inhuman singing that was intriguing and foreboding all at once. Astrid glanced over to see a finned woman was making the beautiful sounds with her mouth.

"A siren." Valentina explained, seeing the confusion on the smaller demon's face.

The houses on the surface weren't large but were comfortable. Most of them seemed to be made from palm trees, but some were constructed of rocks with pearl and seaweed decorations. Fruit trees grew in abundance and the bright sun shimmered overhead, radiating off the white, sandy beach.

Amidst all of this were several tall lookout towers with soldiers positioned at them, peering down over the sands. A single tower hosted more guards than all the others combined. It was pearlescent and had a building at its base.

"What's up with all that?" Astrid waved her hand at the towers and soldiers and they pranced around and continued about their business, ignoring her. "You guys expecting some trouble?"

"Most kingdoms have posted guards." Calder stated as though it was obvious. He quickly adjusted his tone when he caught Valentina's eye, feigning professionalism despite his disdain. "As I said before: powerful demons are reborn over and over, retaking their form in another life when they expire, almost always with no memories of the time they had before – no thoughts of allies or foes. That's why the shrines call out to the demons, so that they may reawaken their full strength and find their kingdoms. In the meantime, the kingdoms wait, hoping to have things in a satisfactory manner for their overlord's return. That could mean having a slaves, sacrifices, or even a feast of flesh. Each demon enjoys something different and each incarnate is different. It's a gamble and some are willing to kill to please."

"Yeesh. That's a bit excessive, don't you think?" Astrid cringed at Calder's words.

"It's a common practice so we must be prepared to protect our people from those who would use them in nefarious rituals." Calder signaled at a passing guard, bidding him to approach. "Soldier, this is our liege – Lady Valentina," he cleared his throat before half-heartedly adding, "and company."

"Madam–"

"Valentina." The pirate captain corrected monotonously, clearly growing weary of the titles. "My name is Valentina. Don't call me 'lady' or 'leige' or any of that crap or I swear on all the oceans of this realm and the other that I will slap a bitch with a damn lake."

"She really likes titles if you didn't notice." Astrid feigned a whisper as she spoke to the soldier. "You should totally just refer to her as 'Mistress of the Happy Rainbow Fish Kingdom' or something. She'll love it. Trust me. Nothing can go wrong."

"Kid, don't encourage this nonsense."

"But I wanna watch you slap someone with a lake." Astrid faked a pout, but couldn't hold back her own smile.

The soldier cleared his throat, regaining the attention of the two demons. He smiled somewhat nervously before addressing his leader.

"Valentina, we're pleased that you have rejoined Atlantis. We have gifts prepared in your honor."

"Oh," Astrid raised her eyebrow in skepticism. "Kinda' like the gifts Calder was just condemning the other kingdoms for preparing? Shocking that it's okay for you all and bad for all the other people."

"They're in the armory." The soldier continued, giving Astrid a disapproving look. She stuck out her tongue and held up her middle finger at the man, turning away from him.

"That's great!" Valentina quipped, ignoring the exchange. "We love presents!"

"I'm actually more of a 'let's not kidnap people from other kingdoms when we say it's such a bad practice' kind of girl, but to each his own." The smaller demon sighed, shrugging.

"Oh, c'mon, kid! If they're not dead then maybe they'll want to be part of the crew!"

"What if you don't need them for the crew? Also, what if they're a demon from another kingdom or something and then we take them into the other realm and they kill a bunch of people? Do you really want to be responsible for that? Just have them put whoever it is back."

"Pretty sure that won't be how it works, but I promise I'll try if it's a person." Valentina smiled sweetly, patting Astrid's horns as she spoke.

"Either way," the soldier interrupted, clearly annoyed that he'd been ignored by his leader for this long, "we'd have to be giving you a person for any of that to really matter." He smirked slightly.

"I kind of hope they just give you a tiara or something." Astrid whispered to Valentina as the soldier gestured for them to follow him to the armory.

"I would hate a tiara." The pirate whispered back.

"I know." She laughed.

"Ladies," the soldier opened the door to the building as he spoke, "after you."

The inside of the building was dark and damp. It housed a small pool in the center, but nothing else. The depth was indiscernible. The only light they had to help them was the square that illuminated the room from the doorway. Astrid glanced at Valentina, realizing by the look on the pirate's face that they were going back underwater. The soldier gestured for them to head under, affirming the thought.

"Are you ready, kid? I know this is all really uncomfortable for you, but I don't want you alone."

"Pretty sure I could murder Calder in two seconds flat if he tried something, but okay. I'm not happy about it, but I'll go." With that, they began to head under, the soldier close behind. "Calder coming?" Valentina asked the man, noting the man's absence via the lack of arguing.

"He's staying up top to ensure you're not interrupted."

She snickered slightly, as they headed into an underwater tunnel, the bubble of air washing away the water around them. The tunnel was illuminated by bioluminescent fish and foliage all around them. "I'm going to have to teach you Atlanteans a thing or two. You don't seem super threatening, but you sure have a talent when it comes to making things sound like a trap. 'He stayed up top to make sure we're not interrupted!' That sounds a lot like, 'he locked us in and now I'm going to murder you two in this scary, glowing, seaweed covered cave.' Don't ya think?"

The soldier's eye twitched, but he said nothing. After all, Valentina wasn't wrong. This tunnel seemed more like a dungeon than anything and the darkness, though slightly remedied by the bioluminescence of the life around them, made it the ideal place for a prison or torture chamber.

"There." The soldier pointed toward a building constructed of seashell-like material. It stood alone at the end of the cavern, sparkling and shimmering in the light of the life around it. They headed inside, the fish darting away as their bubble consumed the building.

"What is this place?" Astrid asked the soldier as she glanced around the room. It was adorned with various types of weapons, each in pristine condition and glistening in display racks. Swords, bows, and spears lined every inch of the walls.

Buckets of arrows were stacked in corners. Maces were displayed in cases.

"Armory." He answered shortly before facing the two demons. "Valentina, being a demon of your caliber means having a powerful weapon – one that belonged to your predecessors before you and one that will now be yours." He nodded towards a pearl coated door at the far end of the room. Astrid and Valentina shrugged at one another before heading over, pushing it open and peering inside.

Alone in the room was a single weapon rack with a shimmering blue trident displayed on it. The prongs were twisted on either side in spirals, but the middle prong was straight, sharp and ready to pierce flesh. A string of pearls twisted down the handle and at the bottom of the weapon was a single large, glistening pearl reflected more colors than Astrid had ever seen on a singular object. She suddenly understood what Valentina had meant by being attracted to this place. She felt it now. It seemed like this object had the same aura as the water demon – they were the same somehow.

Slowly, the water demon approached the weapon, the sound of her boots clicking against the seashell floor echoing throughout the armory with each step. She paused, eyeing the trident with a deep breath before reaching out with a shaky hand and grasping the handle.

The water around them reacted immediately. Small whirlpools formed, whipping around in controlled but powerful circles. The tide roared, waves crashing against the bubble violently as Valentina turned, a satisfied smile on her face. The soldier gave a bow from the doorway.
"Your weapon, My Queen."

Chapter Seven:

Valentina flinched as the trident suddenly melted into sea foam, sliding down her hand to her middle finger. It clenched around it, hardening into a silver ring with a rainbow pearl. She stared dumbly at it before raising her eyebrow in confusion.

"I sorta miss the trident." She pouted.

"It responds to your demon power." The soldier stated. "It will reform when you need it. It takes a more portable form other times. All the demon weapons do it."

"They all turn to rings?" Astrid asked with a grimace. *Seems like something that could be lost pretty easily,* she thought.

"They aren't all rings, no. It's based on the demon."

"This is amazing!" Valentina chirped. Astrid crossed her arms as she watched the sea foam switch between the trident and the ring rapidly. Maybe it was just because the weapon shared the same energy as Valentina, but the pirate certainly had mastered it quickly.

"It's not a toy." Astrid chided. She was ignored as Valentina continued transitioning the object for several minutes. Finally, the soldier saw fit to interrupt and lead them back to the surface where Calder was waiting.

"Hey." Astrid nodded at Calder half-heartedly. "Miss me?" He opened his mouth to answer but was cut off. "Yeah, thought so. I know how much you *love* having me around after all." She grinned widely and plopped down on the sand.

"Oh, ignore her." Valentina instructed. "She can't swim." She leaned over to Calder and whispered, "All this water probably puts her in a bad state of mind."

"You...can't swim?" He raised an eyebrow. "How can that be? Is that common in your realm?" Calder sat down beside Astrid as she pushed some sand into a tiny lump.

"It's common if you don't live near water and I didn't. There was a lake in a forest near Crimson Barrow, but that was it. We couldn't even get to it cause the forest was deemed 'too dangerous.' I never had the chance to learn. Anyway," she stretched her arms above her head and yawned lazily, "it doesn't matter."

"I see." Calder was silent for a moment, fidgeting for a moment. Astrid glanced over at his hands to see a book. It was old, bound in leather and rather musty. He took in a deep breath and handed it to her. She raised an eyebrow as it was placed in her hands. "I had someone retrieve this while you were in the armory. I thought it would be helpful as neither of you seem to know much about this realm."

"What is this?" Astrid flipped the book open. The page displayed a sketched picture of the mirror they had passed through. She glanced over at Calder, wide-eyed. "Is that…?"

"It's the portal." Calder confirmed. "That book has information in it about this realm." Calder looked Astrid up and down before sighing and adding, "You look like an apex demon. It would be against everyone's best wishes for me not to acknowledge that. If you are, you should focus on finding your weapon."

"We should." Valentina agreed. Astrid glanced up at her. The pirate looked a bit more serious and thoughtful than she normally did.

"Calder," Astrid closed the book and turned back to the man sitting beside her, "I don't suppose you could tell me if the demon energy of all apex demons works on all the mirrors or just the ones associated with the demon. I mean, if I was one of these apex demons, could I activate Valentina's mirror?"

"You should be able to, yes." He confirmed. "Though, if a portal is to a kingdom of your opposite, you won't be able to activate it."

"What do you mean by that?" Astrid stood up, brushing the sand off the back of her pants.

"For example, Valentina will never be able to activate the portal of a fire demon. If *you* happen to be a fire demon…uhm…," he paused, grimacing as he struggled to find her name on his tongue.

"My name's Astrid."

"Astrid. If you happen to be a fire demon, Astrid, you won't be able to activate the portal – apex demon or not."

"I mean, I feel like I'd know if I was a fire demon, right?" She looked to Valentina who nodded with the reassurance she was seeking. "I'd be doing stuff with fire…and I'm not." She turned back to Calder. "Mostly people just die. Violently." She rubbed her arm. She felt naked speaking about her powers so casually. She scarcely had the chance to speak about them before and now she was telling someone exactly what they did. It was as though she was airing her darkest secrets, her innermost thoughts and feelings to a complete stranger. It made her stomach turn.

"That sounds like more of a darkness demon." Calder stated, hopping to his feet and taking the book from Astrid's hands. He flipped rapidly through the pages until he found what he was looking for, turning the book toward Astrid to show her. "See?" He pointed to a sketch of a dark-haired woman with large black wings, sleek horns, and a tail that wrapped around her body. Her eyes were solid black, and her veins seemed visible beneath her skin. "This was the darkness demon of last incarnation."

"Wow." Valentina remarked, having appeared behind Calder to examine the picture. She looked from the picture to Astrid several times before remarking, "It's uncanny – the resemblance I mean. You could be twins if your eyes were black."

"You should try that portal." Calder shrugged.

Astrid nodded just before Valentina grabbed them both by their wrists. She yanked them along behind her despite several complaints, dragging them to the ocean's waterline. A bubble formed around them as they proceeded into the depths. The merfolk stared as their queen pulled the two through Atlantis.

"Valentina!" Astrid stammered as she was dragged. "Where the hell are you taking us?"

"Isn't it obvious?" She beamed brightly at the two. "To find your portal!"

"It doesn't have to be right now!" The smaller demon argued as they made their way back through the castle. The citizens of Atlantis whispered in confusion as their queen marched back to where her portal was located.

"Maybe not," she grinned mischievously, "but don't you wanna get out of this water?" A small drizzle began to fall from the top of the bubble like sand in an hourglass. A puddle rapidly started to form on the floor, eating away at what little air they had as they stood in front of the mirror.

"Valentina!" Astrid's voice had gone up a pitch or two in panic, warranting smirks from Calder and the pirate captain. "You can't just *drown* me!"

"I'm not drowning you. *You're* drowning you if you don't go through the portal so we can find your weapon."

Groaning at the water that was now pooling around her feet, Astrid turned toward the mirror, extending a hand toward the glass. She took a deep breath, focusing her energy in her hands. Her reflection distorted as her fingers touched the glass, the cold surface rippling before her. Apparently, the effects hadn't been there just because Valentina had touched the mirror in the other realm first.

"An apex demon." Calder reaffirmed. He sounded shocked, as though he had only half believed it before. "But if your powers are as you described…."

"What about it?" Valentina asked. Beside her, Astrid gestured angrily to the water pooling around their ankles.

"She's just a demon that could be very…dangerous." The man continued, ignoring Astrid.

"No shit." Astrid rolled her eyes. The idea of her being dangerous was nothing new – she'd known that for essentially her whole life. "Anything else you wanna tell us? The sky is blue? Grass is green?"

"Astrid, your being the darkness demon is no joke." He scolded. She didn't pay him much mind. She was still busy waving a hand in front of Valentina's face and pointing to the water that was around her knees.

"Was I laughing, Calder? I know it isn't a joke!" She glared at Valentina and gestured again to the water. "And neither is *this*!"

"I meant no offense," Calder continued as though Astrid wasn't about to drown, "I just mean that the realm of darkness is dangerous."

"Doesn't matter." Valentina stated, a cocky smile on her face. She exuded confidence as she stood, hands on her hips, completely unfazed by Calder's ominous warning. "We need the kid's weapon. We're going. It'll only be worse for us if you don't tell us everything you know, so just spill." He bit his lip and rubbed the back of his head. Sighing, he accepted defeat on the matter.

"Fine, but you must be careful."

"Psht! I'm *always* careful!" Valentina laughed.

"Not when you're almost *drowning* someone!" Astrid screamed. The water was around her waist now. Finally, the water demon glanced over at her.

"So, we're going, right?"

"Like I have a choice! You're gonna drown me if I don't!"

"Whoo-hoo!" The water drained away as the pirate cheered. Calder merely groaned and reopened the book.

"If you're going, then here. This chapter is on the darkness kingdom – Purgatory."

"Sounds like a *delightful* place." Astrid murmured, rolling her eyes. Of course *her* kingdom was called 'Purgatory.' It couldn't be the kingdom of sunshine and rainbows after all. No way. It had to be all about death.

"Oh, don't pout about it!" Calder scolded. "It's one of the most powerful kingdoms in the demon realm." He turned back toward Valentina and added, "It doesn't say where the weapon is, but I'm sure it's guarded. Getting it won't be easy."

"Uh huh." Valentina's seemed disinterested. She yanked the book from Calder's hands and began to look it over. She flipped through the chapter, glancing at the sketches before apparently seeing what she had been searching for. "This is it, eh? This is the mirror?" Calder glanced at the page and nodded before Valentina slammed the book closed and nodded toward her own portal. "I'll be back eventually. Astrid and I have a weapon to get." With that, the water demon pulled Astrid through the glass, waving half-hearted as they left Calder standing in the hall alone.

"Goodbye, Valentina." He muttered, reaching out to touch the now solid glass. He sighed once more before returning to his duties.

* * *

Much to Astrid's pleasure, Valentina hadn't forgotten about the bubble. No, this time there wasn't even a moment of suffocating wetness as they entered the other realm. She could breathe.

"Well, that was eventful." The pirate remarked, eyeing her new ring and the book in her hand. "I think we scored some nice treasure on that little adventure, wouldn't you say?"

"I would hardly call that soggy old book treasure, but you're right about your trident." Astrid began the march out of the small underwater building and back into the lake as

Valentina followed. "Do you feel better now? Does it feel like you're still being called here or whatever?"

"Well, not really. I feel like I could definitely find this place again though. I know it sounds weird, but I feel attached somehow."

"Well, it's good that you're not being subconsciously drawn somewhere anymore." As they walked out of the water, Astrid bit her lip and gave Valentina a concerned look. It seemed as though quite a bit of time had passed – almost a full day since they'd gone through the mirror. "Seems we took a bit."

"It does seem that way, kid. We should head back to the ship. Davy'll be in a piss poor mood. He's not much for waitin' around."

Astrid nodded though inwardly her heart danced. She was jubilant at the words, but she wasn't sure why. Because this meant they could go back to The Clover, her new home? That wasn't it. She shuddered as the shiver of excitement grew.

As they reached the beach, Astrid grabbed ahold of Valentina's arm, forming her wings and taking to the sky. *Why am I so excited?* Slightly more used to her wings, she navigated more gracefully, gliding above the water like a bird. *If it's not The Clover, then what is it?* She bit her lip as she replayed Valentina's words in her mind. 'We should head back to the ship.' *No.* 'Davy'll be in a piss poor mood.' *Davy.* She felt her heart flutter. *Since when do I care about seeing him so much? I mean, he's cool and all, but...,* she fluttered higher in the sky as they approached a dark shadow in the water, putting them well out of the reach of the kraken that breached the surface. *Do I really like him so much?*

Before long, they could see The Clover and, on the top deck, a pacing pirate – Davy. He was chewing his cheek and gripping his bicep. He turned sharply each time he ran out of room to pace in one direction to stalk off in the other. Occasionally, he ran his fingers through his black locks or tapped his foot.

Astrid chuckled. *He's sorta' cute when he's panicked.* She paused. *Wait. What the hell am I thinking right now?!* She shook her head. She had only ever had thoughts like that about Dane. Back in Crimson Barrow, Dane had been the one to roughly grab her and pull her in alleyways away from guards. He had been the one to stop her and pin her against walls to tell her how much he enjoyed her attire. He had been her closest friend and the only hope she had at a future with someone.

Dane was gone though. Forever. Now, there was Davy. Soft, sweet Davy. Davy who made suggestive comments to watch her become flustered. Davy who was gentle and made every effort to protect her. Davy who was pacing the deck, worried because she and his captain had been missing for a full day. Davy who cared.

"Where the hell have you two been?!" Both demons jolted as Davy's voice rang across the deck the moment their boots touched the boards.

"Funny you should mention hell in that question, Davy, because we're totally going there." Valentina virtually sang the words out as she happily trotted over to her fuming first mate. She was ignored, however, as he pushed by her and approached Astrid.

"Where were you two? It's been a whole day!" He paused. Frustration seemed to mate with embarrassment and concern in his eyes. "I was…er...," He fidgeted for a moment before turning away. "You shouldn't just vanish for that long." He finally spat.

"Davy-boy 'ere were worried 'bout ye." One of the pirates, a man named William who had danced with them during their drunken adventures, added, smirking. "He were whinin' da whole time 'bout how he missed ye."

"I was not!" A blush crept across Davy's cheeks.

"True t'ing it is." Another pirate called out to Astrid. "He been all whiny da whole time yer been away. Cryin' 'bout how he wished yer'd come back soon and how he wish ye'd ne'er gone." He mimicked kissing noises as a couple of other pirates mocked Davy by whining out Astrid's name.

"I never said any of that!" Davy shot a glare toward the crew. "Uhg, whatever. What was it that called Val anyway? You figure it out?"

"It was a demonic mirror portal at the bottom of a jungle lake." Astrid stated, shrugging. "We went to another realm and met a man who only wore this fur thing around him —"

"He was a selkie." Valentina interjected.

"He was a prick." Astrid quickly corrected. "Anyway, so Val got this magic ring that turns into a trident and we got this soggy ass book that's gonna lead us to another portal so I can have a demon weapon."

"Then we're gonna fight the angels!" The pirate captain chirped, clasping her hands together and bouncing up and down happily.

"That's…not what we agreed on." Astrid's words were drowned out by the cheering of the crew.

"Aye!" They cheered. "Let's take down them shimmering pigeons!"

"That's starting a damn war, Valentina!" The smaller demon pulled the pirate close and growled out her words. "Do you really think something like that is smart?!" The taller of the two women shrugged nonchalantly.

"Do you think it dumb?"

"Sort of!" Astrid spat.

"Why?" Valentina crossed her arms and leaned against the railing. Most of the crew was ignoring them, but Davy stayed by their side, eyeing Valentina with scrutiny. He offered no commentary for the moment, but it was painted on his face that he didn't approve. "Do you think they're going to stop?" The pirate captain asked. She didn't wait for a reply. "They won't. Clearly, they want you for some reason. Hell, if they want demons, they want me too. They've already started the war, Astrid. We're just defending ourselves." She sighed before patting the smaller demon's horns. Astrid's tail drooped as she glared. "I get where you're coming from – I really do," Valentina assured, "but I've thought about it. It's a good idea." She glanced out over the waves, flicking back her brown locks as they danced in the ocean breeze. "This can't be avoided. They're coming. If we're prepared is up to us."

Reluctantly, Astrid resigned herself to the words. *I don't know anything about what they want. They could be ransacking towns looking for demons now. They could be killing thousands of people as we speak.* She shuddered at the thought of all those corpses being piled up to be burned – everyone who would die to the angels. *If they're after demons, they won't stop. Valentina is right about that much. I don't have much of a choice here.*

"Even so," Davy interrupted, "you said you need a weapon that you need a portal to get to, right? Do we even have any leads on where to go to find that?" Valentina nodded, flipping open the text they had taken from Atlantis.

"This is it." She said, pointing to the mirror as she showed Davy.

"That's all well and good, but where is it?"

"No clue." Astrid admitted. "How exactly are we going to go about finding it, Valentina?" Silence fell in their midst for a moment as the pirate considered the question.

"Er, well, let's look at a map to start." She stated, smiling at her first mate, her eyes begging for his assistance. Though Valentina was the captain, Davy was much better at planning. That had become apparent during the escapade with the repairs to The Clover. While Valentina had barked the orders, Davy had made the plans behind the scenes. He taught members of the crew everything they needed to know for their tasks – including Astrid.

He scoffed, pulling out a map and slapping it down on the deck as they knelt around it. "You're a darkness demon according to Calder, so we need to find something that fits that." Valentina stared inquisitively at the map. "Now to find somewhere that leads to Purgatory." Her first mate blinked blankly at her for a moment before sighing.

"Val," Davy groaned, "There's literally a lake right near Crimson Barrow called Hell's Lake. If Purgatory's portal is somewhere thematic, I'd say it's there."

"Excellent thought." She praised as though it had required an immense amount of brain power. "Though, wouldn't that be too obvious?"

"That's where I would put it." Astrid shrugged. "Everyone in Crimson Barrow talked about the lake in Samba Forest being super haunted and cursed. Lots of howling and dying happened around there. So, if I wanted to keep someone away from my magical portal, I'd pick the haunted lake."

"Haunted?" Davy squeaked. "Like, as in–"

"As in everyone who went was never heard from again." Astrid affirmed. The pirate glanced over at Valentina, the color slightly draining from his face. *Is he seriously scared,* she wondered with a smile. *The big, bad pirate is scared of ghosties? Oh, this is going to be a riot.*

"Sounds super ghosty to me." The water demon shrugged, smiling widely. "Better bring some holy water."

"Val!" Davy squealed. "Stop it! It's *not* haunted!"

"It might be." Astrid teased. "I suppose we won't know."

"Oh, we'll know." Valentina giggled. "You and Davy can do a little paranormal recon while I study this book."

"Wait! What?!" Davy jumped up, almost falling over the banister as he recoiled from the two deviously snickering demons. "I ain't havin' no part in this!"

"Then," Valentina continued, ignoring her first mate, "you can just come get me after you find the portal. I'll help with the demon stuff and lover boy can help with the spooky."

"Nooooo!" Davy whined. "Let me help with the demon stuff and *you* help with the spooky!"

"This is such a great plan." Valentina chirped.

"This is a *horrible* plan!"

Chapter Eight:

"Are we even sure there *is* a lake?" Davy muttered as he and Astrid hopped down from a small ledge. They landed on the grassy forest floor, glancing around at their surroundings. The dark foliage of Samba Forest brought back familiar memories – memories of running from Dane, of the massacre in Crimson Barrow, and of the first angel attack, but Astrid tried not to show any of it. She remained straight-faced as they trudged on. They had been hiking through the trees for hours with no sign of any body of water and complaining about her life wasn't going to make the task at hand any easier. "Maybe it's more of a puddle." Davy suggested.

"I don't think so." Astrid ducked under a branch, Davy following closely behind her. He grimaced and waved away a pixie that fluttered around his face. "Besides," she continued, "I can't see anyone making a big deal over a haunted *puddle.*"

He groaned, cutting down some of Samba Forest's drooping foliage with the sabre in his hand, muttering something about needing to return it to Valentina when everything was said and done. "So, everyone just vanishes?" The pixie had returned, but he merely slapped it away with the blunt end of the steel. It grumbled, fluttering off.

"Apparently." She shrugged. "I've never been so I can't say whether it's true or not." He sighed as they entered a small clearing. Still no lake.

"What would you say about turning back?" He offered. "It's almost dark and we've found a whole lot of nothing."

"That's not true." Astrid commented, feigning shock. "We found all these trees." She gestured widely to the forest behind them. "They're *such* a rarity, you know. Especially in a forest! How can you say we've found nothing?" Her sarcasm earned her a snicker as Davy plopped down in the grass.

"Oh, yeah. I'm sure Val will be quite impressed." He leaned back, looking up at the sky. He crossed his legs and closed his eyes as he asked, "So you seriously never went looking for this mysterious lake? Seems like a game kids would play. Ya know? Like, 'last one in the woods is chicken shit.'"

"Never." She confirmed. "It never seemed all that bright since everyone who looked for it died. I never dreamed of leaving town until Dane…" She paused, biting her lip. She turned away, looking back at the forest.

"Who's that?" Davy's smile faded and his blue eyes landed on her. They were filled with something. Confusion? Jealousy? Maybe even both? He stared directly upward, but Astrid couldn't help but feel some kind of pressure in the air. She squirmed, unsure of what to do with herself. "Who's Dane?"

"He was this guy I knew before I left Crimson Barrow." *Was that all he was? Wasn't he more to me? I guess it was never official, but still.*

"Oh?" His eyes narrowed as he glared up at the sky. "A guy, huh? Was he cute?"

"What?" Astrid nearly fell over as she whirled around to gawk at Davy. *Not particularly. Nothing like you, Davy.*

"How'd ya know 'em?"

"He was a member of the city guard and I was a thief." She sighed. "Mostly he was getting me out of trouble though. Well, until…," she paused, looking down at her tail as it wrapped around her legs.

"Until he found out you were a demon?" Davy sat up. His glare had faded away and now his ocean blue eyes were gentle, kind. *You're nothing like Dane. You're so much better, softer, kinder.* Her heart fluttered as he continued to gaze at her. Her eyes locked with his for a moment. She took a seat beside him in the grass, glancing over at a burgundy flower beside her.

"He ran me out of town and chased me to Doewood." Thoughts of Dane returned. *He hurt me. He bruised me over and over. He slammed me against walls.* She could still picture the fire in his eyes when he had seen her – the hatred burning inside of him. Her tail flicked behind her, a thought finally forming in her mind – one that she had never given a moment to before. *It wasn't okay. I didn't deserve that.*

On the other hand, Davy sat beside her, his dark locks blowing in the breeze. His eyes shimmered like the ocean at sunset. She had no bruises that needed healed from the pirate – no pain that would take time to dissolve. He didn't even mind her demonism. She smiled, picking the flower she had been staring at and putting it behind her ear before turning back to the man beside her. Her cheeks warmed at the sight of him.

"I would kill him for you, you know." Davy's words pierced her thoughts, tearing her back to reality. "Dane." He stated. "If he tries to hurt you again, I'll kill him." She noticed that, at some point, the pirate had taken her hand in his own. He was warm like the sun on the ship. His grip wasn't tight, yet it was possessive – like a hug.

"You would?"

"Yeah."

Astrid stared at the pirate in awe for a moment. She cocked her head to one side. *But why? Why would you do that for me?* Davy stretched lazily, before widely smiling and turning back to Astrid.

"If we camped here, we could go farther tomorrow." He gripped her hand, pulling it closer to him. "We wouldn't have to tell Valentina."

"Not tell Valentina?!" She was in shock at the suggestion. "But you're her first mate. Won't you get in trouble or something?"

"She doesn't have to know. We're adults after all." He winked. "We just need to hike to the nearest town to get some supplies. It'll be better than going all the way back to The Clover."

"We don't necessarily have to hike." Astrid smirked deviously as her wings formed behind her. "How about we fly?"

* * *

Astrid hadn't considered where the closest town was. She hadn't even thought of how Crimson Barrow was nestled in Samba Forest; how it would be closer than Doewood. Now, hiding behind a tree and waiting for Davy to reappear with a cloak from the market place, she was aware. She twitched at slight movements and the loud squeals of children. She flinched every time a guard passed by the edge of the forest. Swallowing hard, her tail drooping down behind her as she leaned back against a tree. She felt nauseous and dizzy.

Just when she thought she would vomit from the waiting and anticipation, the pirate reappeared with an extravagant red cloak draped over his arm. Embroidered into the trim was an elaborate vine of flowers, their golden thread shimmering in the evening sun.

"What is this?" She asked, narrowing her eyes.

"A cloak. That's what you need, isn't it?" He handed it to her, presenting it much more unceremoniously than the garment deserved.

"Yeah, but this is expensive!" She squealed, gesturing to the extravagant embroidery. "You coulda' just got a burlap one—"

"No. You're *not* wearing burlap." He asserted. Astrid squeaked slightly as Davy forced the cloak onto her body, hooking the golden button together and pulling the hood over her head. "Besides, look how well it suites you!"

"But it's so expensive!"

"Please. You're forgetting: I steal treasure for a living." He grinned. "I've looted enough to have the coin for something like this." He patted her cloaked head before taking her hand and leading her into the bustling street. "C'mon, sunshine."

It was an odd feeling. She hadn't been back in Crimson Barrow in quite a while. She had expected something different upon entering the streets. She had expected panic and death, but now, with Davy, her anxiety was melting away. *How does he do this to me? He makes me feel so…normal.* A smile formed on her face as she laced her fingers between his and moved closer to his body.

So much had been rebuilt in Crimson Barrow that one might have forgotten about the angel attack almost two weeks prior. The towns' people had been hard at work, clearly. They had removed the corpses and most of the buildings were either close to being finished or had at least been started on.

"This way." She whispered, procuring the lead and dragging Davy down a labyrinth of alleyways. They ducked down passage after passage until they reached a bustling outdoor market. She took in a deep breath, biting her lip as she remembered the morning before she had turned into a demon – how she had caused chaos in this very place. It was filled with people on this particular day. Some familiar, others strangers. Merchants sold their goods; food and clothes and oddities from afar. It was bright compared to the rest of Crimson Barrow. She glanced over, grimacing at a stand offering demon repelling charms. She scoffed after a moment. *Well, that's clearly not working.*

"Very nice." Davy stated, patting Astrid's head. "This market is going to be perfect." He pulled her close, holding her by his side, his arm possessively wrapped around her shoulders as they walked through the crowd. "Where do you want to start?"

"What all do we need?"

"Everything we have is on the ship so we should probably grab blankets, food, and a bag to carry all this shit in."

"Fair enough. Let's start with the food."

For the next hour they darted from stall to stall purchasing supplies. Occasionally, Davy would suggest something such as a necklace or a ring that Astrid might like, but she quickly reminded him that there was no need for things like that in the forest. At some points she would cite his having bought her such a flamboyant cloak as reason enough to refrain from purchasing any further trinkets. He groaned several times during their exchanges, usually just waiting until Astrid's back was turned and buying the items anyway.

"We really need to buy that bag you were talking about." Astrid stated as she noticed how full Davy's arms had become. She reached out to help him but he pulled away.

"Go pick out one you like then." He nodded toward a stand with intricately designed bags. Astrid grimaced.

"Or, and here's a thought, we could stop wasting money and get one from a cheaper stall." She smiled widely while making the suggestion, but Davy merely rolled his eyes.

"You get what you pay for in these situations, sunshine."

"All you're paying for is glitz and glam though, but that won't help when we're camping in the middle of the woods. We should get something else."

"Just come look at them."

"Looking isn't buying. I hope you know that." She muttered as they approached the bags. They slowly perused the bags, discussing the extravagant threading and designs on each until Astrid felt something familiar. Eyes peered at her from across the way – the eyes of a young girl. They were familiar; eyes she had seen before.

She felt awkward, as though some part of her had been exposed. Why was this child staring at her with such intensity? Why were they fixated on her and nothing else? She paid Davy no mind as he purchased a rather costly bag and packed their things into it. Her heart sank as she realized where she had seen the eyes before.

It felt as though her heart had migrated to her head. Every beat was so clear in her ears as she watched the horror appear in the little girl's face. "We need to leave, Davy." The pirate glanced up, noticing the looks being exchanged between the two.

"Shit." He muttered before taking Astrid's hand. He pulled her along behind him, ducking quickly into an alleyway. "We need a place that's not as crowded." His words had barely left his lips when a scream echoed through the air. He quickened his pace, taking her away from the area as cries of someone having seen the "demon woman" filled the air. "You seem to have made quite the impression on them." He stated, pulling Astrid closer.

"I guess being a surprise demon tends to do that."

They burst from the alleyway and into another crowd. The people were unrecognizable blurs as they passed by. Another alley. Their boots pounded the ground, splashing in puddles. Astrid's heart raced. Another scream. She winced at the sound, but didn't stop. She should have felt like she had when she was running from Dane; she should have felt fear, but she didn't. Her heart was racing and she felt a surge of energy, but it wasn't fear. It was excitement that roared up in her as she held Davy's hand and sprinted through some place she shouldn't have been. She couldn't help but smile.

They reached an almost deserted part of town before Davy saw fit to slow their pace. They stopped, panting in front of a rickety house. The pirate bent down to catch his breath as Astrid's smile faded. She took in the sight of her old home, vandalized and ransacked.

"Let's go, Astrid. We can head back now." Davy called.

"Uhm. Oh, yeah." She muttered, still staring at the shack. Davy looked between Astrid and the building. He sighed, stalking over to it and pushing open the door. He gestured for her to enter.

"After you." He smiled sweetly as he held open the door. The darkness within blocked their view of what was inside, but Astrid couldn't help but to stare into it, memories of her days at home replaying in her mind. "Don't you wanna go look around?" He asked, gesturing again for her to enter.

"Yeah." She murmured, taking a step forward. She paused, looking back at him. "But we don't have time."

"We'll make time, sunshine." Davy kissed her forehead, earning a squeak from the demon as she turned away with a blush. "Go ahead." He urged, gently nudging her toward the entrance. She slowly stepped inside, glancing around.

It had definitely been pillaged – everything of worth was gone. Her mattress had even been turned out. She kicked over an overturned drawer that had been thrown into the middle of the room. "Seems like they took everything," she sighed, "or at least everything of worth."

"Nah." Davy said, waving the thought away as he lifted a board that had been pulled up. "I wouldn't say that. I mean, you had much more here than just stuff."

"Not sure I follow." She glanced under the board, realizing that the citizens had pulled up her floorboards in search of more evidence of her demonic wrongdoings. She groaned. What did they hope to find? Dane had known that she had to steal just to eat so surely some other soldiers knew the same. Why even bother with the stupid floorboards?

"I mean, you lived here." Davy continued.

"If you want to call it living." Astrid interjected, recalling what little time she had spent in the cramped little building, most of it after something had caused her to panic or whenever she had to sleep or eat. It was always the smallest portion of time possible. Nonetheless, she couldn't help but feel violated by the intrusion. She felt naked by having someone tear through what few belongings she had.

"It was still your home – your safe haven in this place." She paused, glancing over at him as he grimaced at the state of the room. "Though it doesn't look like much now. They must have really worked the place over." She smiled at him and his sentiment.

"I suppose it *was* the safest place I had in town. You're right about that. I may not have felt the best here but at least I felt safe." The conversation ceased as a voice echoed in the distance – someone saying they should check the outskirts for the demon. Astrid rolled her eyes. "I guess it's time to go." Davy nodded, gathering up their things and leading her outside.

"This way." He said, leading her into the forest.

She shook her head and dragged him back out of the foliage. Her dark mist swirled around her, forming her wings on her back. Panic roared up in the small group of citizens who emerged in the street as Astrid's cloak whipped around her and her wings stretched out widely. The townsfolk stared, some screaming in horror as she took Davy by the hand and gently lifted him into the air. He smiled softly, staring into her crimson eyes as they ascended higher and higher, a gentle breeze blowing by them as the citizens below tripped over one another to escape the demon above them. *He's absolutely gorgeous,* she thought as she fluttered through the clouds, hand-in-hand with Davy, leaving Crimson Barrow behind for an adventure with Valentina's first mate.

* * *

Setting up the tent took almost no time with Davy's help. It wasn't a skill she would expect a pirate to know, but he certainly showed some prowess with it. She supposed it had to be a skill a pirate would know for when they journeyed inland, far from their precious ocean.

He bent down, setting their bedding in the tent as Astrid started their dinner over the fire. She had to do a double-take upon a realization creeping into her mind. *Is he only setting up one bed space? What is he thinking?!* A blush crept onto her cheeks and her body trembled. Her tail flicked around wildly behind her.

"What're you grinnin' about?" Davy teased as he joined her by the fire. He stood over her, beaming down at her with the sunset at his back and a wide grin on his face. A warm sensation washed over her as he took a seat next to her. *What the actual hell is going on?! Why do I feel like this?*

"I didn't really realize I was." She admitted with a meek smile.

"Ah, well, you were." He yawned lazily and for a moment Astrid thought he might wrap his arm around her. He recoiled, however, clearing his throat and silently looking up to the sky. Silence plagued them for several moments, each fidgeting. "The sky's real nice, huh?" Davy broke the silence. "Especially at this time – just before it's dark when it's not so bright that you can't see the stars." A silence fell between them again as they watched a few more twinkling lights appear overhead. He patted his hands on his legs for a moment, looking to the side. "So," he cleared his throat again, "uhm, yeah. Let's eat or whatever."

The silence persisted as they bit into pieces of rabbit. Her heart pounded as she chewed each bite. *Why do I feel like this?* She glanced up just in time to see Davy staring at her, but he quickly turned away. She blushed, taking another bite of her dinner. *Why's he staring so much? Is there something wrong?* Her tail swished behind her as the pirate inched closer, his hand landing atop hers. The last bit of sunlight faded away from them, leaving them with only the light of the fire.

"So…," Astrid muttered awkwardly after becoming painfully aware of how long they'd just been sitting there, watching the fire dance, "you, uhm, like being a pirate?" He blinked dumbly at her for a moment before bursting into laughter.

"Do I like it?"

"Uhm…yeah?" She blushed a bit more deeply. *What a stupid question!* She mentally scolded herself. *Of course he likes it! He loves being a pirate!*

"It's the most free a man can be, so I suppose I do."

"Free?" Astrid scoffed. "You're trapped on a boat in the middle of the ocean more than half the time. I'd hardly call that free." He smirked in Astrid's direction. Had his smile always been so entrancing? Her tail flicked over behind him, wrapping around his waist.

"I suppose someone who can't swim *would* say that, but, honestly, is it really so bad now that you know how to control your wings?" Astrid thought for a moment. *I can fly off whenever I want to.* She bit her lip. *But I don't want that. I don't want to leave The Clover. Everyone has been so nice. It's been like having a family – like having people I can rely on.* She glanced over at Davy. *And he's there. I don't want to leave.*

"I dunno." She muttered as she watched a bat flutter around overhead, catching the bugs that fled from the smoke of their fire. "I wouldn't want to leave on a whim anyway."

"Yeah." Davy agreed. "I don't like the idea of that either." Astrid gulped as she felt his fingers lace between her own, his gaze piercing into her. "Some things are worth sticking around for, after all." Her heart felt like it would burst as it pounded against her chest.

"Dav-" Her words were cut off by Davy's lips pressing against her own. His sea breeze scent seemed to engulf her, enrapturing her, tying her to him as she wrapped her arms around his neck and pulled him closer. He tasted sweet, like apples, and his muscular arms wrapped around her hips secured her like nothing she had felt before. She leaned closer, her tail flitting around behind her in an excited spasm.

"Astrid…" His breath, warm and moist in her ear, was hypnotizing as his hands slipped down her body, stroking her skin. She moaned as the pirate lavished her body with affection, kissing and sucking at her exposed skin.

He pulled her onto his lap, pressing himself against her as he stroked her body. She drew in a sharp breath as he squeezed her thigh. As his hand glided inward, she felt a chill run up her spine.

Astrid squeaked, pushing away from Davy and sending both toppling over.

He cleared his throat, smiling. "We…uhm…we should head to bed." She nodded, squirming in place. Her body was hot and she felt flustered. Her heart still raced in her chest and the sensation of Davy's hand on her thigh still danced in her mind.

The pirate doused the fire before leading Astrid to the tent, holding open the flap for her before following her inside. He was inches away, but it felt like miles as Astrid's brain screamed out in frustration. *Why did I push away? Damn it! I'm such an idiot!*

She flinched as she felt the pirate shift, inching closer to her until he his body was pressed against the back of her own. "Goodnight." He whispered in her ear. Her tail flicked around his leg, holding him close.

"Goodnight." She replied.

Chapter Nine:

The morning sun was intrusive. It flooded into the tent and shone down onto the two travelers. Astrid nuzzled against Davy's chest. She took in his scent, felt the sculpted curves of his muscles, the warmth of his touch. She could hear each thump of his heart behind his flesh. It was music to her ears as she sighed contentedly. She could have stayed there with him all day, but that wasn't the plan. The plan was very different and she was reminded of that as the pirate shifted. He pet her horns as her tail swayed happily behind her. She didn't open her eyes. Instead, she snuggled closer, letting out another heavy sigh as she made herself comfortable again.

"I know you're awake, sunshine." He gave her head another pat. "Your tail betrays you." Astrid opened her eyes as the pirate beamed down at her. He kissed her forehead as she yawned lazily, finally resigning herself to her fate as she climbed out of the tent and out into the pervasive sunlight. The two of them packed their things in silence. She wondered if he replayed the memories of the night before through his mind endlessly as well. She wondered if it made his heart flutter, if he shook with anticipation when he thought about it, if he missed every touch and secretly begged the universe for another shot at it. She glanced over at him. He had just finished packing. His blue eyes shimmered in the morning light as he smiled down at his work, satisfied. *He's amazing.*

Astrid watched every step the man before her took. She watched the subtle sway of his hips as he took step after step through the greenery. Her heart felt full as she touched the reddened blotches on her neck, the memory of his kisses dancing through her brain. He had tasted like apples. She licked her lips. She longed for him to touch her again, but they had a mission – a job to get done. Reluctantly, she shook the exchange from her mind and allowed her fingers to slide down from her neck and to drift back down to her side.

They trudged along, pushing through branches and vines, missing the empty clearing they had slept in. Each step took them deeper into the forest, deeper into the mass of crimson flowers and lush trees. Minutes quickly became hours and, as they searched and searched, finding nothing, Astrid found her mind wondering back to the kissing and touching from the night before again. She blushed as she watched Davy push through another mass of weeds and branches with the sabre he had nicked from Valentina. She fidgeted as she thought of the way his hand had felt against her thigh.

"Do you hear that?" He asked, turning to her with a large grin.

"Hear what?" She asked, shaking the thoughts from her mind again. She tried to seem as though she had been paying attention the whole time despite how distracted she had been.

"That." Davy said, gesturing in the direction of a distant noise – the sound of splashing water. He turned toward her. "The lake!" He declared. Astrid grabbed Davy by the hand and darted through the foliage, pulling him along with her, racing off in the direction of the sound. The trees thinned more and more, eventually vanishing and leaving them with nothing but the sight of the glistening lake water before them. A trio of deer glanced over at them from the shallows. They pranced off upon making eye contact, hiding in the dense forest.

The water was like a black void, darker than any water Astrid had ever seen before. Its systematic tide wasn't what she had expected from an inland body as it clawed at the shore, dragging in sticks and shells. Its collection was relentless, taking all it could drag into itself, consuming everything that wasn't powerful enough to resist it.

A chill crept up her spine. Her body tingled and she felt her muscles twitch, longing to move. She was shivering, an anticipation inside of her festering. She glanced to the center of the lake. Her crimson eyes locked onto a hazy island in the midst of the black water. It was shrouded in fog, but the silhouette could still be made out. *I need to find it.* She flinched at her own thoughts. *What? What am I thinking?* Her eyes didn't drift away from the island. *I need to go there.*

A howl slithered out of the veil of fog, raping the air. Finally, she broke her stare at the mass of land to look over at Davy. He shot her a nervous smile.

"Yay. We found the haunted lake…." He feigned a celebratory 'whoot' before groaning at the dark waters. "This should be a *lovely* adventure, huh?"

"Shouldn't we go back to get Valentina?" Astrid made the suggestion, but not even she wanted to follow it. She wanted to fly over right now. She wanted to find whatever it was that she needed to find – whatever was causing her body to shake and for her mind to wander.

"That'll take us another two days." Davy pointed out. "Plus, it'll take two days to get back here. We should probably just go ourselves." He grimaced at the foggy island. "Haunted or not." She nodded as Davy glanced around.

"No boats. Not even a dock." He observed.

"Guess I'm flying over."

"*We're* flying over." Davy corrected. "You're not planning on leaving me, are you?" A silence infected the air, engulfing them.

Astrid hadn't even considered it until she heard the words. She thought about how even Valentina had been reluctant to take Davy with her on her journey to find her weapon – how she had purposely waited until she had found another demon because her human first mate would be in mortal danger otherwise. He lacked the resilience of a demon. He lacked the abilities and the fortitude that they had. He was likely to die if he went.

She thought of the night before, biting her lip. He had made her feel loved. He had made her feel special in a good way. She didn't want him to die. She couldn't allow it.

I have to leave him. I would've died in Atlantis without Valentina and I'm nowhere close to as powerful as she is. I can't protect him. I have to go without him. Her muscles tightened. *I have to do this alone.*

She flinched as Davy gripped her hand, pulling her closer and locking her gaze with his own. They were like stormy waters, ready to engulf her. She swallowed hard as he restated, "We're flying over, Astrid." She bit her lip. *I have to give him the slip.*

"You're right." She lied.

"Glad to see that I can talk you out of bad decisions. I was worried for a minute. Geez." He released her hand, stretching as he looked back over at the island. "Where'd that idea come from anyway—" He paused, blankly staring at the winged figure that fluttered over the water, headed straight for the island. He turned back to where Astrid had previously been standing, cursing under his breath at the void space. "Damn it! You *just* said you wouldn't run off without me!" He fumed. No response came as Astrid vanished into the fog. "I can't believe she left me. Damn it…."

* * *

"Well, it's good to know that just mindlessly flying away works." She muttered as she flew into the thick fog surrounding the island. "I hate this, but it's for the best. Tough or not, he's still just a human." As she landed, she looked down at the beach around her in awe. The sand, much like the water, was pitch black. It was like nothing she had seen before. She shuffled up the beach, flinching when she heard Davy's voice calling out for her from the opposite shore.

He sounded pissed. *Oh well. At least he's going to be safe.* She stomped up the beach and started into the looming forest, reminding herself periodically that Davy's staying behind was what was for the best despite her longing for his sea breeze scent and the comforting embrace of his arms wrapped around her. She gripped her sleeve as he called out again. *It's all for the best.*

* * *

"Dammit!" Davy spat as he sliced into a small tree with the sabre. He angrily kicked it, assisting it in falling down to the sandy ground. "I can't believe her!" He all but screamed as he stripped the tiny branches from the mass. He pulled a rope from the bag at his side and tied the log to several others.

Snickering, he proudly took in the sight of his makeshift vessel before pushing it into the rough waters of the lake and hopping aboard. He paddled away with a large branch, eyes locked on the island. Letting out a laugh he muttered, "Guess the joke's on Astrid. I'm helping whether she likes it or not." He cackled loudly as he continued to close the distance between himself and the island.

* * *

Astrid glanced around as howling permeated the air. It was clearly much closer than it had been when she had been with Davy on the opposite shore. She bit her lip but continued on, trying her best to ignore the sound. She couldn't help but think about the guardians Calder had warned about near demon shrines. *Maybe that's one of them,* she thought. She shoved by a branch. *I wonder if it's giant like the eels in Atlantis. Either way: it's bad news for Davy. This was the right call.* She couldn't help but wonder if maybe she was trying to convince herself in his absence, but she shook the concern from her mind as a familiar thought crept into her brain. *Find it.*

She understood what Valentina had meant now. She understood the feeling of having something demonic call to her. It was like having eaten too much sugar. She felt hyper, eager, and happy all at once. She felt she needed to keep moving, like she couldn't keep still. She fidgeted with her hands as she walked. The entrancing force dragged her through the forest, pulling her through the foliage.

The plants around her adopted darker hues. They were like nothing she had ever seen. Instead, the leaves around her seemed almost black. The petals on the flowers were a deep burgundy and she could've sworn she had seen some of them moving. She shook it off, persisting on her path.

The howls of the creatures didn't perish. They seemed to grow the closer she came to the center of the island. They surrounded her, transforming into yips and barks. She thought maybe she heard a laugh or two in their midst, but that seemed so unlikely that she ignored it. She twitched as she noticed the sickly sweet smell of blood drawing her deeper into the island. The trees began to look more decrepit, deader. Their leaves were few and all around her skeletal figures littered the ground. The same burgundy flowers wrapped around the remains, their roots tangled in the bones. Some of the figures looked as though they had been running from something, but from what she had no idea.

* * *

Davy huffed as he trudged through the shallows, making his way onto the black, sandy shore. He sighed, allowing himself to catch his breath for a moment. His determined gaze shot up, staring into the forest before he darted in.

He staggered through the foliage, his wet boots having trouble keeping traction on the mossy roots and stones that he stumbled over. He noticed the howls from earlier had grown, multiplying and amplifying. The source wasn't far off.

He groaned, hand on hilt as he continued. It was like a maze of blood colored flowers and black leaves. Ravens squawked overhead, mocking him as he almost fell over a particularly large root. He gritted his teeth, yanking out the sabre and slashing through branches.

"Astrid!" He called out. Silence. He kicked a low branch in frustration, breaking it before stomping onward. He stopped only when he noticed that the trees seemed to have fewer leaves. The pattern continued the deeper he went into the forest. "They're dying? That's not a good sign…." There was silence all around him.

Why had the birds stopped? He glanced up, catching their beady red eyes staring at him, watching his every move as though he was part of an extraordinary show. Their heads twitched from one side to another as they silently stooped. "What…the hell?" A chill crept up his spine as cackling pierced the air. It was close. It could have been right beside him. He turned on his heels, his sabre at the ready as he scanned the area. The sound of scampering feet caught his attention from not one area, but many.

"Shit…," he muttered as he looked around. He shoved his blade back into the sheath and ran towards the center of the island, the unseen creatures following after him, their laughter and yips chasing him.

* * *

Astrid turned, glancing back towards the forest and raising her eyebrow at the symphony of cackles that filled the air. Ravens flew in circles above the trees, squealing at the ongoing hunt. She wasn't sure why part of her suddenly felt torn. She wanted to follow her senses towards what called her but something was making her heart feel heavy – something made her want to turn back. Concern was washing over her like a wave. She glanced from one direction to the other. She had come here for a reason and that reason wasn't to explore senseless concerns that originated from unknown places deep in the forest. What was she even going after? Astrid shook her head.

"This is so stupid. I need to get the —" She paused. It felt as though a voice was whispering to her, chanting the same word in her ear over and over again, penetrating her brain as the chorus of laughter danced through the air. *Davy.*

She turned so quickly that she tripped and had to stagger back to her feet. "Is someone here?" No answer. The voice had felt external – as though someone had stood beside her and, with an icy breath, whispered into her ear. Astrid gritted her teeth, clinching her fists. Her eyes scanned every inch of the skeleton-littered field, catching sight of only bones and dead trees. This couldn't be right. Someone was here. She knew it. There had to be someone or something here.

* * *

Davy panted as he pushed through the undergrowth, his gaze shot back to the large, black creatures racing after him. They were hunched at the shoulders, covered in wiry fur. Their eyes glowed red and their paws were home to dagger-like claws that tore into the ground with each pat against the earth. Sharp fangs exposed themselves as the creatures cackled.

He could have mistaken them for some breed of ravenous wolf or hyena had it not been for the tails. Long and whip-like, with a spade tip – they matched Astrid's perfectly. They were demonic. He cursed, clenching the hilt of the sabre. Every one of the demon hounds looked ready to rip him apart.

He grunted as he tripped over a large rock in his path, rolling down a drop-off ahead of him and into a huge hole filled with mud and bones. The sabre flew from his hand as he collided with the ground.

"Damn it!" He rushed to his feet but slammed back down by two large paws landing on his back. A cackle filled his ears as the creature's claws dug into him, piercing his flesh. He gasped in pain as blood sprayed out onto the ground. He grunted as he shifted, but managed it nonetheless. His elbow collided with the creature, sending it toppling away from him with a yelp. Three more creatures surrounded him, grinning widely.

They prowled closer, forcing him back as they snapped and snarled. His blood dripped down around him, painting the ground. The creatures lapped at the drops, sick smiles on their faces. A slick, steep wall of muddy dirt pressed against his back. He flinched as it caressed his wounds. There was nowhere he could go. There was no more room to recoil.

"Davy!" The pirate confusedly stared at the hounds as he rapidly ascended into the air. They stared back at him, perplexed. A few jumped, snapping at him, but it was all for naught. They couldn't reach him. Smirking, he looked up to Astrid.

"What? You miss me or something, sunshine?"

"Oh, shut it!" She growled as she dragged him through the sky.

"I don't understand. If you knew I was going to follow you, then why bother leaving me?" He chuckled lightly, a cocky, mischievous sparkle in his eye. "Or did you just want me to chase you?"

"You do realize I could drop you, right? Do you *want* to fall to your death?" She loosened her grip on his coat, allowing him to dangle a few inches lower. It didn't seem to matter. Davy merely laughed at her threats.

"Eh. You wouldn't drop me."

"Says who?" Astrid allowed her grip to slip to the edge of his coat. He only seemed to grow smugger, however.

"Says me. Actually, I think you might have a little crush on me." He gave a wink.

"What?!" The word came out as a squeal, a blush forming over Astrid's cheeks. Her hands recoiled as she instinctively tried to distance herself from the claim.

"Shit!" She squeaked out as she realized she had actually dropped him. She darted through the air, grabbing him by the coat just before he collided with the ground. He gawked in disbelief as she sat him down in their new, safe location.

"Well, shit…I stand corrected."

"It was an accident!" She groaned as her wings vanishing into mist. "Besides, you're not even supposed to be here! This wouldn't have happened if you had just stayed on the shore!"

"Pft. Clearly you didn't think I'd stay away. You wouldn't have been looking for me otherwise."

"Actually," Astrid started, remembering the voice that had chanted Davy's name in her ear, "I didn't know you had followed. I didn't expect it. Something on the island told me."

"What?" He raised a skeptical eyebrow. "What do you mean something told you? I swear…if you tell me some of the demon dogs can talk, I'm gonna lose it…." Astrid shrugged.

"I'm not really sure what it was. I didn't see it. I just heard it. It knew your name though." She cringed, noticing the wounds on his back. "That looks bad." She pointed to them with a grimace on her face.

"Eh," the pirate smiled nonchalantly, "it's not too deep. I'll live. It mostly just needs cleaned."

"That's a lot of blood, Davy." Astrid helped him remove his coat, revealing his pierced, ripped flesh. Fresh blood poured down his shirt, glistening as it washed down his body. It smelled seductively sweet to her, entrancing and beautiful despite the wound. She drew in a deep breath as her crimson eyes remained glued to the liquid. Delicious.

"Astrid?" She jolted back to reality. Davy stared at her, confusion painted on his face.

She shook her head and smiled reassuringly before digging through their resources and pulling out the blanket. She tore it into strips and motioned for him to remove his shirt. He obliged, allowing Astrid to fall into another trance of fascination. His body was lean, slightly tanned and glistened with blood and sweat. She gulped as she gently dressed his wounds to the best of her ability. Her hand brushed against his warm flesh. A shiver ran up her spine as she glanced down at the blood on her finger.

"That'll have to do for now." She stated, tying the last of the blanket-bandage as quickly as she could and sucking the blood from her finger while Davy's back was turned. "You can get better medical attention once I fly you back." The pirate pulled back on his shirt and coat, crossing his arms at his demon ally.

"What? Now?" He grabbed her by the shoulders, forcing her to face him, to look awkwardly into his eyes. "We've come way too far! Let's just grab the weapon first. I'll be fine until we get it and then we can pick up the pace on the way back."

"Or you might bleed out." Astrid pointed out as the more obvious ending to the quest. She lifted one of Davy's hands off her shoulder and dropped it unceremoniously. "We can try again once you've healed."

"Astrid. I'm going with you. I don't know why you left me on the shore before but we're going together so we might as well go now. You're not leaving me behind." He smiled sweetly. "I want to help you."

Silence fell between them for a moment as his ocean blue orbs stared into her blood colored eyes. She groaned, seeing the determination in his stare. He wouldn't relinquish his position, she knew it. She stomped around in a tantrum before turning back to him and accepting the situation for what it was.

"Whatever. Let's just go." She motioned for him to follow her as they started down the path littered with skeletons once more. Davy beamed and followed with pride in his gait. He was victorious at last.

They stepped over the bones, staggering through the field of skeletons as they headed further inland. The flowers and corpses were becoming more common. The petals looked as though they were pulsating, beating like hearts.

"Are you sure it's this way?" He asked, glancing around with a grimace.

"Pretty sure." The feeling inside of her had returned and finding the right path had once again become as easy as following the impulse. They were getting closer. It was roaring inside of her, growing stronger with each step. It was entrancing, a force of nature inside of her that chanted in her mind, find it, find it. Davy grabbed her hand suddenly, pulling her away from the edge of a large drop-off carved into the rocky ground. It went down for what seemed like miles.

It was dark enough that they couldn't see anything below, but Astrid knew that was where they were headed. She could feel the voice inside of her screaming to jump down into the darkness and search for the thing. "Here." Her wings formed behind her and she picked up Davy. They slowly descended into the darkness below, their vision completely obscured. She flinched as something fluttered by her.

"It's just a bat." Davy assured as the creature squeaked and moved on. Astrid bit her lip and did the same until, after several minutes, they reached solid ground.

Davy seemed eager to stand on his own as Astrid sat him on the stone floor. He let out a sigh that she couldn't blame him for. She had been nervous flying down, flinching over every tiny movement, jarring to the side regularly and even bumping into the walls at some points.

"See anything?" Davy asked. He didn't sound like he expected a positive response. Astrid did see something, however. Amidst the darkness, the glow of a blue flame danced a ways off. She fondled around in the darkness for a moment before finding the sleeve of Davy's coat and pulling him to view the specter. "What the hell is that?"

"It looks like a lantern or something." They took a few steps towards the light, testing the ground each time, making certain there were no unexpected drop-offs. Every inch was something new to panic about.

As Astrid took another unsure step forward she noticed the return of a familiar cold breath in her ear. *Go.* She jolted around, frantically searching for whoever had said the word to her, but the darkness that surrounded them obscured her vision. *Go to the flame.* She turned again. Nothing. She bit her lip as she tightened her grip on the pirate's sleeve.

"Did you hear that?" Davy asked, his voice a bit shaky.

"Wait. What?! You heard it too?!"

"The whole 'go to the flame' thing? Yeah. Is that what you heard earlier? Was that the voice you were talking about – the something that told you I was here?"

"Yup. It knew your name. It even knew you were in trouble."

"Great…a ghost knows my name." He scoffed. She could feel him shaking. She smiled softly. He didn't want her to know. He was trying to come off as moderately annoyed if anything, but she knew he was filled with fear.

"I don't know that it's a ghost," she stated, "but I promise to protect you if it is." They were closing in on the light by this time, able to recognize their surroundings by its illumination.

The flame was flickering inside a decorative post. It glimmered, giving off enough light to show off a small building inside of the cave. Two pond-like masses adorned either side of the structure, but, rather than water they were filled with a red liquid. Astrid bent down to examine them; the smell and texture confirming the liquid's identity. "Blood." She said, turning to Davy. "What…the actual hell?" She stood up, glancing around. "This must be the shrine to the demon realm, but it's so…," she paused, but the pirate gave her no time to finish.

"C'mon. Let's go." Davy gestured toward the building. The blue glow of the flame illuminated the dark, wooden door before them. It was the only way inside; no windows or other doors adorned the structure. "You see a handle on this thing?" Davy asked as he searched around the door, ignoring what had caught Astrid's eye – a skull adorning the wooden mass, affixed with melted silver. She shuddered.

"Nothing." She responded. "Can it just be pushed open?" Davy shoved his body against the door, pushing with all his might. It was to no avail, however. The door didn't move.

"Doesn't look that way," he groaned. "I'll be back." The pirate sighed in frustration. He stepped away and began searching the buildings base, eyeing the boards around it and pressing on them as though he thought one would be a hidden button.

"Whatever." Astrid leaned against the door, glancing over at the skull. "I bet you know how to get in, huh?" She groaned, sliding down to the floor. "What are we gonna do if we can't find a way in?" Davy opened his mouth to answer but was interrupted by a faint sound. A barking emanated from the darkness. Both froze, remembering the demon creatures who had chased them before.

"Fuck." Davy muttered, returning to Astrid's side. "Do you think they followed us?" Another series of barks sounded followed by a playful cackle emanated through the cave.

"Maybe," Astrid muttered, "but it sounds…I dunno, different?"

"Are you sure?" Davy reached for his blade instinctively. "Shit." He muttered, remembering that the sabre was out in the muddy hole that the creatures has chased him into.

They could hear the pitter-patter of paws as the demon hound slowly approached. Davy shoved Astrid behind him. "Stay back. I'll handle it."

"You dummy! What do you think you're gonna do?! The last time you 'handled it' you got your back torn to pieces!"

Astrid fell silent, staring blankly ahead of them. Davy's arms dropped to his side and his mouth fell agape.

"What the actual hell?" He muttered.

"Awwww!" Astrid cooed, shoving by the pirate and running up to scoop up the three-headed hyena pup in front of them. It wagged its demon tail as she hugged it tightly. "He's a widdle cutie!" She stated, kissing one the pup's noses. "Yes he is!"

"It's a demon hyena! Put it down!" The pirate scolded, slapping his face with his palm. "Don't you *dare* think you're bringing that on The Clover!"

"Oh, just ignore him." She chirped, rubbing the pup's stomach. "I'll take you wherever I want and there's nothing that sea rat can say about it."

"It probably has fleas! Demon fleas!"

"He's just jealous cause you have three cute little faces to snuggle with." Astrid hugged the pup again. It yipped happily, licking her with all three of its tongues. "You're just perfect aren't you, sweet baby?" It cocked one of its heads to the side and playfully barked. "He's so adorable!"

"Noooo! Stop liking it! We can't take it with us and you're just gonna end up disappointed." Davy whined. The pup cocked a head at him before barking and hopping out of Astrid's arms. It wagged its tail and bounced around Davy's boots, growling playfully. When the pirate scoffed and crossed his arms, the ears on all three of the pup's heads drooped and its tail fell downward. It whimpered softly, sitting in front of him. "Tch." Davy bit his lip, looking away from the large, red eyes that stared at him. He glared at a wall for what seemed like forever before letting out a frustrated groan.

"Uhg! Fine!" He bent down and scratched behind one of the six ears, earning an excited howl from the creature. As the sound entered the air, the skull on the door began to shimmer, its mouth falling open and spewing out a mist identical to

Astrid's. The door shook, opening with a loud clunk and revealing a sea of darkness within the building.

"Good job, Cerbi!" Astrid praised, patting one of the hyena heads.

"No!" Davy spat. "Don't name it!"

"Too late." The demon smiled. She lifted up the three-headed hyena and sat it across her shoulder. "I named him. I love him. He's mine now." She reached up and scratched behind the middle head's ear. "Isn't that right, Cerbi?" Astrid glanced over with a cocky grin but realized the pirate had already gone inside, leaving her with her new pet. She smirked, following as she and Cerbi wagged their tails.

Davy had already taken to looking around, searching the room. Chests had been opened, exposing fabrics like none that Astrid had ever seen. Jewelry was strung about, crystals and stones adorning them. There were skeletons and statues wearing gowns and jewels in corners of the room. Everything was extravagant, beautiful – like the items in Valentina's shrine, but lacking aquatic appeal. She picked up a bracelet with a crimson jewel on it, putting it on her wrist and smiling at it before restoring it to its proper place.

Ba-dum! Astrid perked up, looking around in confusion. *Ba-dum*! It sounded like a heartbeat. She whirled around, staring in the direction of the noise. It was coming from the back of the room. She and the pirate exchanged confused and concerned looks.

"Is that a heart?" Davy muttered.

"Can't be." Astrid shook her head. "It's too loud." As they stared through the darkness, they caught sight of on oval shaped object under a silky, translucent fabric. It seemed to move ever so slightly, pulsating with the beating. She glanced over at Davy, unsure of how to approach the matter.

However, before she could relay any concern, Cerbi jumped from her shoulder. He bounced over to the object, gripping the fabric in his teeth and tearing it to the floor. A mirror. Its border was made of what looked like muscles and flesh, pulsating as blood flowed through it, exposed veins bulging with each beat. Atop the grotesque mirror was a crimson jewel that glistened as though it had blood trapped inside of it. Astrid's heart beat faster as she stared at her reflection in the mirror. The force in her head was screaming madly. Her whole body tingled. There it is.

"This is it." She said, reaching towards the mirror. She stopped short of the glass, remembering how the portal reacted to Valentina's touch. She looked back at Davy. "The portal will open if I touch it. We should get the others first – Valentina and the crew. Plus, you're hurt." Davy rolled his eyes, grabbing Astrid's hand.

"Don't worry so much." He pulled her forward, forcing her hand onto the glass. It rippled at her touch, just as Valentina's mirror had. Davy released his grip on her, reaching through the mirror for a moment before pulling his hand back into their realm and staring at it. "Well, look at that. It works."

"Yup. Sure does. It's just like Valentina's." She paused for a moment, reevaluating the mirror. "Well, I mean. It works the same way. It looks nothing like her mirror."

"Yeah, well, you're not Valentina. Your mirror should be different, right?" Cerbi barked in what seemed to be agreement but Astrid simply shrugged. She wasn't sure if they were supposed to look the same or not, honestly. "Let's go. We have a weapon to snatch."

"But–" She tried to object, but the pirate flashed her a huge smile and cut off her words.

"No buts! We can do this." He gave her head a pat before taking her hand. "We'll do it together, okay?" She blushed slightly, giving in to his desires with a nod. She took a deep breath before bending down to Cerbi.

"You watch things out here, okay? We'll be back." The demon hyena gave a bark, curling into a ball and yawning as Astrid and Davy headed through the mirror.

Chapter Ten:

Astrid let out a squeak as she fell from the mirror onto a stone floor. Davy crashed down beside her, rubbing his head before climbing to his feet and offering her his hand. She accepted, hopping to her feet as he pulled her up. They glanced around, dumbfounded. It was nothing like Atlantis. Cold, grey stone made up every inch of the room except for a wooden door. There was no pearlescent coating that shimmered in various hues and there were no decorations or windows to add color or light – just the door and the mirror. She glanced over at her companion. He seemed unsettled, restlessly fidgeting as he approached the door himself, holding her behind him. *He's scared,* she observed. *He has every reason to be. He's a human and we're in the demon realm now. He could be killed.*

The door opened with a long, loud creak. Before them was a spiraling staircase scarcely illuminated by the flickering flames of torches that hung on the walls. Taking in a nervous breath, they started down. Every step echoed as their boots tapped against the stone. It seemed endless, as though the stairs went on forever. Every step was the same, the view unchanging for what felt like hours. They pressed on, eagerly anticipating the end. Astrid stared at the smooth movement of Davy's body as they walked. His normally sure gait seemed unsure now; his calm exterior broken as his hand slightly shook. She bit her lip. *He should've stayed behind where he'd be safe. If he gets hurt more, it's my fault for letting him come.* Finally, the end appeared.

Again, there was nothing but a single door. It was identical to the first – made of dark wood that was barely distinguishable from the darkness. Davy shoved it open. Another stone corridor.

It was infinitely different from where they had been, however. Beautifully elaborate stained glassed windows glistened, their colors painting the halls as the faintest amount of light shimmered through them. They were not adorned with pictures of love or of beautiful oceanic scenes as those in Atlantis had been, but of scenes of violence, plague, and death.

Davy and Astrid paused, noticing one particular window in the hall. They stared at the woman in the artwork. She was pale with long, black locks. Her figure was petite yet busty. She looked almost exactly like Astrid other than the eyes. The figure had dark, ebony eyes as opposed to Astrid's crimson orbs.

She could be my twin, Astrid thought in horror as she looked over the work. Corpses were scattered around the woman, their skin marred by blackened boils, blood gushing on the ground around them. Some were being burned, some buried, some carted off by figures wearing bird-like masks. Faceless children watched the fires. They all wore ragged clothing, but there was one thing that made everyone uniform. They all wore flowers, pansies, on their clothing. They were pinned to them and overfilling pockets everywhere in the picture.

"Beautiful, isn't it?" A voice asked.

Astrid let out an involuntary scream and fell to the floor. Davy had instinctively tried to draw his blade but was quickly reminded of the empty sheath. He cursed, placing himself between Astrid and the cloaked figure that had appeared behind them. The stranger ignored him, ducking around the pirate to help Astrid to her feet. She glanced between Davy and the stranger with uncertainty as the figure began to speak again with an airy, spectral voice. "Your past life." The stranger said, gesturing to the woman on the glass. "I served her eagerly. She was supposed to be immortal. I thought she would be. There's always the one way, though."

"The...one way?" Davy repeated, joining the others below the window, all gazes on the figure in the glass.

"The one way." The stranger affirmed. "It's the one way she could die. They don't die, you know. Not usually. They live. They live long lives, the demons do. The apex demons that is."

The stranger paused before abruptly turning and leaving the two to their antics. Astrid watched as the stranger in the black cloak vanished. For a moment, she thought she saw a skeletal face, but she decided she must've been wrong.

"Well, that was weird." Davy stated as he took Astrid's hand and began leading her down the hall. "Let's hurry up and get your weapon so we can get out of here. I'm done dealing with the haunted lake and the haunted…," he glanced around, realizing he didn't know where they were, "here."

Astrid glanced back at the mural, shuddering. *What the hell am I? Can I do something like that?* Proceeding down the hall, they noticed that many of the windows were of the same nature. Vicious scenes of violence played out on their glass, forever immortalized.

"I wonder if all these people are past lives." She pondered aloud.

"I don't know." Davy stated, shrugging. "They could be – this is your kingdom after all." He glanced up at one of the windows. Thousands of frogs were descending over a sandy village as a woman flew overhead, large black wings spread widely. "Try not to let it bother you though." Astrid rubbed her arm nervously.

"Easier said than done." She admitted after a moment. "Did you see that woman? I look almost identical to her. It was like seeing myself cause all of that." Davy fell silent for a moment. Their footsteps echoed in the air. *Does he think so too? Can he really bare to even look at me after seeing that?* She sighed.

"Yeah, but it wasn't you. I know you and you're not like that." She paused for a moment, watching the man's back as he checked around a corner for more unwanted encounters. *He really thinks that? That I'm not like that? Does he believe that?* She fidgeted for a moment. She hoped he believed that.

They continued through the building, narrowly avoiding citizens and soldiers clad in black metal armor who stomped through the halls. The last thing Astrid wanted to do was run into a demon or some other creature while Davy was with her. After all, she wasn't sure that most magical creatures didn't just consider humans food. She craved blood, so who was to say that other beings in this realm didn't crave the same?

They slipped through rooms, hiding behind furniture and taking in the sight of everyone who passed through. Davy recognized some of the beings as they traversed the innards of the building, slipping to Astrid in whispers their names. Banshees, pontianaks, and wendigos all roamed freely, gliding through the halls like ghostly visages.

"Are those bad?" She asked as they hid from another ghostly figure.

"They're not good." Dragging her along with him as they darted down another hall. "Most of them are rumored to be beings of death; harbingers of it or something like that." Astrid groaned as they made their way over to an open window. *Exactly what I need: a bunch of creatures of death when I'm trying to not get Davy killed. Stellar.*

The two peered outside, looking out over the mass of people that scurried along the streets below them. They glanced around at the structure they were inside. They were clearly in a castle. She looked over at Davy, but he seemed unfazed.

He was much more distracted by the two armored figures who trudged down the hall, only barely missing sight of them. He sighed, taking Astrid's hand and dragging her down another flight of stairs. *Stay.* A familiar voice rang in her ears. She brushed it away, following the pirate closely. They needed to get out of this place and find somewhere where they could blend in. They darted out a door, finding themselves in the street they had seen below.

Davy shuddered at the words that the merchants yelled out. They bragged loudly about their deals on human flesh and eyes as Astrid and Davy made their way by them. The demon

and pirate gazed around in awe at the ridiculously bloody wares
that were sold at the stalls by talking skeletons, undead corpses,
ghosts, and the like. Davy groaned, inching closer to Astrid as
they passed by one of the spectral figures.

"Hey." They jolted, their spines stiffening at the sound
of a deep, raspy voice from behind them. They turned, nervous
smiles on their faces. Staring down at them, more than double
Astrid's height, was a distinctly cat-like creature. Its legs looked
as though they had been ripped from a giant spider and attached
to it, holding it up so that it could glare down at them. Its face
was a dark tone, but had accents of orange, complementing its
fur. "What exactly are you?" The creature asked, his spider legs
bending as he lowered down to put himself at the level of
Davy's face. "You're bleeding and you smell...human." The
pirate glanced nervously over at Astrid.

"Oh! Him?" She laughed, "He's a...he's a...vampire?"

"A vampire?" The creature repeated skeptically.

"Yup. Sure is. He's a vampire and I'm a demon. We're
new here. We're looking for weaponry. We're going to be on the
road for a while and you know how dangerous that can be,
right?" She pulled Davy close, spinning him around and
pointing to his injured back. "I mean, look what those nasty
humans did to him! He was just trying to eat them. It's like
they've never had a vampire kill countless people in their village
before, right?" She smiled sweetly as the lies left her lips. She
may have felt out of place doing a lot since leaving Crimson
Barrow, but as a thief, lying was no problem. The creature gave
her an incredulous look. She lifted part of the red cloak around
her body and wiggled her tail cutely, dropping the hood to show
off her horns. "See? Demon." It seemed to placate the being as he
cast her a smile, nodding.

"There's a blacksmith in town." He answered. "You'll
have to request something and it'll take some time." His
booming laugh startled the two. "So you better get comfy."

"There's nothing that's premade?" Davy asked.

"Nah, but you should be just fine, little vampire. Vampires are welcome here in Purgatory." He paused for a moment before asking, "By the way: what clan are you from?"

"M-my…clan?" He glanced over at Astrid. The demon twitched slightly, her tail drooping.

"Yeah. You in the Von Drac clan?"

"Uh, yeah. Sure. That one." Davy agreed as quickly as he could.

"Ah! You're in town for the cotillion then?" Davy glanced at Astrid. His face wore a calm expression but his eyes screamed for assistance. He turned back to the conversation.

"Yup. That's it alright. That…thing. Yup. Here for that."

"That's right." Astrid chirped in agreement. "It's a pretty big deal after all! A vampire wouldn't want to miss that…er…thing."

"Right, right!" The being nodded. "Anyway, you should have plenty of time to get your weapon made, little vampire. The cotillion lasts several days, after all." He smiled widely, exposing the fangs behind his lips. "You all following tradition?"

"Oh, uhm, yeah. Definitely. Vampire traditions and stuff." Davy lied, unsure of what to say. There was a silence between the three for a moment before Davy gestured in a direction. "So, uhm…that way, right?"

"Right." The creature affirmed. "Don't get lost now. Your clan would go on a murder spree if they lost one of their little vampires."

"Yeah. That'd sure be…somethin'." He took Astrid's hand, slowly leading her in the direction of the blacksmith. "Anyway, we gotta go, so…yeah. Uhm, thanks for the directions. You have a lovely day, sir, and we're just gonna get outta your…fur? Web? Anyway! Bye!"

"Bye!" Astrid waved sweetly before they ducked into an alley and out of the creature's sight. "Well, I'd say we're getting through this pretty well."

"You have *got* to be kidding." Davy was sweating and gripping his chest. He looked pale.

"It's fine." She assured as Davy leaned against the stone wall. "He bought it, right?"

"Yeah, yeah. It's fine *now*, but did you hear what he said?"

"That the vampires are having some kinda' party here?"

"Uh, no." Davy crossed his arms and rolled his eyes. "That there even *are* vampires."

"Oh, yeah. I heard that. That's, in your words, somethin'."

"You seem awfully relaxed about this." His eye twitched as he spoke. He was shaking all over. *I'm trying to be calm because you clearly aren't*, she thought. *One of us needs to have it together, Davy. That's got to be me right now.*

"I guess the idea of vampires just doesn't scare me much. After all, have you seen what my blood does when I lose control of my demon powers? I don't think it'd be all that appetizing for them." She shrugged as Davy sighed.

"Yeah, yeah."

"Is the big, bad pirate really afraid of some humanoid leeches though?" She teased. *He's terrified and rightfully so. He could die.* She wanted to scream and drag him back to the mirror, to take him away. She knew he could just follow her again though and she might not be with him the next time – he could be killed.

"Ha. Ha. You're hilarious." He muttered before glancing out of the alley towards the crowds.

"We should try to avoid them." Astrid contributed, leaning out to look at the bustling street with Davy. "For your sake."

He gave a nod as they exited the alley, walking along with the people, blending in with the crowd thanks to Astrid's horns and tail. She glanced around. The structures were metal and stone, shades of grey, crimson, and black painting everything around her. The blood-colored flowers from the island snaked their way up buildings. The most intriguing, however, was a river that cut through the street.

"Look at that." She pulled on Davy's sleeve as she spoke.

"It's decoration." He stated plainly.

"Oh, yeah," Astrid chided, "cause this place definitely seems as though it's concerned with its decoration. I'm sure the skeletons are falling over themselves to have the prettiest window garden in the city. Oh! And did you see how concerned that spider guy was with accessories? I'm sure he didn't run off to kill someone or anything. He's probably skipping off to get a new bow for his hair or something, right? It'll probably be red, ya know, to go with all the blood that'll be dripping off his lips after he devours someone."

"Your sarcasm is noted, sunshine, but cities do things like that for aestheticism all the time. Trust me." Astrid rolled her eyes, dragging Davy through the crowd. Maybe the city did have a few flourishes, but a stream cutting through the street? She doubted that it didn't have a function. "Astrid," Davy interrupted her quest, pulling his arm back just as they managed to make their way close enough to the stream that she could peer at it by standing on her tip-toes, "we need to find the weapon. This stream isn't even important to our miss—"

"It's got people in it!" She gasped.

"Wait. What?" Davy raised an eyebrow. "People in it? Are you drunk, woman?"

"Look!" She dragged him over to the stream's edge, pointing into what they had thought was water. Washing toward the castle was a shallow flow of ghostly figures, glowing faintly. They looked to be in agony as they went by. "For decoration, huh?"

"What the hell is this?" He bent down at the edge beside Astrid. He grimaced at the faces as they washed by.

"They kinda look like ghosts." Astrid remarked, reaching down toward them. The pirate quickly smacked her hand away.

"Don't touch that."

"I just wanna know what it feels like." She pouted out her words, crossing her arms and glaring at the pirate.

"Death. It probably feels like death." He sighed, pulling Astrid to her feet. "Besides, what if you fell in? You can't swim."

"Can you even drown in ghosts?"

"I don't know! Maybe these are the questions you should have been asking the tiger-spider-demon!"

"I don't think you can drown in ghosts." Astrid decided quietly.

As they continued on, a chill crept its way up her spine. She shuddered, glancing around the crowded street. She felt as though someone was watching them but she wasn't sure what or from where. Looking around the area didn't yield anything – it was too crowded. *Go back to the castle.* She bit her lip as the voice invaded her brain again.

"Hey." She flinched as Davy's voice pierced her mind. "You're quiet. What's going on?" His hand was grasping hers. "You feel something?"

"Yeah, but I don't know where from." She admitted.

"It's not that calling or whatever?" He glanced over at her, catching her concerned gaze. He dragged her along behind him, his pace quickening into a sprint.

"Davy!" Astrid panted out her words as she was dragged through the street. "Where are we going?!"

"I don't know. To the blacksmith's shop? We're getting out of sight."

"Yeah, but why are we running?!" She stumbled a bit, prompting Davy to drag her back up to her feet. He hoisted her up, throwing her over his shoulder as he continued to run down the street. "D-Davy!"

"Look, I'm unarmed and we're surrounded by things that'll want to rip our heads off if they find out one of us isn't who he says he is. I'd rather not stay near whatever has become curious of us long enough for it to find out what I am."

Me either. I want you to stay alive. They stopped in front of a stone building. There was a small engraving on the doorway of two crossed swords and a soft glow emanated from within its depths. Davy plopped her down beside him before leading her inside.

"This is the blacksmith's shop." She observed, glancing at the display wares.

"Seems to be." Chunks of metal decorated the tables all around them. A kiln glowed in the back of the room, casting a soft, orange sheen over the shop. The light seemed out of place compared to the rest of the kingdom's darkness. They looked at each other for support as the rhythmic clanging of a hammer striking metal filled the air inside the building.

The woman causing the noise looked at home as she struck her target. She hadn't acknowledged them at all when they had entered, simply continued pounding away at her work. She was taller than either of them, muscular yet lean. Sweat was pouring down her pale skin. Even in the orange glow of the room, her flesh had a blue tint, as though she had been deprived of oxygen for quite some time. Her hair, bobbed so that it was shorter in the back than in the front, reached only to the bottom of her jawline and stuck to her sweaty face in messy strands. She wore a dingy, terracotta colored bandana on her head. Her hands were protected with black gloves that matched her baggy pants. The only thing that seemed sized appropriately on this woman, for that matter, was her shirt. It was the same thick, black material, but it clung to her body and was much more form fitting than the rest of her outfit.

"Uhm…," Astrid began, debating just how close to get to this woman and the heated metal she was beating into submission, "excuse me. You're the blacksmith, right?" No reply greeted her. Astrid mentally kicked herself for being so socially awkward before starting again. "We need to place an order with you if you're not too busy."

"An order, eh?" Her voice seemed a bit more chipper than Astrid was expecting it to be. She had expected someone working in Purgatory to be melancholy at least but this girl sounded not only content with her station, but genuinely happy to be doing what she was doing. "What cha needin'?"

"Er…," Astrid paused for a moment. They were here for the demon weapon first and foremost. "I'm looking for a specific weapon."

"Ain't got nothin' premade. I do made-to-order weapons." Astrid bit her lip at the words.

"Okay, then. We need a blade."

"You know what kind you're wantin'?" The girl asked without looking up. Astrid glanced back at the unarmed pirate and gestured for him to answer, mouthing that he needed a weapon. Davy stepped in front of her as the demon turned away, busying herself with looking about the room while he finished their order.

"A cutlass."

"Anything else? Specific metal or just whatever I think is best?"

"You're the blacksmith. I trust you'll make a good one." He glanced over at Astrid as she poked a black metal and glanced over at Davy in confusion. He shrugged, mouthing that he'd never seen it before.

"A'right then. I've gotta get this order done first, but, if you've gotta week, I'll have it done for you."

"A week?" Davy all but screamed. He cleared his throat and squirmed in place, adding, much more politely, "Can't you get it done any sooner?"

"Sorry, but nah. I need time to make it and to finish the other orders too. No offense, but it's not like you're royalty. I can't just drop everything for ya." She glanced up at them for the first time since they had entered the shop to cast an apologetic smile. Her eyes shimmered the color of heated metal, a drastic juxtaposition to the rest of her almost colorless visage.

"It's fine." Astrid interrupted before Davy could protest any further. "We're going to be hanging around here anyway." Her hand was the one to take Davy's this time, pulling him out of the shop with her as she cheerfully called back her thanks to the blacksmith.

"You really think we're going to be here for a week?" He asked as they reached the street.

"I don't know, but we have absolutely no leads on this weapon so it's a possibility. We had help in Atlantis, but we're trying to keep a low profile here." She looked over at him, glancing at his back for a moment. "Ya know, so you don't die and all that." She sighed, adding, "We won't be able to just search everywhere and everything because of that. Besides, we don't even know what we're looking for. Sure, it's a weapon, but we have no idea what kind and, even if we did, Valentina's can turn into a ring. What if this one is in another form? It could take a lot of time."

"No," Davy interjected. "That'd be impossible. By that logic, it could literally be anything. I hate to say this, especially considering the nature of the situation, but we're going to need some help." He glanced around at all the inhuman creatures filing through the street. "Trouble is…where do we find it?"

"Brother!" Astrid and Davy jolted at the happy greeting. They turned, nervously gazing at the man who approached them. Astrid raised an eyebrow at Davy who shrugged in

confusion. The man was pale – much too pale in Astrid's
opinion. His hair was pitch black, well kept, and styled perfectly.
His eyes seemed inhumanly blue. They were unsettling – the
color of someone suffocating. His clothing was all black and
decorated with golden thread. He wrapped his arm around
Davy as though he had known him for years. "I was told that
you may have lost your way."

"Lost…my way?" The pirate sputtered.

"Right. The cotillion is being held at the mansion, but
you're new here. I can see where the problem would arise. It's
quite different than Hail Isle." The word 'cotillion' pierced
Astrid's ears. She felt nauseous as she realized who and what
this man was. She glanced over at Davy. *Does he realize what's
happening right now?* He did. Shock was buried deep in his
expression, hurriedly painted over with a false happiness. "The
good news is that I'm here now." The man wrapped one arm
around Davy's shoulders and one around Astrid's waist, pulling
them along with him. "Come, come. We're all going to start soon
and I wouldn't want you or your little guest to be excluded from
the festivities."

They were moving quickly thanks to the man pulling
them along – inhumanly quickly. Everyone in the street ducked
out of their way while they were in the vampire's arms. Astrid
watched them whisper as he walked by, some even flashed him
false smiles and hazarded a friendly wave in his direction. *A
whole city of monsters and they're all afraid of this one vampire.* She
bit her lip as the words crept their way into her thoughts. Was
she even capable of fighting him if it came down to it? She had
never fought a vampire before. She had never even *considered*
fighting a vampire before. Her blood was enough to save *her*, but
this was different. It wasn't just herself that she had to worry
about. No, Davy was trapped in this man's grasp as well and he
didn't have demonic blood. He was human, and he wasn't even

an armed human. She glanced up at the man, chancing a sweet smile.

"So, he hasn't told me much about the cotillion." She said, gesturing to Davy with a pout. "Maybe you can enlighten me on what exactly we'll be doing at your mansion?" *And also where the emergency exits will be located*, she mentally added.

"Didn't tell you?! How rude. Excuse him." He turned, smiling at Davy, his sparkling white fangs exposed and glistening. "Isn't that right, brother?"

"S-So…right…." Davy agreed with a forced laugh.

"Anyway," the man continued, "you'll find out soon enough. It'll be a nice little surprise."

"Well," Astrid smiled nervously, "I hope the surprise isn't that demons are on the menu." There was a silence as the vampire feigned thoughtfulness at the statement.

"Hm. You never know. Maybe that *is* the surprise." Astrid laughed at the comment, but internally she was screaming. What if they asked Davy to drink her blood? Surely, he would object to it, which would be the first issue that might get him killed, but, besides that, if he *did* drink her blood, he would die! She glanced over at Davy, hoping that he was forming some sort of plan, but, much to her chagrin, he seemed about as lost as she did. "Here we are." The man chirped out as they reached a large metal fence surrounding a field of bones and half rotted remains. The same crimson flowers from before grew there like an elaborate garden, piercing corpses and breaking through bone and flesh.

"Do you like it?" The man asked, mistaking their expressions for awe.

"It's beautiful." Astrid muttered. The flowers certainly were, but she wasn't so sure about referring to the rest of the area as such.

"Yes. The Bone Garden is the work of generations and generations of the Von Drac clan." He stepped forward and opened the gate. "After you, my lady." He gave a slight bow to Astrid, gesturing for her to head in before them.

"Oh, thanks." She glanced around at the flora that decorated the area. It was like an infestation. The flowers seemed to have veins pulsing in their petals. Roots actively moved, draining the liquid from corpses. "I…uhm…we don't have these flowers where we're from."

"Well, I'd imagine you wouldn't. Hail Isle isn't very flower friendly, now is it?"

"No," Davy interrupted, "it's not…what with all the ice and snow there." He directed the statement at Astrid, emphasizing what she didn't know about the area they were allegedly from. Her tail flicked up as she realized that Hail Isle must have been a place in the other realm – somewhere the pirate had been.

The vampire led them down a trail so obscured by the flowers that Astrid doubted that she would've seen it without his help. In fact, she doubted they could've managed their way through the maze of flowers at all without him. They were utterly at his mercy.

"The flowers," he smiled at Astrid as he spoke, content to discuss his clan's garden, "are blood blooms."

"Blood blooms?"

"Yes. I'm sure you can guess why they're named thusly." He said, gesturing to one of the plants as it aggressively tore apart a fresh corpse. Her tail stilled as she realized all of the corpses in the area were fresh, newer kills. She bit her lip as the thought of Davy being torn apart entered her mind. "They feed on meat and blood and root themselves in their food. They aren't like the plants of the other kingdoms in that regard. They don't need light or soil – only death." He turned toward his guests, his smile still painted on his face. "A bit poetic, wouldn't you agree?"

"A bit." Astrid muttered. "It's nice to know that something so pretty can come from something so…"

"Destructive." Davy pulled Astrid out of the man's grip, forcing her to walk in the middle, as far from the deadly flowers as he could put her.

"So, she's your inamorata then?" The vampire asked. "Ah. I thought she may have just been a friend or perhaps a pawn, but this makes much more sense." He nodded knowingly. Davy raised an eyebrow at the man. "I did think that cloak was a bit too lavish for a servant."

"Yeah, no. She's definitely *not* my servant." Davy spat. The vampire laughed.

"Perhaps we will have a wedding during the cotillion as well then." Astrid squeaked, turning blood red and burying her face in Davy's chest. Ignoring her, the vampire snapped his fingers, cuing a wall of blood blooms to scurry away and reveal a mansion. Astrid wondered how they hadn't seen it from the gate, but, upon glancing back, she realized that she couldn't even see the gate from where they were. The vampire had moved them so quickly, covering much more ground than she expected. "This is it." He announced. "Welcome to our clan's Purgatory base."

It was huge, imposing even. Astrid would put money on it being the second largest building in Purgatory, only barely being beaten out by the castle. It had large columns and elaborately designed railings. The windows were placed pointedly, carvings resembling flowers in their seals. Gargoyle statues loomed at the top of the building, casting foreboding shadows over them. Even the doors were huge, bigger than those at Saffron's fortress.

Before even knocking, they were let in by a pale girl. She looked to be in her teen years and was dressed in a tight, pencil skirt and a button down white dress shirt. Her brunette locks were pulled back into a tight bun atop her head. She looked exhausted and sickly, barely shifting with each movement.

"Good afternoon, Alma. Hope we haven't missed much." The man addressed the girl in a chipper tone as he sauntered inside with his guests. She seemed ready to faint as she shook her head. She led them through the pristine halls, portraits staring down at them as they found their way deeper and deeper into the mansion, the exits vanishing from view. "The cotillion hasn't started yet then?" Another shake of the girl's head. "Excellent!" The man chirped. "Alma, why don't you take our brother's little inamorata somewhere to change? She'll need some fresh clothing for the cotillion." The idea of being separated from Davy was like a stab in the stomach that shot panic all throughout Astrid's body. *What if I say the wrong thing? They could find out he isn't a vampire. They could kill him.* She cast a glance over at Davy. He was pale, sweating, and, worst of all, still bleeding.

"I'd rather help her to get ready myself." Davy spat out. The desperation was obvious to Astrid, but she hoped it had been lost on the vampire and his servant. "She's my…uhm…you know, so I would prefer her help to come from me." He glanced over at the girl. "I don't know Ms. Alma here and I wouldn't want there to be any misunderstandings between her and my guest." Silence fell between them. The vampire had lost his smile as he looked over at Alma and then back to Davy.

"I see. Are you worried about what a human might try? Makes sense. I heard you were attacked on the way here." He gestured to the wounds on Davy's back, but it was a word that seemed to bother Davy. Human. It hadn't occurred to Astrid that Alma might have been human. *Where did they even get her from? This is the demon realm! There should be no humans here. Can they use the mirrors or something?* She stepped closer to Davy. This could be his fate if they found out – walking around the house, dressed up like a doll, drained of blood, and too fatigued to even fight back. "We don't have such a good relationship with the humans, eh, brother?" He smiled reassuringly before adding, "I can promise that Alma here is perfectly content to assist you, however. No one here would attack that sweet faced demon of yours."

"I'd prefer to go with her." Davy resolutely restated. He shifted. It was slight, but a very intentional movement. He shifted himself between the two. He put himself between a vampire and a demon. It was beyond the limits of stupidity and yet Davy had done it. He was protecting the girl whose blood would literally melt the vampire if he drank it. It was gloriously dense and, somehow, it made her insides flutter. Her stomach wanted to do a backflip and she wanted to squeal with excitement. Her tail wagged behind her, the only bit of her happiness that she couldn't contain. "I don't want anyone else with her, *brother*."

"Oh, my. It seems we've offended you." The vampire sighed. "Well, I suppose we'll just have to make amends for this little mishap, now won't we?" He turned to the human girl who immediately began to sob and beg for Davy to let her help Astrid dress. Their vampire guide wagged a figure at her disapprovingly. "Now, now, Alma. Our guests have already said that they want you nowhere near them as they prepare for the cotillion. You're only making a fool of yourself." He grabbed her by the back of her neck and pulled her closer to his face, his blue eyes colder than before. His expression wasn't the happy-go-lucky one he had been playing up any longer. "Honestly...it's so undignified...it's pathetic." Astrid let out a squeak as he tightened his grip on the girl's nape. A loud crack echoed through the room as Alma's neck snapped and her body fell limp. He dropped her corpse unceremoniously on the floor, allowing it to land with a 'thud' against the tile.

"I...didn't mean...for you to–" Davy started, eyes fixed on the dead girl. He pulled Astrid closer, holding her tightly. He was trembling as he took her face in his hand and forced her to look away. His arms wrapped around her, the only warmth and comfort that could be had in the moment.

"Oh, it's nothing for you to concern yourself with, brother. Just more food for the blood blooms." He snapped his fingers and two more humans had appeared, sickly looking and dressed up in much the same manner as Alma, to cart off the corpse. The vampire motioned for them to follow as he started through the mansion again.

For a moment, Astrid didn't move. She stared, her stomach in knots, at the door the servants had carried Alma through. She wanted to puke. She wanted to run. She wanted to be far, far away from this man – this monster. Her breath was shaky and her heart raced. She couldn't quite hear what the vampire was saying as he walked on, but she felt Davy's arms tighten around her.

"Calm down." He whispered. "It's okay. I'm here." She glanced up into the blue eyes that stared down at her. Her tail wrapped around him and she snuggled her face into his chest.

"Did you see what he did to her? How can I be calm?"

"He'll kill us if you aren't." She bit her lip, wiping away tears from her face and nodding.

"I know." She could barely breathe now. Her chest felt heavy and her lungs burned. Her heart felt as though tiny needles were being shoved through it. She gritted her teeth.

"I'm here." He assured again, petting her horns as her tail fell limp. "I won't let anything happen to us. Astrid," he lifted her face to meet his gaze, "I'm going to protect you." He smiled. "We're going to protect each other. Right?" She nodded, feeling her heart slowing. Her tail wrapped around his leg as she gripped his arm.

"I'll protect you." She mumbled.

"And I'll always protect you." He promised.

The vampire led them down a long hallway, lined with doors. He went on and on about the history of the mansion, catching their attention when he mentioned that the leader of Purgatory had always been close with the Von Drac clan.

"The leader of Purgatory?"

"Yes. The darkness apex demon." He continued on. "She provided our clan with quite a lot in her last life." He paused for a moment, turning to Astrid. "She actually looked a bit like you." Astrid laughed nervously.

"Haha. Weird." She muttered nervously. They stopped when they reached a door decorated with gold coated blood blooms. "This will be where you get ready." He pushed it open to reveal an elaborately adorned room.

The pirate and thief both twitched, catching each other from the corners of their eyes and holding each other back. They feigned disinterest in the jewels and lavish treasures, glancing up at the ceiling and whistling nonchalantly.

"Th-This'll do, I suppose." Davy muttered as he shoved Astrid into the room. "Thanks and all that…uhm…brother." He didn't wait for a response before slamming the door in the man's face and letting out a sigh of relief. They were silent for a moment, giving the vampire time to vacate the area before they began ransacking the room in search of exits.

Astrid groaned. It appeared that the single door leading to the hallway was the only way out. She flung her arms into the air before collapsing into a chair and allowing her hands to cover her face. This was going incredibly poorly. All she wanted was this stupid demon weapon and now Davy was going to have his throat ripped out by a vampire. Valentina didn't have problems like this in Atlantis. It hardly seemed fair.

"You think they have the hallway guarded?" She didn't uncover her eyes, but she could hear Davy opening the door and muttering out an awkward 'hey' to someone before closing it again.

"Uhm…yeah. It's guarded."

"Vampires or humans?" She asked.

"Pretty sure they're vampires." Davy stated. "So…we're stuck." It sounded even worse when the words were in the air.

"Yup…." Astrid groaned. "Guess we're going to a vampire cotillion."

Chapter Eleven:

Astrid patted Davy's wounds with a wet towel, dipping it into the basin of water that had been left for them in the room. She winced at each touch, but Davy didn't move. Instead, he pondered their escape aloud.

"Do you think I could take that vampire outside?" He asked.

"Not a chance."

"Think we could outrun him?"

"A vampire? I doubt it."

"What about flying?"

"We're in a room with no windows. I can only fly as high as the ceiling."

He groaned, slapping his hand over his face. She dabbed a salve on his back, thankful that the vampire's had provided it. She could already see him healing thanks to the supernatural gunk, although just slightly. She gently wrapped fresh dressings around the pirate's back, careful of each gash in his flesh.

"All done!" She announced after a few moments. She beamed, satisfied with her work.

"Thanks, sunshine." He stretched, flinching as the movement tugged on his mangled flesh. "What're we gonna do?" He looked over at the clothing that had been left for them – a leathery ball gown and a matching suit, each adorned with crimson flower accents. "We're not going to be able to fight as well as we normally would in those."

"No." Astrid agreed. "We aren't, but what else are we gonna do? Not accept? I doubt that'll go well."

The pirate groaned again, hoisting up the dress and passing it to Astrid in defeated acceptance. She held it against her body as Davy dropped his jacket and shirt to the floor.

"At least we'll look nice when we die." She offered. Davy snickered, turning away as Astrid peeled off her shirt and pants and draped her cloak over a chair.

The two dressed slowly, trying to bide their time until they found a chance to escape. There was none. They found themselves almost ready for the party with still nothing akin to a plan.

"Ready for this?" Astrid asked as Davy laced the back of her dress. His fingers stroked the pale flesh under the crisscrossed ribbon when he had finished. A chill of pleasure ran up her spine as his flesh touched hers. She held her breath as memories of the night before raced through her head. Why had she stopped him? She wished she hadn't now that this might be their last night together. She wished she had let him do what he pleased.

"Hardly." He muttered, his hand finally resting on her hip as he whispered the word in her ear.

"We'll be okay." She assured, not even believing her own words. She took a deep breath, trying to accept her lie. "Besides, we clean up pretty nice." She gave a twirl in the dress, a large smile on her face.

"Hopefully we don't look good enough to eat." He joked as they headed out of the room and down the vampire-lined hall. Each step echoed off the walls as they passed couples dressed in similar black dresses and suits. Vampires and their dates. A servant pushed open a large, golden door as they reached the end of the hallway, revealing a white, marble ballroom. Bits of gold accented the walls and furniture. Gold plated blood blooms snaked up the walls. A gemstone adorned dome shimmered above them, the jewels reflecting light like stars. Music filled the air around them as a sea of vampires waltzed.

"It's a dance?" Astrid wondered aloud.

"Apparently." The pirate shrugged as they were waved inside, instantly swallowed up by the ocean of twirling gowns and suits. Davy took Astrid into his arms, starting their waltz together as he scanned the room for exits.

"Didn't realize pirates could dance like this." The demon teased. Davy scoffed as he pulled Astrid closer to his body.

"I've sailed hundreds of places and you assume I can't waltz?"

"I didn't realize you went for dance lessons. I can see I was wrong though." He faltered, almost missing a step as she snickered. A blush crept over his cheeks.

"I went there to loot and pillage and do pirate shit!"

"Didn't know you could loot lessons." She shrugged before glancing around the room, scanning the area around them. "More importantly–"

"I haven't seen any way out yet." He interrupted. "There's too many of them around to just make a break for it." He glanced around at the other twirling couples – pale skinned figures with smiles exposing their fangs.

The music faded during their examination, the mass of figures halting and applauding as a slender man with slicked back dark locks walked out onto the golden balcony overlooking the ballroom. He was dressed in a solid black suit like the others. His eyes were bleak, void of emotion as he gazed out over the crowd. They were sunken into his skull as though he was a walking corpse. His skin, like that of the other vampires, had a deathly paleness to it. He held himself regally overtop of the crowd, looming like one of the gargoyles outside.

Beside him stood a woman wrapped in a fluffy, fur coat. It slumped off of her shoulders, her breasts peeking out of the top of her form-fitting crimson gown. Her hair, blond and neatly kept, was pulled in a bun atop her head, secured with crimson flowers and golden chains. She had more color to her flesh than any of the vampires at her side. Her cheeks were rosy and her skin, although pale, seemed alive.

In that moment, Astrid realized many of the creatures in the crowd shared this trait. Their cheeks were pink with life and some of them even lacked the prominent fangs that the vampires sported. She glanced over at Davy but he seemed distracted by something different. He was staring up at the two beings who loomed over them on the balcony. A group of children had appeared behind them, staring down at the crowd with icy, unfeeling eyes. They were definitely not human.

"Brothers! Sisters!" The man began, spreading his arms widely. "We are humbled by your presence!" Astrid cringed as the crowd cheered, wondering what exactly they were in attendance for. On either side of the room, doors had opened. Servants dragged in beaten and battered humans who were chained together. They were led to the center of the room and forced down onto their knees.

Many of the vampires were eyeing them, nodding in approval and whispering amongst themselves. Some of the humans tried to fight against their restraints but it was clear that their efforts were wasted. They were stuck. "We are a proud clan," The man above them continued. "Proud of who we are. Proud of what we are. We are proud of our home, proud of our brothers and sisters." He paused for a moment, bending down to one of the children, a girl with blond locks and cold blue eyes. "Most of all," he continued, his hand in the child's, "we are proud of our children." The crowd roared even more enthusiastically this time. The vampire children beamed, glowing with pride. They smiled widely at one another and then at the crowd.

Davy elbowed Astrid's side as he nodded in the direction of an opened door – one that the servants had used. He lightly tugged her hand, leading her through the crowd with him as the man, followed by his swarm of children, started down the staircase to the ballroom below.

"Today is the day when they become true members of the Von Drac clan." He announced. Astrid ignored his theatrics in favor of watching the woman looming over everyone. She wondered why someone so alive was so important to the Von Drac clan – to a vampire clan.

Davy's eyes were fixed on the children as they slowly surrounded the bound prisoners. "Our children: the future of the Von Drac clan shall make their first kills tonight. We shall celebrate and partake in their joys as they truly become one of us."

Astrid flinched, feeling a hand gently touch her own. She glanced over to see a younger boy, about fourteen, smiling up at her. He had long, dark locks pulled back in a ponytail and eyes that sparkled as though they had a thin coating of ice over them. His flesh wasn't dead and he didn't have fangs that invaded his smile. He seemed slightly out of place despite his matching clothing.

Astrid narrowed her eyes at him, confusion clouding her mind and blocking out Davy's nudges and encouragements to 'hurry up and move it.' A sweet smile slipped over his lips as he looked up at her horns.

"You two aren't supposed to be here, are you?" The words were soft like fresh snow, but easily as dangerous as an avalanche. He knew. Screams radiated through the air as Davy pulled Astrid close, hiding her face in his chest. She could hear the children laughing as they ripped into the humans' throats, tearing open flesh and spilling blood over the floor.

"Come with me." The boy beside them offered his hand. "Before anyone else finds out."

Nervously, Astrid accepted the offer, allowing him to whisk them away through a nearby door. They followed closely as he hurriedly led them down a hall identical to the one their room had been in. He pushed open a door, revealing a matching room. Astrid shuddered. This place was really like the worst type of maze.

"What's your name?" The boy asked as he plopped down in a chair. He directed the question to both of them at once, but didn't wait for even one answer. "I'm Eider. I'm like you." He stared at Astrid's tail with a twinkle of joy in his eyes. It drooped under his stare as Astrid recoiled behind the pirate somewhat.

"Like me?"

"Oh, right. Let me show you." He chirped. A white mist shimmering with flecks of snow and ice surrounded his body. Large, angelic wings appeared behind him, but, instead of a halo, the remainder of the mist formed a long, slender tail, the tip of which popped into the shape of a heart. Astrid could have screamed. She didn't know if she was horrified or elated, but her heart was racing and energy filled her. *A demon. He's a demon.*

"Are all of them demons?" She asked abruptly, glancing back at the door and remembering the hundreds of living looking beings dancing with the vampires. "The ones who aren't vampires I mean."

"Nah." Eider shrugged. "Mostly they're incubi or succubi."

"What?"

"They're creatures of lust. The Von Drac clan has a branch here in Purgatory. That branch is mostly vampires, but they have a few succubi and incubi. It's reversed on Hail Isle. That's where mother and I are from." He paused for a moment before adding, "My mother is the leader of the Hail Isle branch."

"The woman in the fur?" Astrid asked, crossing her arms as she remembered the voluptuous woman who loomed above during the cotillion.

"Yeah. That's her." Eider confirmed excitedly.

"So, are you how the vampires are getting the humans to feed on?" She asked. He shook his head.

"Nope. There are other ways to get out of the realm. They don't really need my mirror, per say. It just makes it easier." He paused. "How did you know I could travel between realms though?"

"Lucky guess." Davy interrupted. Eider smirked and his tail flicked playfully as he leaned forward.

"How'd you get here?" He asked.

"Mirror." Astrid confirmed automatically. The boy's eyes lit up further. Davy threw his hands into the air and fell into an adjacent chair.

"Okay, cool. Let's just tell him everything." The pirate muttered, pressing a pillow over his face.

"I knew it! You really are like me!" Eider cooed as the two demons ignored Davy. "We're both apex demons!" He looked her over and smiled. "I bet you're the darkness demon – you're here for Purgatory, right? I rule Niflheim – it's the ice demon kingdom. What's your vice? Or maybe virtue?"

"Huh?" She cocked her head to one side, her dark locks flopping over as she gave a confused look.

"All of us have dominion over a virtue or vice – all of us apex demons I mean. I control lust. You have…?"

She sighed, remembering what her mist caused; how rage consumed everyone it infected, driving them mad and urging them to kill in a bloodlust induced fury.

"Wrath."

"Fitting." He chirped. "Man, Vlad and mother are going to flip when they hear you're here." Davy threw the pillow across the room with a squeak.

"M-Maybe we don't tell them just yet?" He offered, ignored again by Eider.

"What's your name?" The tiny demon asked, fluttering close to Astrid's face.

"Astrid. Eider, can we keep this between us though. I don't think they'd like my–"

"Human?" He smirked. "Yeah, they won't mind him once they know he belongs to you, but they would maul him otherwise." He winked. "It'll be a secret for now."

"What do you mean?" Astrid asked as Eider landed once again, frolicking to the door and poking his head out. He motioned for the two to follow him back down the empty hall. They obliged, making their way back to the ballroom. It had been emptied out, the guests heading off to someplace else within the mansion leaving only a large, crimson pool of blood that seeped into streams as the servants tried to catch the trickles in rags.

Eider ignored the scene, leading them to the back wall and pressing on one of the golden blood blooms. With a loud creek, the wall split open like two large doors, revealing a hidden passageway just beyond.

"Are you serious right now?" Davy growled.

"I feel your pain." Astrid muttered.

"Why don't you people just use normal doors like everyone else?" The pirate screamed.

"I dunno." Eider shrugged. "This is a Purgatory branch thing. I think it's so the humans don't find a way out while the family is trying to feed, but you'll have to ask Vlad if you really want to know."

"Who's Vlad?" Astrid inquired as they passed through the doorway. The walls were crimson with white flowers, roses. Portraits of regal looking vampires hung on the walls and tapestries draped down neatly in their midst.

"He's one of the head members of the clan. He's over this branch." Eider stated as he gestured around at the mansion – the maze they might die in. "Vlad is the one who gave that speech today." He snickered, glancing back at Astrid before adding playfully, "He's a real blowhard."

As they finally reached the front door, the servants allowed them out without question, opening the door to the Bone Garden. "Here's the exit." Eider confirmed. "It's straight on from here."

Astrid paused for a moment. "Eider, I don't suppose you know where the demon weapon is around here, do you?" The icy eyed boy thought for a moment before smiling widely. He fluttered just above Astrid, his tail excitedly wagging.

"I might have an idea, yeah!"

"Oh, yeah?" Davy perked up. "Where's that?"

"Midday. She's the counselor to all of the darkness demons; she's an immortal so she's served many of them. She would know the exact location."

"Midday?" Astrid muttered as her wings formed behind her. Eider gasped lightly, evaluating the new furry appendages while their owner ignored him. "Where do we find her?"

"The castle." Eider stated as Davy held him back from petting Astrid's wings, scolding him and lecturing the younger boy about a lady's personal space.

"Right. Of course. Why wouldn't it be exactly where we started at?" The darkness demon groaned, flying up and grabbing Davy's arm.

"Wait!" Eider called. The two turned to him in confusion. "I, uhm…I've never met another apex before."

"Oh." Astrid blushed slightly, looking to the side. "Uhm, well sorry I'm underwhelming, but–"

"You're not!" He argued. "It's just that," he paused for a second, joining her where she was in the air, "maybe I could help you more?" Astrid smiled sweetly at the boy.

"You want to be friends?" She asked. "Is that what you're getting at?"

He nodded, smiling before looking down at Davy who stood on the ground, hand on hip. "And with you too. Please let me." Scoffing, the pirate shrugged.

"I guess."

Eider's eyes lit up as he looped around in the air before fluttering in front of them, tail wagging. They turned to leave, but were stopped as the ice demon cut them off again.

"I could be your guide!" He offered.

"Well, we could certainly use one." Astrid shrugged. She turned to Davy. "And you did say we needed help."

"I suppose it would be okay." Davy agreed. Eider cheered.

"Yes!" He chirped. "You two won't regret this! I'm gonna be the best helper!"

Astrid carried Davy through the air as Eider led them through the Bone Garden and back to the streets of Purgatory, safe from the dangers of the mansion. It was awkward to fly in a ball gown, but Astrid soon got used to it.

They quickly made their way back to the castle, navigating Purgatory with much more skill thanks to Eider's expertise. From the air, Astrid could see more of the kingdom; how the stream of ghosts flowed into the castle, how witches flew about in the air, and how the kingdom was surrounded on all sides by a huge, stone wall. She flew by one of the stained-glass windows of the palace, a familiar face looking back at her. It was the same mural she had seen before – the woman, the children, the flowers. She grimaced at the boils and rotted flesh in the piece, the death and the blank faces of the lifeless humans.

"Eider," Davy called out as Astrid sat him down, "you know enough about Purgatory. What can you tell us about those murals?"

"They're past lives of the darkness demon." He shrugged, floating down beside them as they circled the castle, looking for an appropriate door to enter from.

"We know that much." Davy stated.

"Well," he continued, "the woman you two were gawking at was the last life – before our life. I hear she used magic."

"Magic?" Astrid asked as they fluttered down in front of the main door, casting a glance at the guards. The huge armored beings did not move other than to turn and face the group.

"Yeah." Eider confirmed. "Scary, huh? I hear she nearly caused an apocalypse."

"How?" Davy asked. He directed his words at Eider, but he glared at the guards as though he dared them to make a move.

"Plague." The trio jolted at the airy, spectral voice that came from behind them. They whirled around, coming face-to-face with a pale looking woman in a form-fitting black gown. There were slits on either side of the dress, exposing the woman's corpse-like long legs. Her eyes looked to have a milky coating of something over them and her lips matched the veins that Astrid could see through her flesh – blue. "She started a plague." The woman reaffirmed, gesturing to the stained-glass window. "The masks were what the humans used to try to keep it away. They used flowers for the stench of the corpses." She turned back to them with a smile. "But where are my manners, my lady. You must be famished." A snap of her pale fingers cued one of the mountainous guards to shift. He lumbered over to the stream and plucked out a soul from within in. As it touched the air around them, its figure shifted, melting into an apple-sized orb. The guard knelt before Astrid, presenting the glowing, blue object.

"Eat, my lady." The woman encouraged. Astrid stared at her, frozen in place. The woman sounded just like the voice she had been hearing before – just like the ghostly voice that had instructed her to go back for Davy. "Oh, dear…," The woman rested her cheek in her hand, "you seem perturbed."

"Midday," Eider interrupted with a giggle, "she doesn't even know you." The woman looked shocked for a moment before sighing.

"Quite right. I suppose it's been a while since an introduction was needed. Forgive me, my lady." She gave a deep curtsy. "I am Lady Midday – your humble and loyal counselor as well as the gatherer of souls."

"Midday?!" Astrid and Davy jolted upright, both exclaiming the woman's name in unison.

"You're who we needed to see!" Davy stated. "We need the demon weapon!"

"Your weapon?" Midday stared at Astrid as she spoke. "Ah. I have kept it safe for you – as requested." She flicked back her waist length black locks and pulled down the collar of her dress, exposing a shimmering crimson pendant on a silver chain. "It's been on me every second that you were away, my lady." She secured the necklace around Astrid's throat before leaning close to her ear and whispering, "If you don't eat, you'll lose control. You should consume that soul."

A shudder ran up the length of Astrid's spine and she fingered the blood colored jewel in the center of the pendent. Her crimson eyes shot back up at the hand extended before her, at the glowing orb. Thoughts of death permeated her brain – thoughts of losing control. She bit her lip, taking the soul in her free hand as she thought about what it would mean if she did lose control on the ship. Valentina, Davy, the crew – they could all be killed. She pressed the mass to her lips. It was cold, airy. Crunch. It was soft. Crunch. Sweet. Crunch. Delicious.

She licked her lips, staring back at the blind eyes of the woman who smiled at her. She felt somehow calmer and her desire for blood had finally, for the first time since being in Purgatory, waned. Astrid raised an eyebrow at the woman.

"How did you know?"

"Because I have served you many lifetimes over. I know what a darkness demon needs." She glanced at Davy. "Though I must admit that this is new." She circled the pirate, smirking. "Usually you kill humans by now."

"I...," Astrid paused, looking back at Davy and considering her words carefully. "That's not who I am." She finally decided to say.

"What is he to you?" Midday inquired, looking the pirate up and down.

"That's none of your business." He spat, glaring at the woman.

"A lover then." She concluded.

"He's not a—" Astrid was interrupted by Eider's giggles.

"Ooh! A demon and a human! The scandal!"

"Shut it, frosty!" Davy snarled. "Anyway, we were only here for the weapon. We're leaving now."

"Wait!" Midday grabbed the pirate by the arm, but looked at Astrid as she spoke. Her eyes seemed desperate, pleading and her voice had shot up with urgency. "You've only just arrived!"

"We've been here long enough." Davy shrugged off Midday's trembling hand.

"But I've been waiting so long for my lady's return. Please," she stepped in front of the pirate, "please stay for one day at least. I implore you."

"Why's it so important to you that we stay?" He asked, pushing her aside and taking Astrid's hand just in time to see the vampire who had led them to the cotillion pushing through crowds before them. He was searching for something. His brow was furrowed and his fangs gritted as he threw a skeleton out of his way. His lips inquired about something Davy couldn't quite make out, but he *did* recognize one word: human. He twitched, turning back to Midday. "On second thought, why don't you show us around the castle a bit?"

The counselor looked over, smiling at the scene as the man pushed his way through more of the crowd. She nodded, gesturing for the trio to follow her as Eider winced at another individual being thrown to the ground.

"Faust looks mad." The ice demon muttered before following them through the door and into the large front door of the castle.

"Quite so." Midday agreed, leading them onward.

* * *

The main hall of the castle was decorated with murals, but, rather than stained-glass, there were banners that dangled from high up, draped down the walls in cascading waterfalls of expensive fabrics to tell tales of Astrid's past lives. The woman was there again – the magic user. She wasn't depicted with a plague this time. No, this time was worse. This time she had a boiling pot that tiny hands stretched out of. Children tried to climb out, but her hand was outstretched, pushing them back in. Her other arm dumped a spoonful of the stew into her mouth. Her teeth were exposed, showing off the double canines that Astrid also sported.

"She ate children?" She asked Midday as they continued down the hall.

"She ate humans." The counselor confirmed. "That depiction is merely of a certain time when she took away all of a town's children as punishment for trying to burn her at the stake." Midday turned, a smile on her face as she gestured to the piece as though she were giving a tour. "She used her magic as a witch to bestow a flute with hypnotizing powers. Only the children could hear and they followed her into the woods."

"And she ate them." Davy finished.

"And she ate them." Midday confirmed with a nod. "It helps to add to the immortality, you see. The darkness demon has a very specific healing ability: the demon can cure itself, heal, or even prevent death, but, in exchange, it must give up some of its life. To restore this, the demon can absorb the lives of others by killing them." She smiled at Astrid. "The soul you ate was ended early."

"What do you mean?" She asked, suddenly feeling a little sick.

"I killed him." Midday chirped. "About a year before his time. Not long, really."

"Long enough…." Astrid muttered, holding her stomach and trying to stifle the urge to vomit.

"He was a murderer." The darkness demon perked up at the words.

"What?"

"He killed his two children. He left them in the forest to starve after he and his wife couldn't afford them anymore. I thought the world would be better without him." There was a pause as Davy and Astrid exchanged unsure looks. The demon felt somewhat relieved. At least she hadn't consumed a good, hardworking soul who didn't deserve to die. On the other hand, however, she *had* consumed a soul. She wasn't sure how to feel.

"This," Midday continued on, pushing open a door, "is where the ruler of Purgatory hosts audiences with their subjects."

"You!" The trio flinched as a familiar voice broke into their tour.

"There's Faust." Eider whimpered, recoiling behind Davy who instinctively attempted to draw his blade. He groaned as he realized, for the second time since entering Purgatory, that he was unarmed.

"Fucking human!" Faust spat the words. He was nothing like he had been when he had thought Davy to be a vampire. His hair was disheveled, his eyes were flickering like blue flames, and his nostrils flared. "Piece of shit!"

"Buddy, c'mon. Can't we just talk about this?" Davy smiled innocently as he backed away. "I mean, you called me your brother right? We're bros and, you know what they say, 'bros before murdering people for accidentally getting mistaken for a vampire and wondering into a cotillion.' Am I right?"

The vampire tore up a large stone table, tossing it through the air at Davy. He squeaked, grabbing Eider and Astrid and jumping out of the way as it collided with the floor.

"Disgusting! Disgraceful! To think we may have never known if it wasn't for your blood-soaked clothes."

"Yeah, if I could have those back, that'd be–" Davy was cut off by a flying chair. He ducked down, narrowly avoiding it as it smashed against the wall behind him.

"Shuddup! Shuddup! Shuddup! You made me look stupid!" Faust screamed.

"Nah, man. That's all on you." The pirate muttered, pushing Astrid and Eider over to Midday before rolling out of the way of another airborne chair. Faust lifted another table, but, just as he was about to throw it, a white mist encircled his body. It shimmered before solidifying into a sparkling tower of ice that trapped him up to his neck.

"Eider!" He growled. The demon winced at his name being called so aggressively. He gave Faust a nervous, meek smile.

"No." Midday interrupted. "I instructed him to freeze you. Don't blame him when it's my commands that did this to you." She stepped forward, glaring at the vampire and wagging a disapproving finger in his face. "You'll leave the human be, Faust Von Drac. That means no biting or killing or even maiming."

"Yeah!" Davy called out mockingly. "Leave the human be, ya glorified leech."

"You're not helping." Midday scolded before turning back to Faust. "He's the lover of our queen."

"The queen isn't here." Faust argued, squirming in the ice. It didn't budge or crack and Eider seemed unconcerned that it would. He yawned lazily, fluttering his wings and making small spurts of snow appear.

"She is." Midday gestured to Astrid. "The darkness demon has returned, Faust."

Chapter Twelve:

Coronation. The word pierced Astrid's mind and triggered her nerves to fire rapidly. Her hands trembled and her heart beat faster with excitement and uncertainty. A coronation. For her. She shuddered. The moment Midday had suggested it, all eyes had turned her way. She didn't seem the coronation type – not to herself or to anyone else, but she was anticipating everything with a vigor she didn't expect. The spectacle, the crown, the dress, the kingdom – all hers. She wiggled as Midday adjusted said dress against her body, lacing the back of the revealing bodice and fluffing the bottom of her dress. Her pale legs were exposed in the front, but the fabric flowed like a ball gown in the back.

She pulled Astrid's hair back in tight braids that circled a neat bun atop her head, fixing it in place with ribbons and crimson jeweled pins. Astrid felt the part, the part of royalty as Midday painted her lips a deep crimson and lined her eyes with an onyx colored material. She helped her into leathery, thigh-high boots and smiled at her work.

The demon eyed herself in the mirror. She had never felt so pretty and formidable looking at the same time. She smiled widely at her reflection before giving a twirl and hugging Midday.

"Thank you! I love it!" She squealed.

A knock at the door cut the interaction short as soon as it began as Davy sauntered in, dressed in a black, leathery duster, matching pants, and a crimson, form-fitting top. He stopped short, looking Astrid over. His mouth fell agape.

"You look…," he paused as he took a step closer to her, eyes wide, "like a goddess." She blushed, turning away with a smile.

"Thank you. You don't look bad yourself, Mr. Pirate." He laughed.

"Impossible when you're ravishing the whole room. Nothing could come close to you right now."

She squeaked, turning toward Midday who automatically spun her back around to face Davy. He was so close now, staring down at her. He was inches from her face. She placed her hand on his chest. She could feel his heart racing beneath the tight material. "Absolutely stunning." He assured again, leaning forward. His lips pressed against hers. His sweet taste engulfed her. She pulled him closer. His arms wrapped around her waist as his tongue slipped into her mouth.

Just then, Midday cleared her throat. The two tore away from one another as quickly as they had come together. Davy wiped the smudges of crimson from his face, turning away with red cheeks.

"I think it's time." Midday stated, leading both out to the balcony where they were greeted by the Von Dracs – Eider, Faust, and the two heads of the clan, Vlad and a woman Astrid had learned was named Morgana. Valentina and Calder were also there – Midday's doing upon hearing that they were friends of Astrid.

Midday stood before all of Purgatory on the balcony, hands outstretched to the crowd. "Ladies and gentlemen," she began, "I give you, your queen!" Astrid winced as the thundering applause rang out from the crowd below her. Faust snickered behind her but was quickly silenced by a quick jab to the gut, courtesy of Davy's elbow. Vlad placed a black tiara with crimson jewels encrusted into it upon her head. Her heart was racing. Hundreds of eyes were on her, but they belonged to smiling faces, happy people. It was new. It was more than she could've asked for. She glanced over at Eider, standing with his mother, looking bored in his own icy crown. Then, she glanced to her other side. The Queen of Atlantis had been dragged to Purgatory by Midday. Valentina pouted in a flowing gown that looked like it was made of water, her coral and seashell crown atop her head as Calder muttered something about smiling to her. She ignored him.

Astrid felt a firm hand massage her shoulder. Davy. He stood behind her. His hand slid down her exposed back, stroking the base of her wings. He leaned forward and whispered in her ear.

"I'm sure they're all happy to have such a gorgeous, powerful, and resilient queen."

"I'm not sure about all of that." She muttered while smiling and waving to the crowd below.

"I am." Davy assured.

"Why, she's good enough to eat." Faust interrupted.

"The hell?!" The pirate spun around, glaring at the vampire. He merely laughed, however, unfazed by the threat of the man before him.

As they continued their bickering, Astrid and Eider looked over the crowd, catching a glimpse of a dark-skinned man. He looked human other than his fiery orange eyes.

"Who is that?" Astrid asked.

"Not sure." He admitted. "I've never seen him before."

"You think Midday invited him?"

"Maybe. She sent invites to people in all kinds of kingdoms. It wouldn't be weird." The man below her flashed a smile and gave a wave. She returned the gesture with a grin.

"He seems friendly enough."

"He'd be a good ally." Midday interrupted, appearing between the two demons. "He's an apex demon like yourself."

"What?!" Astrid turned to face her advisor. "Where did you find another apex so fast?"

"In his kingdom." The answer was nonchalant and matter-of-fact. "In the castle of Vulcan. His name is Flint. He's the King of Fire. He'd make a good ally against those angels hunting you." She smiled. "He could burn them."

"Another powerful ally *would* be nice." Astrid agreed. "But it's not my place to invite people to join us. Valentina is our leader and –"

"He can come." Valentina interrupted as she pulled at her dress.

"Stop." Calder scolded. "You need to act as a lady."

"No." Valentina turned back to Astrid after denying Calder. "I welcome the fun on The Clover. Plus Midday is right – there's safety with a fire demon around. Just don't let 'um burn up my ship." She looked back over at Calder. "Tell me to behave one more time and I'll throw you over this banister." He clamped his mouth shut, turning away with frustration.

Astrid smiled down at the demon again, waving to one of her guards to allow him inside. The large, armored being nodded, approaching the demon slowly as the coronation party made its way back inside.

They made themselves comfortable in the throne room, waiting patiently until the soldier appeared. With an almost spectral voice he announced the man behind him.

"His majesty the King of Fire: Flint." Flint beamed widely at the three demons sitting before him in thrones made of bones and blood blooms. Davy stood at Astrid's side, eyeing the newcomer dangerously as Cerbi bounced around the pirate's boots.

"Hello, ladies and gents." Flint bounced up to Astrid, taking her hand in his before planting a kiss on it. "It's lovely to meet you."

"That's enough." Davy intervened automatically, pushing Flint back.

"Oh. I'm sorry." He said, grabbing Davy's hand and repeating the action. The pirate blushed fiercely, yanking his hand away. Valentina, Astrid, and Eider burst into laughter as the pirate frantically inched behind the throne.

"What the hell!? No!"

"Oh, calm down." Flint shrugged. "You just seemed a little jealous is all."

"Not jealous!"

"Completely so." The fire demon teased. "Anyway, Astrid is it?" He turned back to the Queen of Purgatory, still smiling widely.

"It is." She confirmed with another giggle.

"I heard you're getting some allies together. Got ya' a lil' angel problem, do ya?"

"They've attacked several towns already while hunting me." She admitted with a sigh. "They've killed tons of people. We can't let it keep happening. That's why Valentina and I need help."

"I agree with all of it." He crossed his arms and nodded knowingly. "And I think I can assist. I can make you some damn fine weapons too. Blacksmith and all that. Worked with some demon ores in my time." Astrid giggled again. Flint spoke as though 'his time' had been long, but, in truth, he was no older than Davy or herself. "I think, though, that you may need to look at this another way." He continued. "What's the best way to protect everyone, Miss Astrid?" She thought for a moment before shrugging.

"I'm guessing you have an answer ready for me."

"I do. The best reaction is no reaction but to be proactive." He went on. "Don't wait for those feathery fucks to come to you."

"You want us to start a *war* with them?!" Davy interrupted in shock. "That could be suicide! We have no idea what their army is like!"

"So we figure it out." Flint leaned against a wall as he spoke. "We infiltrate. Not all the angels are on their side. We can find one to use. Then we garner some access to their forces."

"Good plan except where do we get an angel?" Astrid asked, crossing her pale legs. Davy blushed as he eyed them from behind her throne. He squirmed slightly, his hand slipping onto her shoulder and rubbing her exposed skin. She almost shuddered with joy at his touch.

"Well," Flint rubbed the back of his head, "that's the bit I don't have yet, but I assure you this is a good plan." Before Astrid could retort, Valentina broke in.

"I like it, but I'd like it better if we actually had the numbers to take them on. Look," she paused for a moment before asking, "Flint, was it?"

"Yeah. It's Flint."

"They have loads of angels. Aurora and her brother are bad enough as is and then there's Forfax. That's three that we know of."

"They have more." Astrid assured. "When they attacked Crimson Barrow, they had way more."

"Well," Flint smiled, "we can make our own demon army. We have the darkness, water, ice, and fire demons already." He excitedly leaned closer. "We can find the other apex demons and then we can just go crazy on them."

The two women exchanged looks of concern, staring at each other for a while before turning back to Flint. Astrid bit her lip, glancing at Davy every few seconds. He raised an eyebrow at her, daring her to say what he thought she was considering.

"I think it could work." Valentina said the words for her. "Pending we have the right allies, that is." She paused, crossing her arms. "First we need to do some recon though. I think we should figure out what they want with the demons and how their army operates before we do anything rash." She looked to Astrid. "We'll want to break into two groups."

"We will?" The younger demon was shocked. "Why?"

"Divide and conquer the tasks, ya know? We need to expand our army while also finding the things we need – demons, demon weapons, and an angel. I can work on building our naval forces. I know a few pirates. In the meantime, why don't you work on either finding one or two of the other things we need?" She looked over at her first mate. "Oh, and of course lover boy can go with you. I don't want to send you off alone."

Before Davy could argue with his nickname, Eider burst into the conversation, wings formed as he fluttered overhead, his tail wagging. He flitted around the room, leaving tiny patches of frost everywhere he touched.

"I wanna help with something too!" He chirped.

"Of course!" Valentina almost purred out the words. "You and Faust can head to Niflheim to get your weapon and then meet up with Astrid and Davy somewhere to assist with their mission."

"And me?" Flint interrupted.

"You," the pirate seemed less thrilled now, "will be with me on The Clover. The best place for a new ally is trapped in the middle of the ocean with me since that means I can watch you," she smirked, "and, if need be, kill you. We don't know you that well yet, after all."

"Fair enough." He shrugged. "I'm fired up to get started on this. I have to admit – I've had some issues with them myself." Astrid cast him an incredulous look. He's had issues with the angels?

"You didn't mention that before."

"No reason to if you weren't going to help. Fuckers killed almost everyone in my town." He looked down to the floor, the burning in his eyes seeming less like flames and more like embers that could be snuffed out at any moment. "They kidnapped my sister." He looked up again, conviction raging around him like a wild fire. "That's why I have to stop them – no matter what. I have to get her back." Astrid nodded. She understood the feeling of wanting vengeance against them. She understood some of what Flint must've felt. Rage. Unbridled rage at having something he loved, his home and family, stolen from them.

"It's decided then." Astrid stated. "We're going to start a war."

With their roles determined, the group changed into more fitting outfits. Valentina pulled on a flowing tunic over tight black pants. She slid on her boots, glancing over at Flint's back as he dressed. His harem pants were white and drab compared to his orange, sleeveless top. She narrowed her eyes at him, biting her lip as bubbles formed around her. They popped, vanishing just before the fire demon turned to look at her. He smiled widely.

"Looking forward to working with a water demon." He cooed. "You know…my opposite. Some would say we'd probably not be good together, but I doubt that'll be true."

"Yeah…," she muttered, "I doubt it."
Astrid and Davy, in their own quarters, took their clothing from Midday. Black. It was all as black as night. A form-fitting top hugged Astrid as she slid on the tight, leathery pants and matching boots. As Davy flicked on his duster and strapped on his holster, weapon finally in place, the darkness demon looked at herself in the mirror. She took in a deep breath as she ran her fingers through her dark locks. Images of her long-haired past life ran through her mind. She saw the plague once again, the death she had caused. She looked exactly like that woman in most regards.

"I wanna cut this." She stated after a moment with a sigh. She flipped her hair back.

"Hm? Why?" Davy raised an eyebrow at the sudden decision.

"It's not very practical for a fight, is it?" She lied about her reasoning, but figured it was also a good enough reason to cut off her locks as she remembered being grabbed up by her hair during a fight. "If we're fighting, I don't want to be easy to grab." Before she could say anything further, Davy was beside her, holding her hair at the base of her neck.

"Here okay?"

"Uhm. Yeah, that would be–" She squeaked as his blade slid through the mass. Black hair dropped to the floor. She stared at herself for a moment. She looked less like the woman from the mural now. It was a small change, but a change that mattered deeply. It calmed the storm in her mind when she looked at her reflection. She turned to Davy. "Thank you." She murmured, placing a kiss on his cheek.

The door swung open and they were joined by the pirate captain and the fire demon. Eider followed close behind them in a white tunic styled shirt and black pants that were tucked into his ankle high boots.

"Where's Faust?" Astrid asked.

"He's meeting us at the mirror." Eider shrugged. "He was getting changed when I left him." The group walked into the hall, their footsteps echoing against the stone floor.

"You'd think he'd be faster. I mean, he is a vampire." Davy muttered. He opened his mouth to make another comment, but was interrupted by a loud crash emanating from outside of the castle. The floor and walls shook, sending the group plummeting to the floor.

"The hell?!" Astrid growled. Another crash rang out and screams filled the air. She jumped to her feet, running to the window. Her jaw fell open as she looked down on a scene she had never expected in Purgatory. Her stomach turned and her heart beat faster. *Aurora.*

She shook her head, forcing her panic down. No. Now wasn't the time. If she was Queen of Purgatory, now was the time to help protect her people. She turned to Davy and the others.

"It's Aurora." She confirmed.

"What?!" Valentina snarled. "How the actual fuck is she here? She can't get through the mirror!" Astrid shrugged before climbing into the window, her wings spread widely behind her.

She took a deep breath and leaned forward, falling through the air. The wind rushed by her cheeks and whistled in her ears as she plummeted toward the ground. She spread her wings, allowing them to carry her through the air. She darted through the dust of the destruction, slamming into the pink-winged angel.

"You!" Aurora smiled. "I was *so* hoping to see you." A harsh slam of Aurora's hardened wing sent Astrid flying back, but the angel was quickly assaulted by a stream of water that zipped through the air. She folded her wings in front of her, blocking the attack. Water streamed down the pink feathers as the angel growled. "I guess all of the little troublemakers are in Hell."

"This isn't Hell!" Astrid spat, grabbing Aurora by her hair and throwing her through the window of a store. "This is Purgatory!"

The angel recovered quickly, lunging at her. Astrid ripped her necklace off, a black mist swirling around it as it transformed into a large, glistening scythe. Flinching away at her armed foe, Aurora took to the air.

A barrage of flames assaulted her as she flew upwards. She screeched as her feathers burned, bone exposing itself as the flesh and meat melted away from her wing. She slammed into the ground as Flint jumped from the castle window, using his fire to propel himself through the air until he landed in front of the angel. His flaming hand grabbed Aurora's hair, dragging her to her feet as she screamed and writhed. He smirked, his other hand positioned in front of her face. Just as he was about to blast her with another wall of fire, however, he was smashed into the ground.

Astrid winced as she watched Forfax punch Flint over and over. The fire demon roared, catching one of the fists and throwing his attacker aside before screaming and releasing a blast of fire from his mouth. He let out another war cry, smoky mist burning around him, spitting off ashes until it solidified and formed two horns atop his head and a long red tail that resembled a bull's. An explosion of flames burst around Flint, launching him through the air and after the angel.

"Holy hell…." Astrid muttered before turning to the bleeding mass that was Aurora. She was already being helped by two of her soldiers who eyed the demon with distain. "Drop her." She ordered, holding out her scythe out at them. Neither obliged. Instead, each formed a set of wings. Toxic green haloes appeared over their heads – just like Oran's had looked. Astrid growled, jumping away from the men who charged at her like rabid animals. She flicked her wings, throwing herself into the sky as the two angels pursued. Elegantly, as though she had done so her whole life, she flicked the scythe, slashing open an angel's face. A slight twirl of the weapon and the other was missing a wing.

She winced as she felt something warm above her. Looking up, Astrid saw the fight between Flint and Forfax raging on not far from where she flew. Flames raged through the sky. The angel could do little more than defend. The fire demon shot her a smile and winked, his arm now alight up to his elbow. She nodded, ducking out of the way as he shot flames in her direction. The angel behind her was consumed almost instantly, screaming as the scent of burning feathers and flesh raped the air.

"Nice." Astrid panted as she fluttered beside Flint.

"Thanks. I've had a little practice." He nodded at the scythe. "You're pretty good with that."

She looked at the weapon in her hand. The crimson blood dripping from the blade matched the orb-like jewel embedded in it. The black pole was as dark as her tail, horns, and wings and the blade shimmered a beautiful silver. She smiled. It felt like part of her – an extension of herself.

"Thanks. I've had no practice." The two laughed for a moment before being interrupted by a scream from above.

"Bitch!" Astrid flinched as Forfax dove at her, but the angel was all but instantly consumed by a wave that crashed over him, surrounding him in an orb of water as Valentina loomed from the window. She glared at the angel, her horn and tail formed. He squirmed to free himself, but Valentina held him in the aquatic prison until she was charged at by yet another angel. The orb burst apart as she was tackled back into the castle.

"Capture them!" Aurora screamed from her position on the ground. She stumbled to her feet, her wing dissipating into a pink, shimmering mist as she limped forward. Her back poured blood and her hair was scorched up to her shoulder blades. She eyed Flint dangerously, scooping up a handful of her blood and pelting it at him. It hardened at her touch. A crimson, metallic ball flew at Flint, but was intercepted. Astrid smacked the ball with her scythe, sending it flying back at the angel.

Aurora squeaked as it slammed into her face. A loud crack rang out as blood spurted from her mouth. She fell back onto her rear, groaning as she rubbed her new wound. Blood dripped down her chin as she crawled back to her feet.

"Fucking…demons…."

"You're attacking *my* kingdom and you have the audacity to act like we're a nuisance to *you*?" Astrid scoffed, landing a few feet from her foe. She twirled her scythe, the blood on it flying off and splattering on the ground. "I'm supposed to be queen here. You think I'd really let you destroy this place like you did Crimson Barrow?" She took a step closer. "These people welcomed me; they don't view me as a monster like you or your little comrades. I've looked for something like this my whole life – somewhere where I feel right. You really think I'd let go of it and let you wreck it?"

Aurora opened her mouth, but was slammed through a wall by the sudden impact of two fists to her side. Astrid blinked blankly at Faust and Davy standing side by side where the angel had just been. She looked from vampire to pirate for a moment in confusion before fully processing what had happened. "You two just worked together." She observed.

"Yeah, well, ya know…." Davy shrugged. "We're both pretty supportive of the Queen of Purgatory."

"The Von Drac clan is at your disposal." Faust added. "Purgatory is our home and, though we may not always agree, we support its ruler." He cracked his knuckles. "Besides, I'm not too fond of that bright as hell pink halo. Let's rip it off her. Without wings or a halo, after all, how much of an angel is this bitch really?"

Aurora burst out of the rubble, tackling Davy and pulling a small knife from a holster on her side. She lifted it into the air and plunged it down, only to have Faust kick her in the chin. The knife fell from her hand as she rolled away.

"Damn it!" She coughed out, blood falling from her lips. Before she could move again, Davy gasped loudly. Faust and Astrid spun around. Forfax had taken up the knife and it was now sticking out of the pirate's chest. Davy gagged on the blood that sputtered from his lips.

"Davy!" Astrid cried, running to his side as Forfax grabbed Aurora and darted away through the crowd. "No!" She wrapped her arms around him as he fell to his knees. His hand gripped the handle of the blade. He winced and yanked it from his chest. Another cough splattered blood over Astrid's chest. "No!" Tears welled up in Astrid's eyes as she pulled him closer. "You're a badass pirate. You can get through this."

"He can't." Faust muttered, joining Astrid at Davy's side and placing a hand on her shoulder. "Astrid, he really can't."

"Shut up! Yes he can! What do you know anyway?! You're like dead or something already!" Tears rolled down her face as she turned away from the vampire, lip quivering. She pulled Davy closer, his blood pouring over her body. "It's going to be okay." She assured, brushing her hand through his hair. "I'm here."

"Astrid…it hit his heart." Faust reached out to touch the demon's shoulder, but she pulled away.

"No!" She screamed. "He's gonna be okay!"

Another gag and more blood poured out. Davy gripped Astrid's hand, pulling her closer. His sea-like eyes were glazing over. Astrid's heart pounded in her ears. "You're going to be okay." She lied. "There has to be something…something we can do…." She turned to Faust, her face soaked in Davy's blood and her own tears. "Please say there's something we can do! You're a vampire! Can't you make him one too?!" She pulled Davy closer, sobbing into his shoulder.

"I…don't have that ability. Only Vlad does." Faust muttered.

"Please, please, please don't die! Please! I'm begging you, Davy!" Faust ran his fingers through his hair with a sigh and bent down to the two.

"Let me see him." He tried to pull Davy away from Astrid, but she didn't relinquish her hold. "Astrid, I won't hurt him – I promise, but I need to see him to help him." She sniffled, releasing her hold on the cold body in her arms and allowing Faust to take Davy into his own.

"Faust is going to help you, Davy. It's going to be fine." She gently stroked his cheek, blood smearing over his face at her touch. "It's gonna be fine."

The vampire pulled a small vial filled with silvery liquid from his pocket and forced open the pirate's mouth. Instantly, Davy began to writhe and twitch as though he was in agony. He coughed and gagged on the liquid, but Faust covered his mouth, holding the pirate close as he shushed him.

"Shh. Shh. Just swallow. Swallow." He instructed as the pirate squirmed, blood dripping down from his wound onto Faust's lap. "Just swallow." Faust's voice was soft, kind, even more so than it had been upon first meeting him. He was patient as he forced the pirate to comply with his demands, releasing his hold only when he had been obeyed. Astrid reached out and pet one of Davy's hands. He was icy to the touch. She recoiled. Her warm, ocean-breeze scented pirate was no more. He was cold and reeked of blood now.

"He's so cold, Faust." She barely got the words out through the sobs. She leaned into the vampire, holding Davy with him.

"Because he's dying. Let the serum take effect."

The pirate twitched. He gagged. He choked. His eyes changed from an oceanic blue to a crimson red – from sea water to blood. His canines extended slightly as he snarled and wriggled in agony. He screamed loudly, sending a chill to Astrid's core as convulsed. She lunged toward him, wrapping her arms around him and holding him close.

"It's okay. You're going to be okay." She looked up at Faust. "He's going to be okay." She stared at him for a moment, longing for confirmation. "He's…he's going to be okay?" Faust took in a shaky breath before nodding.

"He's going to be…," he paused, "alive."

Chapter Thirteen:

Davy reeked of blood. It coated his chest. It covered his face. It dripped down off of him into the floor. Normally, Astrid would've been entranced by the decadent scent, taking it in while fighting the urge to devour it. Today was different, however.

Today she was watching the pirate struggle to breathe. He was pouring sweat; a side effect of either his wound or the liquid Faust had poured down his throat, though Astrid wasn't sure which. The hole in his chest was slowly closing, but Astrid couldn't begin to guess what price it would come at. Faust hadn't provided much intel and had all but vanished the moment he had finished pouring the goop down Davy's throat. She groaned, leaning back in the chair she had made her perch. Her tail drooped beside her, occasionally flicking when she felt a tinge of impatience.

"It's maddening." Valentina remarked from the corner of the room. Her arms were crossed and her gaze fixed on her first mate. She lacked her normal pep. She was soaked with something else. Anger, concern, dread – Astrid couldn't quite tell which it was, but it dripped from her just as her zeal normally did. It filled her aura like nothing Astrid had experienced from the pirate before.

"You can say that again." She said, leaning on the bed where Davy was sprawled out, shirt open and wound exposed. She flicked back some of Davy's dark locks, sighing when he didn't move or say anything. "Do you think he's going to be okay?"

"Faust said–"

"He said he'd be *alive*." She reminded, remembering the vampire's reluctance to agree that Davy would be anything more. That could mean anything. *That could mean that he's going to regret every second he exists. All being alive means is that he's not dead. It doesn't mean he won't wish he was.*

"Alive is okay. At least for now." Valentina said, taking a seat at the end of the bed. She was silent for a moment, looking down at the blood-soaked blankets and fidgeting before adding, "This makes me think Flint is right. We need to be proactive. If the angels can get into the demon realm too, there is no safety." She glanced up. Tears were in her eyes, but she didn't let them fall. Inside, she bit her lip and looked away for a moment, stifling the expression before continuing. "They're trying to kill anyone we care about." She drew in a shaky breath. "I know we agreed to it anyway, but this solidifies my position. I want to destroy those bastards. I won't allow them to tear my crew apart." She wiped a stray tear from her face, muttering something about being over hydrated.

Astrid silently nodded, watching Davy's chest labor to rise and fall with each cycle of air. Her tail twitched again as she shifted in her seat, eyeing his every movement, every sign of life. She glanced over at the pirate. She was watching her, her leg bouncing as she waited for Astrid to respond.

"I agree." The smaller of the demons finally stated plainly. "We need to be proactive." She hoped that would be enough to get Valentina to turn away, but she could still feel her gaze. She shifted for a moment, hoping the conversation didn't persist. She already felt uncomfortable enough. She didn't want to discuss war right now. No. Instead, she wanted to hold Davy, to smell his ocean-breeze scent and to taste his sweet lips. She wanted the scent of blood to be gone from the air. She wanted to see him open his eyes.

The two women turned as the door behind them opened slowly and Flint poked his head in. He smiled sympathetically at Astrid, but she lacked a response as he joined them in the room. *Great. Another damn person to watch this spectacle. Can't a girl and a pirate get some peace around here?*

"Knock, knock. Hope I'm not interrupting."

"You are, but it's fine. We're about done." Valentina shrugged. She eyed the fire demon, looking him up and down before adding, "Good job with the fight by the way." Astrid glanced over at Valentina, raising an eyebrow. She could've sworn that the pirate didn't like him only hours ago. After all, she had threatened to kill him if he did anything out of line.

"Thanks." He beamed. "I try my best. Anyway, I hope we're still on for the plan?" He shot Astrid another sympathetic smile. "I know that, in light of the situation, it might be a different answer. Which I'm fine with – I understand if you wanna change your mind after all of this. That fight was crazy. Those angelic assholes showing up in the demon realm was unprecedented."

"Sort of." Valentina interjected. "We're still sort of on. I don't want to send Astrid off alone and Davy is out of commission right now. That skews our plan a bit."

"She can come with us!" Eider chirped, having appeared in the doorway with Faust on his heels. The ice demon hopped inside with a smile on his face. *Great*, Astrid mentally pouted, *more people. We're never going to get a moment alone, are we?* "Besides, she's never seen Niflheim before."

"None of us have except you." Flint pointed out. Eider ignored the comment, running over to Astrid.

"We can take the human realm and look for an angel and other demons along the way. It'll be equal distance anyway." Astrid bit her lip, glancing back at Davy's bloody body.

"I don't want to leave him." She admitted after a moment.

"They're lovers." Valentina added.

"We are not!" Astrid screamed as Valentina laughed.

"The more you deny it, the more true it seems." She paused for a moment, looking from her first mate to Eider and Faust. She crossed her arms and muttered a 'hmm' as she thought. "Do you think you all could manage bringing him with you?" She suggested abruptly.

"What?!" Astrid gasped. "Bring him?! Like this?!"

"I could get him on The Clover, but they might notice the ship. A fight could ensue pretty easily on my end. It wouldn't be good for his recovery. Theoretically, you all would be best suited for taking him if we're going to keep to the plan of taking him with us." She turned to Astrid. "The other option is leaving him here, which I know you won't like." The ice demon nodded before anyone else could respond, bouncing between the two women, his wings forming and fluttering happily behind him.

"Faust'll help us keep him safe til he's fully healed." He offered cheerfully.

"It's the least I can do." The vampire added, glancing over at Astrid. "Has he woken up?"

"Not yet. Should I be worried that he hasn't?" She narrowed her eyes at him, searching for something that would betray his thoughts – something to tell her what to truly believe. For a moment, he gave her nothing to work with, but, under the scrutiny of her glare, he finally gave in.

"What I gave him…," he sighed, "it's a potion. It was bestowed upon the Von Drac family by your previous life."

"The magic user?"

"Right. It causes a painful transformation." He bent down beside Astrid's chair and added with a sigh, "It's going to take away his humanity." She stared at him in horror, her mouth agape.

"Wh…what?"

"It was the only way to heal that wound. It was that or the hole in his heart would kill him."

"Take away his humanity?" Astrid blinked blankly as she stared at him. He groaned as he ran his fingers through his hair.

"Look, normally," he continued as he placed his hand on hers, his cold flesh petting her comfortingly, "we use it to make people into our pets so we can use them to serve us."

"Pets?!" Astrid screamed, jumping to her feet. Faust winced at the sound, grimacing as though he half knew it was coming. "You're turning him into a fucking dog or something?!"

"Not exactly, but close." Astrid crossed her arms at the words. She popped her hip to the side.

"Excuse me?"

"More like…a wolf?" He offered with a slight smile.

"A damn wolf?! You're turning him into a damn *wolf*?!" Astrid paced frantically, her tail flicking erratically behind her as she ringed her hands together and made small, whimper-like noises. Valentina slapped her face with her hand.

"Holy shit…my first mate can't be a damn dog!" She groaned out, slouching into a chair.

"To be exact," Faust interrupted, "it's a monster your past life created."

"I got that," Astrid spat, "and it's a fucking wolf!"

"It's not a normal wolf. He'll be human most of the time – except for when he doesn't want to be or during full moons."

"Weirdest. Potion. Ever." Valentina murmured. "And you just carried that around on your person?"

"We all get a little bit of it when we finish our cotillion." He shrugged. "It's to help us hunt in the human world. While we're stealthy and fast, it's easier when a giant beast is dragging your prey back to you. I just hadn't picked someone to be my pet yet so I had it available."

"You're turning Davy into your fucking pet?! This just gets better and better!" Astrid groaned, collapsing in a heap as she pouted in the floor.

"Oh, it's fine." Eider stated, patting her head. "He'll be a good puppy. Besides, it's not like Faust can just magically control him. He still has free will," he smirked, "and if you get too sad about it, I can always get you a potion and you can be puppies together." She glared at him, pushing him away as she got to her feet. Her tail swished dangerously behind her as she crossed her arms. "Aw, don't be mad." Eider cooed. "Here, I'll give you good news: with those fancy new powers, he should be fine to travel as soon as tomorrow. Better?" She perked up at the words, jumping to her feet and wrapped him in a hug.

"So much better!" She chirped. Her tail wagged as she released Eider and began jumping up and down in joy.

"We should discuss the new plan then." Valentina interrupted. She didn't wait for agreement before she began. She ignored the ruckus, pacing as she made her new plan. "Davy, Astrid, Eider, and Faust will all head together to Niflheim."

"Right." Flint interrupted. "They'll get Eider's weapon and check for an angel to help us along the way."

"And you'll be with me." She added. "We'll build naval forces and see Saffron about help with an army. She's a baroness – she should be able to get us some soldiers from somewhere."

"What about Calder and Midday?" Astrid asked. "They could help too."

"Better not drag them away from Atlantis or Purgatory for too long." The pirate shrugged. "We need someone at our home bases too."

"Point taken." Astrid looked back at Davy. *I guess all that's left to do now is to wait.*

* * *

The night seemed unending as it dragged on. Astrid paced and groaned, checking Davy every few minutes for signs of improvements. She formed and unformed her wings in boredom, fluttering around the room every now and then to have at least something to do.

Eider took to showing her ice demon tricks, forming small flurries in corners of the room. They built snowmen for a while before Valentina started a snowball fight. Faust leaned against a wall all the while, absently staring at the pirate. Soon, it was the early hours of the morning and Astrid found herself the lone survivor of an onslaught of exhaustion. As the others slept, she watched the pirate breathe. He seemed more comfortable than he had been in the hours prior. He seemed to suffer less and less with each breath he took in. She leaned on one hand and huffed. I wish he'd just open his eyes.

She watched his lips part slightly with each exhale. They weren't blue any longer. They looked warm, alive. She leaned closer to him, brushing back his dark locks and taking in his smell once again. Blood. He still smelled like blood, but there was something more. Deep down, under the maddening scent of the sticky red liquid that was caked on his chest, she smelled him. The scent of the ocean peeked out from under the smell of blood. She smiled softly, sighing.

"Good to see a smile on your face." Astrid jolted, her eyes shifting up to Davy's. The oceanic blue had returned to the orbs staring back at her. She drew in a sharp gasp.

"You're alive!" She screamed, tackling him with a hug. She gritted her teeth, but it wasn't enough to hold back her jubilation. Tears rolled down her cheeks as she sobbed into his shoulder. "You're alive! I thought you were gonna die!" He groaned slightly under the weight of her body on his but didn't complain. Instead, he gently patted her head, stroking her horns. "I was so worried." She choked out. Valentina shifted slightly in her sleep as Astrid wailed out the words.

"Shh. You'll wake everyone up, sunshine." He chuckled. He sat up, helping Astrid off of his chest before running his fingers through his hair and stretching. "I remember getting stabbed. Forfax is to thank for that. Then Faust shoved something down my throat." He paused with a grimace. "It tasted like ass. That's all I remember though. What happened?"

"It was a potion. The Von Drac clan has a weird potion. He had to use it if we wanted to heal you." She explained, nuzzling her face into Davy's shoulder.

"What's it do?" He asked. Astrid twitched slightly at the words. She gripped his shirt and bit her lip. "Nothing good." He decided. "Just tell me if I'm gonna wish I were dead."

"I...I don't know." She admitted. "You're not human anymore. That potion made you into something else."

"What?" He asked, gazing at his hands. He flexed them for a moment before shrugging. "I don't feel...I dunno...inhuman? I guess I wouldn't know what that feels like, but I feel fairly normal all things considered." He looked back at her. "If I'm not human though, then what am I? Demon?"

"I don't fully know." She sniffled, looking away and wiping away the tears on her cheeks before adding, "Faust just said you were a monster now. He said it was something my past life made to help the Von Drac clan in the human realm." He took Astrid's face in his hand and turned her back toward him.

"Please just say one thing." His expression was serious as he stared deeply into her eyes. "Tell me I'm still hot." Astrid scoffed, punching him in the arm as he laughed. "What? If I'm not human anymore, can't I at least want to retain my good looks?"

"Shuddup!" She ordered as he pulled her into a hug, still chuckling over his own joke.

"But really: I'm sorry I worried you." He offered. A shiver of pleasure ran up her spine as his lips touched her cheek. Their eyes met for a moment before he pulled her close and pressed his lips against hers. She closed her eyes, leaning into him, wrapping her arms around his body as his hands slid down to her hips. His tongue slipped into her mouth as they fell backwards onto the bed. He tasted sweet, like always. Delicious. She let out a low moan as his hand lowered, squeezing her rear.

"Ahem." The two froze. They glanced over, catching Faust staring at them with a raised eyebrow. "Not lovers, huh?"

"How long have you been awake?" Astrid growled out the words as she glared at the vampire.

"'I was so worried!' 'I thought you were dead!'" He mocked with a grin. "Poor thing. Missing your boyfriend, were you?" He looked to Davy, his expression becoming serious again. "As for you: we have a name for what I made you – for what the monster is called." The two stared at the vampire silently. "We call them lycanthropes." He grimaced as he said the word. "Just be careful. You're going to crave meat the closer we get to a full moon."

"Meat?" Davy raised an eyebrow. "That's not a problem. I love meat!"

"Human meat."

"Oh. Yeah. *That's* a bit of a problem." He corrected with a cringe.

"We'll make do." Astrid interjected. "As long as you're alive, we'll figure it out." She hopped off of him, taking her place in her seat. "You should rest though. We're starting toward Niflheim tomorrow with this idiot," she jabbed a finger toward Faust, "and Eider."

"Rude, but okay." Faust muttered.

"I thought that the plan was–" Davy began only to be interrupted by Astrid.

"It's changed." She beamed happily, leaning in and kissing his cheek. "Now get some sleep." He nodded, laying back on the bed. He stared up at her for a moment before smiling softly. He reached up and stroked her cheek.

"Goodnight, sunshine."

"Goodnight, badass pirate."

* * *

The next morning came soon – too soon for Astrid. She groggily dragged herself from the chair where she had fallen into an uncomfortable slumber. She yawned as Davy sat up and beamed widely at her. Unaware of the happenings the night before, Valentina let out a squeal and tackled her first mate back down to the mattress.

"I thought you were dead!" The admission made Astrid's stomach turn. Even the chipper pirate captain had lost hope for a moment. She had never heard Valentina expect the worst case scenario and, somehow, that made everything about the day before much worse. *It's over now,* she reminded herself. *He's okay. He's going to be fine now.*

"Feeling perfect, actually." He commented with a smile. "It's weird."

"It's not." Faust interrupted. "Lycanthropes have accelerated healing abilities."

"Well, that's good to know." The pirate mumbled while looking at the closed wound on his chest. While the hole had closed, it had left a raised, pink scar.

Valentina looked from one to the other in confusion. Realizing she had missed something during the night, she huffed and turned away.

"I hate being out of the loop." She muttered, pouting in her chair as Davy shrugged, climbing out of bed and putting on a fresh shirt and coat. He attempted to comfort his captain while they got themselves ready, dressing for their adventure.

It didn't take the group long to be dressed and armed, ready to head out. For the most part, many of them were already dressed from the day before when they had prepared. It was merely a matter of those of them soaked in blood changing before they headed to the mirror. Each step through the hall echoed as they had before, but this time their steps weren't a secret. They passed by guards who bowed to their new queen, wishing her well on her journey. The crimson jewel around Astrid's neck dangled just above her breasts, a sign of her clear claim to Purgatory that all eyed as she passed by.

The mirror rippled at Astrid's touch, allowing the group to pass through to the human realm effortlessly. Cerbi bounded through the portal with them, following his master and perching upon her shoulder.

Davy turned toward Eider. "You're leading the way, kid. Let's go to this kingdom of ice."

The ice demon nodded, forming his wings and fluttering slightly overhead as he led the group over the shrouded island. The ominous howls permeated the air once again, but as Davy and the others looked to the area he had been attacked in, the creatures didn't come for them. Instead, they whimpered, running away and hiding.

The pirate raised an eyebrow, looking to Faust for some reaction, but the vampire quickly turned away to avoid eye contact. The trend continued as they made their way back to the edge of the lake. Astrid lifted Davy into the air as Eider shakily did the same for Faust.

"You need to lay off the blood snacks, Faust."

"Oh, shut it!" The vampire spat out with a blush. "It's just cause you're so damn tiny and weak!" They flew over the dark waters, wind brushing by their cheeks until they made their way to the opposite shore. In scarcely any time at all, they found themselves on the edge of Crimson Barrow's border. Having flown had cut their time down drastically. However, now they were all crouched in the tree line, peering into the town as guards marched through the streets.

"We might draw unwanted attention if we fly over this area." Faust stated as Astrid placed Davy down. She hated being back here again, but she knew he was right. If they flew, there was a chance the angels would see them from the sky and they could easily end up fighting loads of them. They had no idea how many of them were still in Crimson Barrow.

She glanced to the side, gaze scouring the streets. It wasn't too busy and it seemed as though no one had noticed them. Eider's demonic appendages evaporated into mist as he gestured for them to follow. Astrid shuddered, remembering the first time she had gone into Samba Forest. It was dark and dimly lit, beautiful but a reminder of how Dane had found out about her demon side.

Davy's fingers slipped between her own, lacing them together as he pulled her closer. She flashed him a smile as he pulled her against his side. He didn't reek of blood anymore. He smelled like the ocean again. He smelled like freedom from the memory of Dane and from the persecution of Crimson Barrow.

"Careful." He said, helping her over a large root that was in their path. She stumbled into him as her feet touched the ground. Her body landed against his. She could feel his muscles beneath the tight black shirt he wore. He winked. "I've gotcha." He pulled her up, helping her to regain her balance before leading on. Her heart fluttered. He was her freedom from everything bad that had happened. He was her new sanctuary.

"What's on your mind, sunshine?" He asked, placing a kiss on her cheek.

"It's just," she paused, rubbing her arm. She had never had a conversation like this with a man before. She had never committed to any relationship, officially or otherwise. Her stomach turned. What if he didn't feel the same?

"It's just?" Davy repeated, urging her to continue as he gestured outward as though the other half of her thought was somewhere before them.

"Why do you act like this?" She groaned at her own question. "I mean, why are you so nice to me?"

"He loves you." Both parties flinched at the sound of Eider's voice chipping in from ahead of them. "Trust me. I can tell." He spun around, causing the party to come to a halt as he stopped. "Lust and love – they're similar creatures and yet vastly different. Regardless, the demon over lust can sense and cause them both. I sensed it from the moment I met you two. He loves you."

Astrid's cheeks burned. She looked up at the blue eyes of the man beside her. She wanted to ask if it was true, but the red of his cheeks and the terrified look on his face answered for her. Excitement raced through her body. She felt numb but in a way she didn't mind. She felt like screaming and laughing and hugging everyone. She couldn't help but smile widely at the pirate. Love. That was something she hadn't expected to find when she had left Crimson Barrow. She leaned up and kissed his lips softly.

"Well, isn't that cute?" The group jolted, spinning on their heels to face the voice that boomed out cynically in their direction. Astrid's heart dropped. Every good feeling dissipated instantly as she stared into fiery eyes filled with rage. She felt nauseous and her whole body shook. Davy pulled her closer, shoving her behind him.

"Dane…"

Chapter Fourteen:

Dane's armor glistened in the light as it always had when he had hunted Astrid down and saved her from persecution, but today was different. Today he stood before her, armored and twirling a sharp, iron sword not as a friend or ally, but as a man wanting to kill her. His eyes burned the same way they had when he had looked at her after her horns and tail had appeared. They were full of hatred, disgust, and bloodlust. It radiated from him, filling the air with a heavy unease. As he took a step closer, Davy whipped out his cutlass, pointing the blade in the direction of his opposition.

"Who are you?" The pirate demanded, holding his weapon at the ready.

"Oh, I'm hurt, demon." He mocked, smirking menacingly at Astrid. "Have you not told your new friends about me? About how I saved everyone from your damned demon magic?" Dane took another step closer, steadying his sword with a tight grip. "You didn't tell them how you caused half this town to die? How you plagued us for more than twenty years? How you caused all the suffering in Crimson Barrow?" Faust glanced back at Astrid. He nodded upward as the demon cocked her head at him in confusion. *What's that supposed to mean?* She wondered. She glanced up, noticing the branches above her.

"Get in a tree. High up. Take Eider with you." Davy whispered.

"But-"

"No buts." Davy scolded. "Just go. I can handle this." She gave a reluctant nod before grabbing Eider by the arm and forming her wings. Darting into the air, she dragged the ice demon along with her.

"H-Hey!" Eider objected.

"Calm down." Astrid instructed as they landed on a high branch, perching at the edge so that they could watch the exchange below them. Astrid folded her wings, her tail wrapping around her legs as she watched Davy confront Dane. *Be careful.*

"Yeah. Just leave the humans to fight, Astrid. What a coward. Run away just like you did before!" Dane bellowed up at the tree with a laugh. "Fucking demons – you're all the same."

"I'm not the one who abandoned everyone!" She screamed back. "You're a guard and you wanted to run away when the angels attacked! You're nothing but a damn coward! You were going to leave everyone to die! I came back for them! I tried to save them!" She growled as he scoffed, rolling his eyes at her commentary.

"A coward, eh? Cowards don't fight. I fight for the justice of Crimson Barrow and for the greater good of everyone. I fight to keep my people safe. What do you do? Steal? Murder? You're nothing but a scourge on this world. You're a monster and you should be eliminated!" He lifted his sword, smiling wickedly at Davy and Faust. "I know what I need to do to get you down here, demon. I'll kill your new little friends one by one!"

Before Astrid could say anything more, Faust charged. He planted a firm punch on Dane's cheek, sending the soldier flying back through a tree with a 'crash.' Astrid and Eider winched as Dane coughed up a mouthful of blood and staggered to his feet. He glanced up to the sky with a scowl on his face.

"Don't just fly there!" He called out. "Help me kill these fuckers!" Astrid's gaze shot up just in time to see a silver blur whizz by her. Faust's victory was short-lived as Forfax fell from the sky behind him, throwing him back into Davy's body. Both toppled to the ground with a groan, rubbing their heads and staggering off of each other.

"Fuck! Forfax!" Astrid jumped down from the tree rushing through the air, charging the angel, but was slammed into the ground by a force landing on her back.

"Hey there, demon." The voice was wicked, seeping with anger and malice Astrid's hands were pulled behind her back and bound over her folded wings. It was a familiar voice, feminine and imposing. *Aurora*, she thought. The angel stepped on her tail, pinning it into the dirt. She leaned close to Astrid's ear and whispered, "We need you alive, but we don't need you in one piece. I'm going to clip your wings just like your little friend did to mine."

"Get off of her!" Davy managed just before Dane began wildly swinging his sword at the pirate. Each slash was closer than the last as Davy bobbed and weaved out of the way, blocking attacks with his cutlass. Clanks of metal against metal filled the air as the two men slashed at one another. Davy kicked Dane back, but to little avail. "Fuck!" He muttered as Dane swung down his blade again, slamming it against Davy's weapon with a loud 'clang.'

Faust snapped at Forfax, but the angel held him still in the dirt. His fangs were just out of reach as the angel laughed at the feral reaction.

"You're not human at all, are you?" He tightened his grip on the vampire's wrists. His knee dug into Faust's stomach causing a whimper to escape his body. "You're a disgusting little monster just like the girl. You're a rabid beast. You know what we do to rabid beats where I'm from? We put them down." He leaned closer, just shy of Faust's bite. "I'll be glad to do it." He laughed. "How would you like to live your worst nightmare? You're going to. That's my power, you see. I can make you experience it." The angel's wings closed around Faust, blocking them off from the world. A faint silver light seeped out from the feathers as Forfax chuckled.

Astrid gritted her teeth as Faust screamed. A drizzle of blood streamed out from under the feathery mass as Faust writhed in pain inside, only distinguishable by the shadows that squirmed in the light.

She turned away, her gaze landing on Davy. He was close to being pinned. Dane loomed over the smaller man, hacking away in a blind rampage. It was all Davy could do to block blow after blow. He winced as the soldier's sword met his cutlass with enough force to send him staggering back.

A crash in the trees caught her attention. She looked up to see Eider pinned in much the same position as herself. He groaned under the weight of the boot by Aurora's brother – Oran.

"Eider!" Astrid screamed, squirming under Aurora. She growled, yanking her arms and kicking as much as she could. Her tail whipped around under Aurora's boot, but nothing was freeing her. "Get off me you holier-than-thou seagull!"

"Not a chance." Aurora's single wing formed. The feathers sharpened like daggers, glowing a faint pink as they pressed against Astrid's back. "Feel that? Sharp, huh? They get like that when I'm hardening my wings. My feathers are going to slice you open and I'm going to make it slow. I'm going to enjoy every second of your pain, demon."

A crash resounded through the air suddenly. Forfax shot by, slamming into the ground and sliding through the dirt, his wings coated in vampire blood. Faust panted, dragging himself to his knees as blood poured from his mouth, nose, and eyes. He shook his head, shaking the liquid from his body like a wet dog. A snarl escaped his body as he glared up at Oran.

"Stay away from my cousin, shithead!" He jumped up, maneuvering through the trees with incredible speed and grace before slamming Oran off of Eider and throwing the angel to the ground. Eider scurried to his feet. He panted as his icy eyes met Astrid's. His wings flapped harshly and, before Aurora could move, she was sent flying back by a mighty gust of snow filled wind.

Astrid flashed him a smile, her tail whipping around excitedly as she took to the air, fluttering beside her demonic ally.

"Tch!" Aurora growled, eyeing them from the ground as a storm of ice and snow swirled around her like a tornado.

"What's wrong, Aurora?" Astrid's voice echoed from all around the angel. She was obscured by the blinding white material that circled around rapidly, blinding Aurora to her foes. "Not gonna fly after me?" Out of the ice a blur of black collided with the angel, knocking her to the ground. As quickly as it had appeared, it vanished back into the white vortex. Aurora spat out some blood, pulling a dagger from the holster on her thigh as she prepared for the next assault.

Davy snarled as he kicked Dane again, slicing through the air with his cutlass as the soldier blocked, laughing at each swing. The pirate growled at his own inability to break through. He was gaining no ground. Frustration morphed to anger as his swings continued to fail, easily blocked or dodged by the larger man.

His eyes flashed red as he growled and slammed his weapon into Dane's. Again and again he tried, but he was constantly blocked. Dane slammed his bracer into Davy's face, sending him toppling back. The pirate's pupils grew large as he watched Dane's sword slice through the air at him. He rolled to the side, barely dodging. As quickly as he could, he jumped to his feet. Another onslaught of failed swings ensued. He snarled angrily, his canines growing long and sharp.

From the corner of his eye, Faust caught sight of the exchange. He cursed as he dodged a blow from Oran, grabbing the angel's arm and slamming him into the ground before darting to the pirate. His knee collided with Dane's gut and he grabbed the man by the hair. He threw the soldier through the air, sending him colliding into a rock several feet away before he turned to Davy. He darted to his side, taking him into his arms.

"Davy! Davy, calm down!" He whispered into the smaller man's ear. The pirate snarled as though he was a rabid, wild animal. "Fuck." Faust muttered as he threw the pirate over his shoulder and jumped through the branches.

He sat the man down before him on a branch. "Take a deep breath." He ordered, holding the pirate back as he snapped and growled. He was foaming at the mouth as he lunged forward, eyeing the area where Dane had fallen. "Try to calm dow—" Davy shoved the vampire off, sending him toppling to the ground below.

Davy gripped his head and whimpered as he fell from the branch, colliding with the forest floor below. Rolling in the dirt, writhing, he howled loudly. Faust crawled over to him.

"Davy you have to—" Dane grabbed the vampire by the ankles and yanked him back as Oran appeared over him. The angel stomped down on his chest. He let out a loud gasp as he watched Davy double over in pain. "No...," he muttered as Dane pushed his face into the dirt.

"You're going to die, monster!"

Astrid and Eider flew in circles around Aurora, concealed by the snow and ice. The angel screamed in frustration. She was blinded by the miniature blizzard around her.

"Damn it!" She cursed, slashing through the air mindlessly with her blade, but missing every blow. Astrid, however had better luck. Her scythe flew by Aurora, slicing open the angel's side and sending blood spraying into the air, coloring some of the snow red. Eider's boot collided with the woman's opposite side. She fell to the ground, gasping for air. Blood pooled below her. She slammed her fist into the bloody, snowy ground. She grabbed a handful of blood and snow, hardening it in her hand with her mist.

"You're not the only ones with tricks." She threw the mass into the blizzard. It swirled around before slamming into

Eider's face. He yelped, falling to the ground as his whirlpool of snow vanished. Blood trickled down his face as Aurora loomed over him, grinning wickedly. She bent down gripping a handful of her blood again and transforming it into a solid mass.

"I'm going to bash your skull in." She snickered, lifting the mass above her head. Just then, Astrid's scythe slammed between the two.

"Forget about somebody?" The demon sneered. She swung at Aurora, pursuing her with a whirlwind of slashes.

Davy screamed in pain as his skin peeled off in chunks. Fur pushed through as though it had always been under his flesh. A wolf-like tail formed behind him, ripping through his clothes. His ears inched up his head, elongating and standing up like a canine's. His clothes tore from his body as he began to grow, his hands and feet transforming into giant paws with huge, imposing claws that shimmered like steel. Saliva dripped from his snout as he eyed the situation around him. He licked his chops, a low growl on his breath.

Faust winced as Oran stomped on his chest once more. He gasped in pain as the boot collided with his body. Above him, Dane lifted his sword, grinning wickedly as the metal shimmered over the vampire.

"Time to put you down." He laughed. The reflection of the cold metal shimmered in Faust's eyes. He clinched his teeth, turning away as the blade dropped toward him, whizzing through the air like a guillotine.

Suddenly, the tension on his chest was relieved. He opened one eye, noting a significant lack of a blade overhead. He stumbled back to his feet, glancing around frantically before realizing what had happened.

Above Oran and Dane loomed a huge, wolf-life creature – a lycanthrope. It roared angrily, throwing the two men aside before charging Forfax. It grabbed the angel in its mouth and threw him into the air, teeth tearing into his chest, sending a shower of blood down on all of them. Aurora yelped as the creature came at her next. Astrid stepped aside almost casually, putting her hands up as the creature dashed by her and tackled the angel through several trees.

"The fuck?" She muttered as she listened to Aurora's cries radiating through the air. She glanced over to Eider and Faust, searching for some explanation.

"It's a lycanthrope." The ice demon stated as the other enemies staggered to their feet.

"Wait." Astrid turned to him. "As in what Davy is supposed to be now?" Eider grinned half-heartedly and shrugged.

"Afraid so." He gestured toward the forest where the lycanthrope was mauling Aurora. "That's your boyfriend mauling your stalker."

Astrid glanced between where the creature had been and where it had gone as roars radiated from the forest beyond her view. Aurora's screams were almost drowned out by the carnal sounds, but they were still there, shrill and full of agony.

"Aurora!" Forfax screamed, darting into the forest after her, his metallic wings carrying him at full speed. "Hang on!"

"That's badass." Astrid finally stated after watching Forfax dive through the trees after Davy and Aurora. "He's taking so many people on all at once. He's so much stronger than he was before." She observed. She looked over to Faust.

"So this is what you meant, huh?"

"Yes." He confirmed. "He's no longer human. This is what he can become. He won't be able to control this during full moons though, so be prepared for this to be *our* enemy as well."

"He wouldn't hurt us." Astrid stated plainly. "Davy would never hurt me."

"He won't know you."

Forfax screamed from within the trees. Scurrying sounded from the bushes as Aurora pushed her way through the foliage, now wingless entirely. Blood poured down her back and gashes marred her otherwise perfect skin. Her halo looked dented, as though it had been chewed, and her clothes were torn. She let out a growl, looking around at the party that surrounded her before turning to Dane.

"Let's go." She finally muttered.

"No." Astrid interjected. "You're not running this time." She lifted her scythe, but was blocked by the soldier. Their weapons collided loudly as they glared into each other's eyes.

Dane let out a roar as he lifted his blade and smashed it into the scythe again and again, blocked each time by Astrid and her scythe. She slipped out of the way as he charged her, allowing him to fall to the ground. They scowled at one another before a flurry of attacks began once more. Slashing and clashing echoed through the air as sword collided with scythe and vice versa. They slammed their weapons together, eyeing each other viciously.

"What's wrong, Dane? Having some performance issues? Not used to me fighting back?" Astrid smirked. Her wings spread wide, flapping up dirt and leaves into Dane's face. He snarled as he choked on the dust, falling backwards and dropping his sword.

"Bitch!" He growled, wiping his face and grabbing for his weapon. It was gone, missing from where it had landed. He screamed in frustration, searching the ground around him.

"Looking for something?" Eider mocked, spinning the sword in his hand as he stood beside Oran. The angel squirmed in a block of ice. He was trapped, stuck motionless in the heap that held him. He shivered, his breath visible as he struggled. "I think I'll keep both of these, thanks." Eider winked, shoving the blade into the ground and leaning on the hilt.

"Piece of–" Dane started, but was interrupted by Astrid's boot colliding with his jaw. A loud cracking echoed through the air. Blood poured from his mouth as he gargled out a scream.

"It's rude to talk to kids like that." She sneered. "You should be acting like a better role model." Blood dripped from the soldier's face as he frantically pulled out a small blade from his belt and pointed it toward her. She kicked it from his hand with a scoff. "You're nothing but a coward, fearing what you don't understand." She took a step toward him. "And you don't even want to learn. You're ignorant." Another step. He shrank back, his back pressed against a tree. She grabbed him by his arm, pulling him forward. "I can give you a reason to fear me if you want." Her scythe inched toward his neck, but, just as it pressed against his skin, Aurora tackled her.

"Let's go!" The angel demanded. The two stumbled through the foliage, darting away to lick their wounds back in Crimson Barrow. Astrid scoffed, climbing to her feet and dusting off her clothes.

"Damn Aurora…." She muttered. From the forest lumbered the great creature that had previously been Davy. It chewed on a metallic halo as blood trickled from its lips. It took a seat behind Astrid, licking its paws. The demon turned to it.

"Davy…you're okay." She smiled.

"Forfax is dead." Faust announced. "I can smell his blood." He paused before correcting himself, "I can smell *a lot* of his blood."

"I say good riddance." Eider shrugged. "He sucked anyway." He turned to Faust. "No offense."

"Haha…you're hilarious." The vampire muttered. The group looked back at Oran, still encased in ice. "What should we do with him?"

Davy snarled, snapping at the angel with his large, glistening fangs. He stood up and took a step toward his would-be prey, but Astrid caught his face and held it in her arms.

"Down, boy." She commanded, rubbing his snout. He huffed, snuggling into her arms as she scratched behind his ear. His tail wagged and his tongue lulled out of the side of his mouth as he panted with pleasure. "Please tell me he's gonna change back." She turned to Faust and raised an eyebrow. "I don't want him to be a dog forever."

"He will. Just give it some time. He just needs to learn to control it is all." He paused, guiltily biting his lip before adding, "It might take a, I dunno, week or so though."

"That'll be fine." She smiled softly at Davy, kissing the tip of his huge, wet nose. "He waited on me to learn. I can wait on him." The lycanthrope sat beside her once more, nuzzling her face with his own.

"Why is his halo an icky green?" Eider interrupted, changing the subject back to Oran as he poked at the angelic appendage. "It doesn't match his wings at all. That's not normal, right? Is he sick? He must be sick." He pulled at the halo, earning himself a glare from the man he was harassing.

"Give me the demon." Oran commanded monotonously. Eider laughed.

"Okie dokie." He hopped in front of the trapped angel and posed exuberantly. "Here I am. Now what?" Their prisoner continued to glare. Astrid leaned closer, staring into the toxic green eyes.

"There's certainly something wrong with him." Faust determined. "He's virtually unresponsive save for battles. That can't be normal." He circled the angel. "His wings must be the true color his energy should be – that powder blue. Something must've happened to him." He turned to Astrid. "You seen this before?" She shrugged.

"Only with these guys. A few of the angels in Crimson Barrow, the ones that attacked us on The Clover, and in Purgatory were like that, but I don't have the slightest clue what it means." Davy nudged her hand, forcing her to continue petting his head. "Needy-ass." She muttered, kissing his snout again and running her fingers through his fur. Faust snapped his fingers in front of the man's face, but received no reaction other than another demand to hand over the demon.

"He's outta it. It's like he doesn't have a mind of his own or something." He announced. "It must be someone's power. Probably an angel…or even a demon."

"Maybe Forfax?" Astrid offered.

"Trust me," Faust muttered, rubbing the blood from his face, "that wasn't his power. He created living, waking nightmares in the pod of his wings. Besides, it would've dissipated upon his death." Davy barked loudly, whining as he laid on the ground beside Astrid and rolled onto his back. His tail wagged as Faust joined her in scratching the lycanthrope's stomach. "It has to be someone else's power."

"It could be someone else in that organization they were part of – the Holy Light or whatever." She suggested as Eider's ice swirled into a block around Oran's hands. Faust grabbed the angel by the sleeve and began dragging him along as they made their way through the forest. "Honestly, that would make sense." Davy hoisted Astrid onto his back, carrying her through the foliage as she spoke. "After all, someone who could brainwash people would be good at forming a group like that and, if they brainwashed a demon, they could get into the demon realm too."

"And it would explain why they want us alive." Eider added. "To use us for whatever they're planning by brainwashing us." He crossed his arms. "You realize we have to find whoever is doing this, right? If we don't, we're always going to be hunted. They'll kill everyone until they have our power."

Astrid nodded, placing her hand on her chin as she thought. *An angel or a demon who can brainwash people is a huge problem. They could turn us against each other. If anyone is exposed, they could be turned into an enemy.* Flint was right. They had to be proactive to save themselves and everyone around them.

"We need to find them and stop them before they take control of everyone we care about." The group nodded as they continued through the forest. "The first step to stopping whoever is behind the Holy Light is to find Eider's demon weapon and an angel to assist us. We have to complete this mission." Her grip on Davy's fur tightened. "If we don't, we're all going to become puppets to the person killing everyone we care about."